A MAN OF HIS TIME

A Man of His Time

by Phyllis Bentley

THE MACMILLAN COMPANY, NEW YORK

813.54
B 44 m.
58166
July 1967

Library of Congress Catalog Card Number: 66-25585

The Macmillan Company, New York

Printed in the United States of America

CONTENTS

IV: TEXTILE

V: END OF AN ERA

I
JONATHAN

I: JONATHAN

1. The Beginning of Change

IT WAS IN 1958, thought Morcar, looking back at it ruefully, that for him things had begun to change.

Morcar had often, when reading history (for he was quite a reader nowadays, Christina had taught him that) wondered how it felt when a period ended, a period began; did people then living recognise the change at the moment of its occurrence? He rather thought not. Looking back at it now, he saw of course that 1958 had been the beginning of the space age; but it had seemed fairly calm at the time. The Bank Rate had come down nicely, and Syke Mills had had an excellent year. There seemed to be only one untoward happening, one thing surprising, one thing a trifle disconcerting, but surely he could have made nowt of that, he reproached himself roughly: boys must be boys, he liked the lad's spirit, Jennifer being a woman had made too much of it, and so on. And yet, after that year nothing had seemed the same.

Up till then he had been pretty well satisfied with his life, at least for its recent years.

True, his optimism at the end of Hitler's war had been excessive; the post-war Labour government had made a mistake, he thought, in not rallying all the forces of the nation to the creation of a new world; instead of that they had remained just a Party; they had talked of *vermin* and *we are the masters now* and *jobs for the boys*, and in general had made half the country feel that they were not to be allowed to participate. Still, the Welfare State had been founded; and if it were not perfect, injustices had been greatly lessened and distribution of wealth improved; nothing was perfect; humanity had set itself tasks beyond its present capacity to fulfil, so what did people expect? It was an improvement on the old mode, anyhow, thought Morcar; gladly—no, not gladly, but rationally accepting the necessity—paying out the thumping taxes and continually increasing wages which the new way of life required. Mistakes had been made by successive governments; but then mistakes were always made by governments; except for the frightful blunder of Suez, he was not too dissatisfied. The slow diminishment of Great Britain's position as a premier world power, though he sorrowed for it, he expected and accepted; we had had our turn, we had sacrificed our power and wealth in a good cause—they'll be hard put to it to find a better candidate for the job, thought Morcar.

In his private life, too, the years since the war had not been too unhappy.

True, he was divorced from his wife Winnie, had been so, by mutual consent you might say—though too late to do him any good, he thought with a pang—for nigh on fifteen years. True, the only woman he'd ever loved, Christina, had been killed in a London air raid with her husband. True, his only son, whom he barely knew in any case, his child by Winnie, was married to an Oldroyd and out in South Africa growing oranges or tobacco or something instead of in Yorkshire making good West Riding cloth. But over the years Morcar had come to terms with these disasters. Winnie his wife he'd put out of his life except for alimony which he made continually more generous with his growing prosperity—heaven knew what she did with all that money; she'd no more taste than a fly, but no matter. Towards his son Cecil he would not allow himself even to feel disappointment, but merely a mild friendly interest in Cecil and his wife Fan—a shrewd little person though you wouldn't think it to look at her, a pretty kittenish blonde. He had bought Cecil his farm and made him a yearly allowance, wrote him a stiff letter occasionally, gave his children handsome presents, and that was pretty well all. Morcar never forgot his beautiful Christina, of course; her photograph, sad and lovely, stood alone on a handsome stand in his bedroom, and in the morning and the evening, as the poet said, with a deep loving pang he remembered her. But he had made a family for himself out of the ruins of his earlier life: Christina's daughter Jennifer, widowed of her husband David Oldroyd by the war, lived in his house with her young son. Morcar's mother, too, though bedridden now except for an hour or two each day, was kept comfortable by his care, and her great age was a source of pride to her.

Then too Morcar was one of the largest textile manufacturers in the West Riding, probably one of the most prosperous, certainly one of the best designers. Everybody knew that. What was more to the point, he told himself with a sardonic grin, he knew it himself. Building up overseas exports after the war had proved a congenial and successful task. He managed his own huge Syke Mills and little Daisy Mill for himself, and David Oldroyd's small neat Old Mill by the Ire for Jennifer and her son, with perfect efficiency, and kept an eye as well on the financial affairs of Mrs. Oldroyd senior—a silly fluttery woman, and very inconvenient living away down on the south coast, but she'd truly loved her husband and her stepson David and still loved her daughter Fan who was Cecil Morcar's wife out in South Africa, and Morcar respected her for that. Lucky for her that he was at hand to husband her small resources. Yes, he was pretty good both in his family life and his business, he thought.

Or rather, he *had* thought. The West Riding had been his and he had freely roved up and down in it, perfectly at home and at ease and sure that whatever he did was right and proper and generally estimable. And now he felt uncertain and ill at ease, and even found himself hesitating about a design. Was that blue pick there really the charmer he had thought? Did it clinch the design? Or was it perhaps a trifle corny, to borrow Jonathan's word, a trifle over-emphatic? He found himself asking the newest, youngest lad in the designing-room for his opinion, and actually hanging on his answer. Of course the lad was embarrassed, but whether because he was being asked to pronounce on a design by the great Harry Morcar, or because he thought the design frightfully out of date but didn't like to say so, was beyond Morcar to discover. And all this, Morcar now perceived, together with much else of a similar nature, had begun in 1958.

In 1958 De Gaulle had risen, Verwoerd had become Prime Minister, Algeria and Cyprus seethed, a monkey was fired into space, scientists protested against nuclear bomb tests. All these things, as could now be seen, foreshadowed troubles to come. Oh, and there was Kruschev too; not that he was a nuisance, Morcar indeed rather liked him. But the real trouble for Morcar was that for the first time, laugh it off how he would, a rift sprang between himself and Jennifer's boy, a lad he had always thought of fondly as his grandson.

Jonathan—it was an effort on Morcar's part to call the boy Jonathan; he always thought of him as David, his young friend David Oldroyd's son, and indeed sometimes, he knew, he still called him David without meaning to do so. He had been quite disconcerted to find that the child's name was Jonathan. In the tragedy of those war times which now seemed so far away—David Oldroyd shot after parachuting to the aid of the resistance movement in Jugoslavia; Jennifer's father and mother Christina killed in a V.One raid; David's father perished in a south coast air raid; Jennifer herself near her time, being hurried out of dangerous London to Yorkshire and the arms of old Mrs. Morcar; all the arrangements caused by these disasters falling on Morcar's shoulders—he had been away from home when the child was born and christened. To himself he called the child Baby David for several months, and was greatly taken aback when Jennifer told him the child had been baptised as Jonathan.

"But why?" exclaimed Morcar, astonished.

"David wished it," said Jennifer.

There was no more to be said. Morcar, who knew West Riding textile history, and particularly the history of David Oldroyd's family, pretty fully, understood well enough why David had wanted his son, if he had one, called after one of his Luddite ancestors—well, a collateral ancestor, David was descended from the Luddite Jonathan Bamforth's sister. The said Jonathan Bamforth was certainly a noble type, reflected Morcar, but after all he had been hanged; Morcar hoped this was not a bad omen for young Jonathan Oldroyd. But for the first fourteen years of young Jonathan's life, this was merely a joke.

For young Jonathan was really a very nice boy. Rather serious, rather tall and thin, with an oval face, a high brow, a clear sallow cheek, a decided nose, and large dark brown eyes to match his dark wavy hair; he had an air of distinction, of nobility, about him from his earliest days, or at any rate Morcar liked to think so. In the years just after the war, when Morcar's heart still bled from his loss of Christina, his best consolation was to stroll round the gardens of Stanney Royd, the home where he had hoped to see Christina as his wife, with the child's hand in his—Jonathan was Christina's grandchild, after all. Jonathan listened seriously to all Morcar said, and occasionally came out with some rather remarkably appropriate comment. Jonathan was a clever boy; Jennifer taught him herself at first (she had an Oxford degree, after all, and took a lot of trouble to learn the proper methods): then he did well at his preparatory school, then he began to do very well indeed at his public school. He was thoroughly kind to everyone he met, very pleasant with old Mrs. Morcar, whom Jennifer taught him to visit regularly, and apparently genuinely attached to Morcar, whom he called *Uncle Harry*, as did his mother; also he listened attentively to Nathan, Morcar's works manager—though Nathan, Morcar noticed, seemed a little timid with him and Jonathan made few comments. Jonathan rode well, and was friendly though calm with dogs; walked a great deal and swam better than most; handled a boat well, was interested in cricket and football but not too passionately; did not talk a great deal but occasionally came out with something neat and witty. In a word, he was a boy after Morcar's own heart, and Morcar loved him—quietly but dearly.

And then one December afternoon in 1958 Jennifer rang Morcar at the mill. It was unusual for Jennifer to ring him at the mill; she had too much sense to worry him with minor domestic details there.

"Uncle Harry?"

"Jenny! Is there something wrong?" he said at once.

"Yes, I'm afraid there may be. The Annotsfield police have telephoned me and asked me to call immediately at the central station."

"Have you been in trouble with your car, then?" said Morcar with a sigh—this was a usual problem for all too many, but he had thought Jennifer a careful driver.

"No. They asked me," said Jennifer—her voice shook a little but she quickly controlled it to her usual cool courteous utterance —"they asked me if I was the surviving parent of Jonathan Brigg Oldroyd."

"Jonathan! Good heavens!" exclaimed Morcar.

Jonathan had not yet come from school for Christmas. He had gone to stay for a few days with a reputable schoolfellow, but was expected to return tomorrow to spend the rest of the holidays at Annotsfield.

"I thought," resumed Jennifer.

"Yes, of course. I'll meet you there in ten minutes," said Morcar at once. "Did they say—anything more definite? Who was it? Anyone we know?"

"It was the Chief Constable. He said it was not an accident and there was no need to be unduly alarmed."

"Well—let's get there and hear what's up."

"Yes."

13

"So you see, Mrs. Oldroyd," said the Chief Constable in a kind tone: "All you have to do is to complete and sign this bail form, and your son will be released forthwith."

"They won't keep him in a cell?"

"No, no. Anyone under the age of seventeen has to be bailed forthwith," said the Chief Constable soothingly.

"Shall I sign it instead of my niece?" suggested Morcar, who was disturbed by Jennifer's pallor.

"It must be the parents who stand as surety."

"I don't quite understand how you come into this," said Morcar aggressively, for he felt a great need to express vexation.

"The police at Norwich communicated with us and asked us to get the bail form signed, so that the boy could be released."

"Norwich! What has Norwich got to do with it, for heaven's sake?"

"It is the nearest Divisional Police Office to Swaffham."

"Swaffham! This gets worse and worse," growled Morcar.

"Swaffham is a rocket base."

"But what has the boy *done!*" exclaimed Morcar angrily. "What has all this to do with Jonathan?"

"He is accused of being on special property without authorisation, and of conduct calculated to cause a breach of the peace."

"Oh, nonsense."

"I'm sorry you should take that line, Mr. Morcar," said the Chief Constable in a harder tone. "The police do not make unsubstantiated charges."

"I'm not taking any line," said Morcar, clamping down his temper. "But Jonathan's a good boy, you know. I can't see him doing any of these things. He can't have thought it up for himself, any road; somebody must have set him off."

"He was accompanied by a schoolfellow, I understand," said the Chief Constable. "But in any case, it's said there were a hundred or so on this C.N.D. protest. Not all of them were arrested, however."

"Oh, it was a march like that Aldermaston affair?" said Morcar, enlightened.

"The same idea, but carrying it a bit further. Civil disobedience this time."

"I see," said Morcar, glum.

"What will happen to Jonathan?" said Jennifer.

"They'll probably hold a special court in Norwich and clear all the accused off quickly, together," said the Chief Constable. "A juvenile must be brought before a court within seventy-two hours, in any case. Still, as he was arrested acting with adults, he may be tried with the rest. We could ask the Norwich police to put him on a train for Annotsfield, but it seems rather foolish to bring him all the way up to Yorkshire and then take him straight back again."

"We'll drive down there at once," said Morcar.

"That would seem best. Mrs. Oldroyd will have to be present at the court. Where will the boy go meanwhile?"

"Can't he wait at the police station for us?"

"No. He must be released at once, on bail. He's under seventeen."

Jennifer gave the address of the friend, Ralph Featherstone, with whom Jonathan was, or was supposed to be, staying.

"It's not too far away."

"The Featherstones may not want to take him after this to-do," said Morcar gloomily.

"We can be there in a few hours."

"We'd best wire him some money, choose how."

"Yes, I think that would be advisable, sir. Not too much, perhaps."

Morcar took out his notecase and threw down a five-pound note. There was a sour taste in his mouth and he could not make himself behave agreeably. His Victorian upbringing made any conflict with the police a horror to his respectable soul, and the thought that a boy in his care, David Oldroyd's son, had actually committed an offence, been charged by the police, would have to appear before a magistrate, gave him awful feelings of guilt, shame and perplexity. Jonathan! That quiet, agreeable boy! What would his father have thought!

"What do you make of all this, Jenny?" he said gruffly as they drove south through the wintry dark.

Jennifer did not turn her handsome face to him, but looked ahead. "He must believe it a good cause," she said.

"Has he said so to you?"

"He hasn't spoken of it to me at all," said Jennifer.

Her voice, though calm and self-contained as usual, held grief, and Morcar understood it. Her son had not confided in her.

"A breach of the peace! The young idiot!" he snorted.

They had a disagreeable interview with Mr. Featherstone, who was much put out by his son's escapade, for which he clearly regarded Jonathan as chiefly responsible. This view seemed probably correct to Morcar; Jonathan had been arrested and Ralph had not, and Ralph now looked red-eyed and repentant, while Jonathan was clearly still full of spirit. He entirely agreed with Mr. Featherstone's view of the lads' behaviour, but could not bear to say so; he left it to Jennifer to express regrets for any inconvenience Jonathan might have caused, thanks for the Featherstone hospitality, and so on. His manner indeed was so gruff that Ralph looked ready to cry again.

"You mustn't be vexed with Ralph or the CND on my account, Uncle Harry," said Jonathan as they drove away towards a Norwich hotel. He spoke amicably and leaned forward with his arms folded on the back of Morcar's driving seat. "Mr. Featherstone is right, really. Joining the demonstration was entirely my idea. I've always wanted to join them since I read about Aldermaston."

"What was your conduct calculated to cause a breach of the peace?" demanded Morcar, grim.

"The police were carrying off a girl by her arms and legs," explained Jonathan eagerly. "It looked horrid, you know. I just struck his arm up, that's all."

"Did they carry you off by your arms and legs?"

"Yes—right into the van. I wouldn't stand up, you see. We sat down all over the road."

"Serve you right, then."

"Oh, I didn't mind," said Jonathan.

"So now you've got a police record. You're too young—they shouldn't have allowed you to take part."

"I'm so tall that I look older than I am, you see," explained Jonathan. "Besides, there was no enrolment or anything of that kind. One just joined as and when one wished."

"You might have let us know—you might have let your mother know—before you embarked on a prank of this kind."

"It wasn't a prank, Uncle Harry. It was a serious protest. I must say I didn't anticipate any trouble of this kind," said Jonathan. "I thought I should come home tomorrow in the ordinary way."

"Anticipate! Enrolment! Protest! How the boy talks. One would think he was thirty," thought Morcar: "They're older nowadays," remembering his own gauche innocence when he was Jonathan's age. "Why did you do it, David?" he exploded suddenly.

"I thought it a duty," said Jonathan.

"What do you know about it? Unilateral disarmament is madness," said Morcar.

"But could you really ever envisage using a nuclear bomb?"

"No. But the power to use one acts as a deterrent."

"How can you tell whether it would deter or not?"

"Everything in life works on the principle of reward and deterrent," said Morcar. "You eat something and like it, therefore you eat it again. You put your hand in the fire and it is burnt and pains you, you don't put your hand in the fire again."

"But if you're only threatened with the fire," began Jonathan.

"Without a weapon you are subject to endless blackmail—and not only you, but everyone dependent on you."

"Someone must begin to take a risk. The possession of such a weapon is morally wrong."

"If your slogan was 'Never the first' to use the bomb, there would be some sense in it," said Morcar, "but unilateral disarmament is madness. Madness!" he repeated hotly. The thought of his beloved England lying helpless beneath threats which she dare not resent, bluff which she dared not call, made him feel sick.

"Don't worry, Uncle Harry," said Jonathan. "Things are different nowadays. We'll manage."

His tone was soothing, affectionate. Nowadays! Morcar glanced quickly back. The boy's face wore a slight smile, his eyes were bright with commiseration.

"Good God! He's pitying me!" thought Morcar. "He thinks I'm out of date."

Morcar, who had always considered himself a decidedly-on-the-left, progressive, forward-looking sort of chap, was dumbfounded.

Since then, nothing had been the same.

2. Son of a Hero

ABOVE THE HEAD of Jonathan's bed hung the insignia of his father's D.S.O. and posthumous bar, with the printed citation, in a glazed frame. They had always hung there; they had hung there since he was an infant in a cot, as his mother had told him, and sometimes he felt as though his whole life were lived in their shadow.

Of course he was proud of his father. He had watched parachutists on television, he admired their courage, he imagined himself leaping out of an aircraft—in the dark, too, and above hostile territory—and knew it would take every ounce of fortitude he possessed to behave in such a manner, if indeed he could ever bring himself to do it. To organize the distribution of arms to a resistance movement of unknown men, over wild and mountainous country, to be hunted for one's life by Nazis, to be captured, interrogated and perhaps tortured, without betraying a single detail, to lead men to their execution whistling an English song—what was it, Jonathan often wondered? the newspaper accounts, which he had privately studied with some care in the Annotsfield municipal library, never gave its name; *Tipperary* perhaps, or *Keep the Home Fires Burning*, no, those belonged to the earlier 1914 war, perhaps it was even that Yorkshire classic *On Ilkla Moor*, it would have been nice to know—to stand up calm and smiling before a machine-gun squad, and give the freedom sign as the bullets rattled: all these were the actions of a brave man, and Jonathan, looking at the fine frank smiling face of his father in the enlarged photograph in his mother's room, gave him a full tribute of respect.

When he was a child he had thought the story magnificently romantic, and yearned to do something as finely adventurous himself; now that he had grown up, read a bit and looked around he still thought it was romantic, of course, but also bloody silly. All these heroic postures, these guns banging, these bombs dropping, simply resulted in heaps of torn and bleeding flesh and millions of broken hearts. His mother, for instance. So beautiful, so distinguished, slender almost to emaciation from continued grief, her fine fair silky hair turned prematurely grey, her wide grey eyes and handsome profile stamped indelibly with its mark —her life was wasted. Of course he was glad when she refused various offers of marriage which came her way, glad to have her to himself; but this was just a normal Freudian process, an Oedipus reaction; looking at the matter as a rational being, objectively, he thought it was a terrible waste of so much good material, so much beauty, so much intelligence, so much capacity

18

for love and happiness. And she was only one; there were millions.

Of course, Jonathan had too much knowledge of himself and of human motive in general not to wonder whether in truth he commiserated his father or was jealous of him. Did his detestation of all violence, of the military life, of these wicked bombs, spring from pity and disgust and moral contempt, or did it spring from a sour feeling of jealousy, a resentful recognition that in the eyes of his mother and of old Uncle Harry, Jonathan would never equal his father in achievement? A recognition that he lived, indeed, in the shadow of his father's heroism? Jonathan admitted frankly to himself that he did not know.

His feeling was strong, however, and his doubt about its origin made it even worse to endure.

Accordingly as he grew into his teens he particularly disliked to be introduced in a manner which revealed his parentage. This operated only in the West Riding, of course; Jonathan was sardonically amused to observe that his father's deeds, his total sacrifice for his country, his outstanding merit as a patriot, were unknown, or at least unremembered, except in one portion of his native county. Falstaff's opinion of honour seemed to him all too justifiable. But the business men, the textile men, of the West Riding, especially those of his father's generation, who had fought at his side, so to speak, in World War II: they remembered.

"David Oldroyd's son, eh?" they said, and they gave him a grave look, of pity perhaps mingled with admiration.

Jonathan sustained the looks with a gravity and dignity which he hoped matched their own, for he would not for anything in the world "let down" his father. But beneath his calm exterior there lurked this hateful ambivalent resentment.

Worse than these introductions, worst indeed of all, was poor old Uncle Harry's habit of calling Jonathan *David* by accident. Nowadays this made Jonathan's blood leap and his skin crawl. He longed almost unbearably at times to break out in an explosion—after all, he was an Oldroyd and had the right to the well-known Oldroyd temper, he reflected, whatever other mollifying genes had entered his blood. He saw the irony of summoning his father's heredity to protest against his father's name, but this vexed him all the more. Once he had actually mentioned the matter to his mother, very quietly of course.

"Why do you dislike it, Jonathan?" said she.

"I'm not my father, Mother, and I can't be," returned Jonathan.

"No, dear, I see that. But I don't like to mention it to Uncle Harry. He was so fond of your father, and he's been so very kind to us."

A burst of temper stormed through Jonathan's brain; he kept it down, but flushed. He did not like the idea of anyone's "being kind" to his mother and himself.

"He's growing older now," continued Jennifer on a note of apology.

That of course was true. The last year or so the ageing process had become, not obviously noticeable perhaps, but observable to a keen eye such as Jonathan's, in Morcar. His broad shoulders stooped a little, his thick hair greyed at the temples, and he had taken, sensibly enough, to wearing spectacles, which at first he managed ill, leaving them about all over Stanney Royd in odd situations, from which Jonathan often had the task of retrieving them. Presently, however, Morcar coped with the spectacle affair, for he had still a great deal of common sense, reflected Jonathan approvingly; he developed several extra pairs and kept them in different rooms and on different levels of the house, and no doubt of Syke Mills too. It was a rich man's solution, observed Jonathan, not open to a poorer man and therefore not wholly to be admired or recommended; still, it served. Thinking this, a picture rose before his mind's eye of Uncle Harry looking over his glasses at Jonathan's latest school report and smiling very kindly, and a responsive friendliness washed away Jonathan's resentment for the moment.

"I shouldn't wish to hurt Uncle Harry's feelings in any way," he said.

"No, dear," agreed his mother, relieved. "We'll leave it then, shall we? Uncle Harry has had so many sorrows in his life I shouldn't like you to add another."

Sorrows, reflected Jonathan. It was difficult, somehow, to imagine people as old as Uncle Harry having sorrows; they seemed so set and stiff. Quarrels, of course; rows, vexations, especially with their juniors; but hardly such warm and poignant feelings as the word sorrow implied. He was interested, however.

"Is the photograph in Uncle Harry's room, of his wife?" he enquired.

"No, no!" exclaimed his mother. "Surely I've told you before, Jonathan. That is my mother, your grandmother."

20

"Oh, yes, I remember. Was Uncle Harry very fond of her, then?"

"He had a deep and respectful devotion to her."

Poor old pet! thought Jonathan, walking away. A deep and respectful devotion, indeed! What a way to go on! Not much in it for Harry, I must say. Well, he was truly sorry for Uncle Harry and for his mother, but they were old. Their life was over, in the past. He was young, his life was to come. He wanted his generation to go on living, not be blown to bits or radiated to deformed pulp in another war. International co-operation, complete disarmament, that was the only way. Someone must give a lead. Why couldn't the older generation see the truth of that?

3. Black and White

THE FOLLOWING WINTER Morcar had a short bout of pneumonia. It came, he decided, from walking out of the hot tentering shed across the sleety cold of the large Syke Mill yard without donning his coat; a daft thing to do. The bout was short, soon over.

"These modern antibiotics act swiftly," said Jonathan, smiling kindly at his bedside.

"You've the constitution of an ox, Mr. Morcar," said his doctor.

Morcar, who did not know what an antibiotic was though he guessed, preferred this latter diagnosis.

"You'll soon be up and about, as right as rain," continued the doctor. "But why not take a little holiday? You can afford it, I suppose?"

This was meant as a joke, Morcar presumed, and he snorted.

"In a warm climate. Sunshine, you know. Haven't you a son in Africa somewhere?"

"Aye. Near Johannesburg."

"Go and take a look at him."

Jennifer pressed this proposed trip so strongly that Morcar supposed either he had been more seriously ill than he thought, or Jennifer believed a visit to Cecil to be his duty. He tried these two theories on his mother, in whose old-fashioned shrewdness he still had a great deal of faith. Old Mrs. Morcar, sitting very comfortably in a padded rocking-chair beside a huge wood fire, and looking neat in the fur-lined dressing-gown and pastel silk nightwear with which Jennifer provided her, smiled at him derisively.

"Harry, she doesn't want you to favour Jonathan above Cecil and his children," she said. "They're your own flesh and blood, after all."

"You're right, as usual, mother," said Morcar. He meditated on this for a moment, while his mother rocked slowly back and forth At length he said: "Jennifer is a good girl."

"She is *that*," said old Mrs. Morcar with emphasis. "Now be off with you to South Africa, Harry, and be sure to bring me some pictures. I don't want Table Mountain, you know, but snapshots of my great-grandchildren. I don't even know their names, not rightly. There's a boy and a girl, I think, but that's all."

"I get a bit mixed with them myself," said Morcar, colouring, a little ashamed, for he had not the faintest idea of the identities of Cecil's children. Cecil and Fan wrote rarely, and his replies were rarer still.

"Ha," said Mrs. Morcar, who knew this very well. "When will you leave, eh?"

"Next week."

"Why not this week?"

"I must fix things at the mills. Now you be sure and take care of yourself while I'm away."

"I will," said Mrs. Morcar grimly.

Fixing things at the mills for an absence of six or eight weeks took longer than Morcar had anticipated, and he had rather a rush to catch the plane from Yeadon to London at the last; in fact he actually ran to the check counter brandishing his ticket, while Jonathan and Jessopp ran beside him carrying his suitcases. However, once he was on the plane from London all went well; an experienced traveller, Morcar knew well all the small details which made for comfort and took delays and setbacks equably. He liked air travel, enjoyed the immense views of land and sea; all too soon, it seemed to him, he was descending, in the middle of a fine morning, at Johannesburg airport. The sky was white with heat, the sun was blazing; the bright colours of the flowers, the white summer uniforms of the officials, the handsome appearance of the coloured attendants, pleased him. He felt that breathing was certainly easier here. A white man stepped up to him.

'Father," said Cecil.

Morcar looked at his son shrewdly. Cecil was much more presentable than of old, he thought. Tallish, much tanned, with very broad shoulders, Cecil still had a rather too mild look in his brown eyes, thought Morcar; his fair hair was greying—he must be over forty, for heaven's sake!—and several deep lines engraved horizontally across his forehead increased an expression of harassment and anxiety; but his hair was still very thick, he held himself well and wore a suit of good tropical worsted and a regimental tie. He did not in the least, thank heaven, resemble any of the Shaws, his mother's people.

"Well, my boy!" exclaimed Morcar heartily, offering his hand.

His heartiness was assumed, for he never felt at ease with Winnie's son, but to see Cecil's face brighten at his fatherly welcome touched him, and the heartiness became more real.

"It's grand to have you here, father," said Cecil. "Really grand. Fan is so pleased you've come."

Something in the way he said this convinced Morcar at once that Fan was not pleased at all, or at least had reservations about her father-in-law's visit. "I shall find out why, presently," he said grimly to himself. Feeling now suddenly cross, grimy and hot, he allowed Cecil to shepherd him through the necessary formalities —not very cleverly, I could have found my way better for myself, thought Morcar—and to his waiting car. This was large, white and handsome, though slightly filmed with red dust; Morcar was pleased by this sign of prosperity, vexed by the dust.

"It's thirty miles," said Cecil apologetically.

"Good," said Morcar.

Cecil was not a particularly agile driver, but once out of the airport traffic made good time. The breeze from their movement refreshed Morcar, and he was in a fairly good temper when they turned down a dirt road and after bumping a mile or two drew up in front of a white house with white wooden pillars and verandahs.

Fan came out at once on to the stoep, as Morcar supposed it was called. She was still an extremely pretty little blonde pussy, thought Morcar, kissing her; face rather thinner, chin rather firmer, claws decidedly sharper, but figure still good and very well dressed in a plain white linen dress. She said "Uncle Harry!" in a very warm tone and throwing her arms round him hugged him so heartily that at first he thought he had been mistaken about her attitude to his visit. But no; looking more closely—her complexion was only slightly less brilliant than of old—he was sure her eyes were red-rimmed; she had been crying.

She took him to a light pleasant room, well equipped with furniture which looked tasteful and surprisingly "period".

"Yes," said Fan, seeing his eyes wandering, "I expect you've seen it before, Uncle Harry. It's good Oldroyd furniture. As mother lives in a hotel she doesn't need it, so she got it out of storage and sent it to us. The freight cost the earth, of course, but we're proud of having furniture from home."

"Ah, yes," agreed Morcar, who seemed to remember an exorbitant item of this kind in Mrs. Oldroyd's accounts ten years or so ago. He did not remind Fan that in the days when the Oldroyd furniture stood in a West Riding house, any Oldroyd establishment had been far, classwise, above his head, quite out of his reach. He disliked men who boasted of their early poverty as much as those who boasted early riches. Fan knew the facts, anyway, if she bothered to recollect them. He changed into a thin suit.

Cecil came and led him to the stoep, where chairs and tables were agreeably arranged and Fan awaited him. An African "boy" in white brought out drinks, and Cecil served them. His actions had the ease of familiarity, and Morcar, remembering his lack of sophistication before marriage, was amused.

The house stood on a slight slope, and the ground rolled gently down away from them. In the blazing sunshine Morcar perceived a short stretch of grass, rows of trees which were presumably an orchard, and to one side a mass of low greenery which looked for all the world like an English kitchen garden.

"What's your main crop, then, Cecil? Oranges?"

"Apples."

Morcar felt vexed. A son growing oranges in South Africa was one thing, but to journey all those thousand of miles to grow fruit which you could grow just as well in Worcestershire seemed silly work. Just like Cecil, however.

"And peas and beans and strawberries and lettuce and tomatoes," cried Fan with a mischievous look, correctly interpreting his reaction.

"They grow well here, then?" said Morcar, forcing an amiable tone.

"Except for pests, cloudbursts, hurricanes and drought, they do very well," said Fan as before.

"Fan!" Cecil reproved her.

"Well, we may as well face facts," said Fan, tossing her head.

Cecil's face changed suddenly, irradiated by a smile. Morcar followed his glance to the doorway, and saw there a very charming little sprite, with long fair hair and dark blue eyes, delightfully clad in a fluffy white frock and neat white socks and shoes.

"Who's this, then?" said Morcar, smiling.

"My youngest unmarried daughter," said Cecil.

The sprite gave a merry laugh—a delicious trill, thought Morcar—and bounding over to her father stood leaning against the arm of his chair. Cecil put his arm round her and they both gazed at Morcar, looking well satisfied.

"Cecil!" said Fan reprovingly.

"But how many children have you, then?" enquired Morcar, bewildered.

"Only two—one boy, one girl. This is Susan," said Fan. "The youngest unmarried daughter bit is just a joke." (And a very familiar one, obviously, thought Morcar, to judge by its unsmiling reception.) "Susie, say hello to your grandfather, dear."

Susan bounded across to Morcar, and saying "Hello, Grandfather," in a small and piping but sweet voice, bent forward and kissed him on the cheek.

"Well, you *are* a nice little girl," said Morcar, delighted. He had not hitherto enjoyed close acquaintance with any little girls and he found her soft warm cheek, her thick lustrous hair, the miniature perfection of her arms and hands and feet, quite enchanting. "Susan, eh? I must take your photograph to send home to—" He paused, made an effort to recollect the relationship, and concluded—"your great-granny."

"Where's Chuff, Fan?" said Cecil, frowning.

"He's not back from the village, dear."

"I told him to be home by noon."

"He'll be here soon, dear," said Fan soothingly.

And indeed almost immediately a big well-grown boy in his teens appeared, hot and panting, in the doorway.

"You're late, Chuff," said Cecil.

"Go and shower and change, Chuff," said Fan. "It's nearly lunch-time."

"How old are the children, then?" asked Morcar.

"Chuff's fourteen and Susan's ten," said Fan with a grimace

which showed what she thought of this disparity in time of conception.

"*What* is the boy called?"

"His name is Charles Henry Francis, but we call him Chuff."

"I'm not surprised."

"Well, Cecil's mother begged us to call him Charles, after her brother who was killed in the First World War," began Fan, a trifle testy. (At once the hideous scene of Charlie's death rose vivid again in Morcar's mind, where it had lain unforgotten for forty years.) "Cecil wanted to call him Henry, after you, and I wanted to call him Francis, after my own father. So we called him the lot."

"Well, you got it all in," said Morcar gruffly. He was touched but irritated to find that the boy bore his name.

"C. H. F. Morcar—it's quite nice," said Cecil.

"Aye, quite euphonious," agreed Morcar. Where on earth he had got this word from, heaven knew: Jonathan, he supposed. What a long way off the West Riding seemed from here.

Chuff now came out, clean and well-brushed, and was introduced. He was a solid boy, reddish fair, well-built, with strong features and keen grey eyes; to Morcar there seemed something familiar about his appearance, and after considering this for a while he thought he discovered what it was.

"He's like your father, Fan. Colonel Francis Oldroyd," he said.

There was a sardonic note in his voice, for Francis Oldroyd, once Morcar's employer and later his Captain and Colonel in the First World War, had never been a particular favourite with him. "What he knew about textiles would go on a sixpence," he grumbled to himself.

Fan, however, as he expected, was pleased.

The next few weeks passed very quickly for Morcar.

First, of course, he had to view the farm, for which after all he had paid the purchase price, at the close of the last war. He noticed that Fan was not very eager about this, but, native of a great industrial conurbation set amid infertile hills, as he was, he knew so little about crops and trees that he had no idea whether it was well run or ill. Cecil employed three native "boys"; the "boss-boy", John, was married to Eva, the household maid, and they lived together in a deplorable hut at the bottom of the garden. On ceremonial occasions—such as Morcar's arrival—John donned white shirt and shorts and served at table. The relations between

26

Cecil and his staff seemed reasonably friendly, Morcar thought, and Eva was delightful, kind, warm-hearted and efficient; but Fan was sharp with all of them.

"You have to keep after them all the time," she said irritably.

Certainly John and the other two seemed to stand about and laugh a good deal, but Morcar was an employer of labour himself and accepted the desire for a break as natural to all men.

Once this inspection was over, Morcar thought rather to Fan's relief, Cecil and his family laid themselves out to entertain him. They took him to a game reserve, where he saw a lioness (unfortunately couchant rather than rampant), impala, zebra, giraffes; they took him to Zulu dances; they showed him weaver-birds' nests and jacaranda trees with their pendent mauve blossoms; they took him out for picnics, braivleis as they called them —Morcar was not one who enjoyed alfresco eating but accepted the custom of the country with easy good-nature. They dressed formally—Susie in delicious white gloves and tiny straw hat—and drove him into Jo'burg, as he learned to call it, to shop, and allowed him a day or two there by himself to visit one or two of his customers. They showed him the outside of a gold mine and told him all the traditional stories. They did not, in spite of his repeated urgings, take him to a native location, Fan urging distance, unpleasantness, lack of permission and finally danger. They offered instead to take him to see Cecil's maternal uncle, Hubert Shaw, who had an orange farm fifty or sixty miles away, but this Morcar drily declined. He remembered Hubert as a fairly harmless, insignificant member of the teeming Shaw household in days of old, but he did not wish to see Winnie's brother, and he thought he saw that Fan was glad of this decision. They declined to accompany him to the Victoria Falls—the distance was much too great, they said discouragingly; however, Morcar went off there by himself, and certainly, though he had seen Niagara, the spectacle was well worth while. When he came back after his week's absence, the family's company manners had worn off somewhat, and he was able to see their relationships more clearly.

These were not too bad, he thought. They fell into a familiar pattern. The daughter turned to the father, the son to the mother. Whenever Cecil came to stoep or room, Susan crossed silently and swiftly to her father's side; the pair exchanged a look of love and appeared content. Chuff on the other hand seemed always in need of Fan's support and intervention. He was rather a sulky boy in

Morcar's opinion, and his manners and speech were not as pleasing as his sister's, though Fan was always scolding him about them. His voice had broken and was deep and manly, and he was always bellowing "Mom!" about the house—for a shirt, some money, or heaven knew what. Cecil was rather sharp with the boy, Morcar thought, but not to much effect, and in return Chuff was apt to be sullen, not to say rude, to his father. Once, indeed, after being commanded twice by Cecil to fetch a map of some kind from another room, and not stirring from the floor, where he had extended another map, the command being repeated Chuff said: "Oh, all right!" in a tone of such surly insolence that Susie flying across to him slapped his face hard. Chuff was astonished and dismayed.

"Why, Susie! What are you about?" he cried, scrambling to his feet and rubbing his cheek. "How could you hit me? I'm your brother!"

Susie, scarlet, burst into tears, and the incident ended in brother and sister falling into each other's arms and kissing. Morcar thought Susie's rebuke deserved, but was glad to see genuine fondness between the pair.

Out of the house, on picnics and so on, Chuff became a different lad; he was skilful with his hands, swift on his feet, and knew quite a lot about African fauna and flora. When engaged about any outdoor pursuits his face brightened so that he became almost good-looking. At any rate, reflected Morcar, there was already more energy, more decision in his young face than in his father's.

Morcar also observed with some satisfaction that although Fan's sharp tongue exercised itself rather too freely in exasperation on her husband, who received it with a mild endurance irritating to his father, Fan and Cecil were still in love or at least still loved each other. Cecil kissed his wife when he occasionally left her for the day, and she expected this and lifted her face willingly to him. She also kept up a loyal façade for him towards the children. A small example of this occurred one day when, on Fan's telling Chuff that he and Susie must eat their supper alone together, as the grown-ups were going out, Chuff said:

"Is Oom Harry going too?"

"Don't let me hear you speaking Afrikaans, Chuff," said Fan sharply.

"Why not?" said Cecil in his mild tones.

"It was only one word," Chuff defended himself.

"Mr. Morcar is your grandfather, not your uncle, in any case," said Fan, changing her position, under attack, at once (woman-like, thought Morcar) to more tenable ground.

"Well, it's difficult to remember, with you calling him uncle and dad calling him father—*I* don't know which is right," growled Chuff.

"Your father is right, of course," snapped Fan.

Through the days Morcar perceived that this loyalty, though often enough illogical in expression, was constant. So that in spite of some sharp marital altercations which drifted to his ears—just the sound, not the words—at night from their bedroom, he thought Cecil and his wife were not too unhappy together. It struck him that whereas in small matters Fan ruled, in large affairs Cecil got his way. In a word, these South African Morcars were a normal family, he thought, with all the blessings and banes consequent on that condition. One could not expect to find the co.⅄. .eous urbanity of a Jennifer and a Jonathan everywhere.

With the outside relationships of the family, however, Morcar was not so well pleased. They had many friends, accepted many invitations to parties of many kinds. It was clear that the men liked Cecil, and the women, though they were a little afraid of Fan, liked her; they trusted her not to flirt with their husbands and respected the way she ran her household. Of these sentiments Morcar approved. But the talk at these parties was always the same: it dwelt continually on the ignorance and inferiority of the black Africans, the merits of apartheid, the disillusionment with England, the iniquities of the Afrikaners, the Boers. At first Morcar listened eagerly to these discussions, anxious to inform himself of on-the-spot opinion on these great questions, but the opinions were always the same and presently he grew weary of the ignorance, the arrogance, the illiberal blindness of people who on other subjects were kind and honest. At first, too, these hosts and guests remembered that he was just out from home, and modified their tone; but presently they forgot his presence, and reproached England bitterly for her desertion of the white cause, which they attributed to all sorts of mean and preposterous intrigues. One day the word *cowardice* was actually mentioned. Morcar started and coloured, and Fan made eloquent eyes of warning. There was an awkward pause.

"I hope we haven't offended you, Mr. Morcar," apologised his host at length.

"You have, as a matter of fact," said Morcar. "But never mind! I can take it."

His host stuttered a little. "It's best for us to say what we think?" he suggested.

"Aye! If I'm allowed to say what I think, too," said Morcar. He glanced round the circle and enjoyed their look of alarm. "But never mind! I won't," he said. His tone was that of a well-feared nanny menacing her charges, and his hearers were abashed.

Only a few days later, however, at drinks in the home of a prosperous Afrikaner farmer—Fan had wanted to evade the invitation, but Cecil accepted—he had to listen to a sudden outburst of hate from his host on the subject of the British at the time of the Boer war, who had enclosed women and children in camps and starved them, so that they had nothing to eat but fungus from the grass.

"Aye! That was bad management," said Morcar. "And some British people said so at the time."

His host proceeded to accuse the British of having inserted powdered glass into their prisoners' soup.

"Nay!" said Morcar strongly. "That's not true, I'm sure. Mushrooms I grant you, but powdered glass, never." Gazing straight into his host's angry face, he added calmly: "We aren't cunning enough, you know."

It seemed that he gained quite a reputation in the neighbourhood for his outspokenness, and, as always with the English—it's their great redeeming feature, thought Morcar—his eccentricity was respected when it was found to be sincere. But he grew more and more tired—sick and tired, as he said to himself—of the unjust, heartless, inhumane arguments, endlessly repeated, which masked an ever-growing fear.

At last the day of his departure drew near. He bought handsome presents for Fan and the children, tipped Eva and John so generously that they laughed with glee. The day came. He packed, he said goodbye to the children; the car—"dirty as usual, but I expect it's difficult to keep clean in this red dust," thought Morcar—was brought round, the luggage loaded; Fan, dressed for town, climbed in.

"There's no need for you to come, Fan," said Cecil. His tone was rough, and more commanding than Morcar had heard it.

"But I want to come, Cecil!" exclaimed Fan. She seemed really hurt, and short of incivility Cecil could not but yield.

They rode in silence until they were almost at the airfield, when Fan, leaning forward from the back seat, said urgently to Morcar:

"You haven't told me much about Jennifer and David's boy, Uncle Harry."

"Jennifer busies herself with cultural committees. She's serene, but still locked in grief."

"And what about David's son? David was my half-brother, after all."

Morcar had refrained from speaking much of Jonathan because he did not wish to reveal the contrast between that civilised, well-educated boy Jonathan and Fan's rather loutish son. So now he said shortly:

"Jonathan's a fine lad. Clever, you know, like his father. Tall. Dark."

"Is he like David in appearance—or my father?"

"Not very."

"He's nearly two years older than Chuff."

"That's right."

"Is he a *nice* boy, Uncle Harry?"

"Thoroughly nice," said Morcar. He remembered the C.N.D. incident. But in this illiberal land it would scare people out of their wits. Best not mention it. "Naturally he has some of these modern ideas," he said hesitantly.

"Naturally," agreed Fan, a trifle relieved, it seemed to Morcar, to find that the paragon Jonathan was not absolutely perfect.

They reached the airport; Cecil parked the car before having the luggage unloaded—a foolish thing to do, thought Morcar, as porters had to be summoned from a distance. Cecil looked white and strained, and Fan too appeared ill at ease.

"Where is your overnight bag?" exclaimed Fan as they stood in the reception hall. "It's not here."

Morcar was at once aware that the small bag in question had lain at Fan's feet in the car, and that to leave it there was a manoeuvre on her part to get rid of Cecil and gain a few moments alone with himself.

"Here it comes," thought Morcar, remembering his first impression on arriving in Africa, that Fan was for some reason uneasy about his visit—an impression never entirely dissipated. "Best hear it," he thought. "No, it's not here," he said aloud, looking round as if in search. I must have left it in the car, I'm afraid. Cecil, will you fetch it, lad?"

Cecil gave Fan an angry glance, but perforce departed.

"Uncle Harry," began Fan immediately as soon as he was out of earshot, "I must tell you. Cecil won't tell you, and he doesn't want me to tell you. We've argued and argued about it."

"Well, get on with it, then," urged Morcar drily. "We've not much time."

"We're in great trouble. We owe a lot of money. We've had two terrible harvests. That's why we couldn't take you up to the Falls. We couldn't afford. We're afraid we shan't be able to keep up the children's schooling."

"How much do you need?" said Morcar bluntly.

"A thousand pounds," wailed Fan, crying.

"All right. Don't fret. You shall have it," said Morcar.

"Cecil will kill me if he thinks I've told you," sobbed Fan. "He's so proud, you see."

"Well, dry your eyes. Don't let him see you crying. Here he comes. We'd best not be talking together," said Morcar, as Cecil appeared in the distance. He gave an explanatory wave to his son and walked off briskly to the men's lavatory.

Luckily he always carried his cheque-book about his person. He drew it out, wrote a cheque to Cecil for two thousand pounds, dated it the previous day, folded it, dirtied the creases a little, and stowed it into an inner compartment of his wallet. Emerging, he saw Cecil looking very white and determined, clearly saying "No!" to a tearstained Fan as clearly imploring him to confide in his father.

"Fan, do you mind leaving Cecil and me alone together a minute?" he asked soberly.

Fan, unable to speak, withdrew to the bookstall, looking frightened.

"Look, Cecil," said Morcar, drawing his son away by a hand on his arm, "I want to thank you with all my heart for your hospitality. You've given me a grand time, and I shall never forget it." Here Cecil smiled with pleasure; Morcar did not know whether to rage at or admire his ingenuous simplicity. "Here's a bit of a present for you," he said gruffly. He drew out his wallet, made a bit of a fuss over getting out the cheque as though he did not remember exactly where it was, and thrust it still folded into

Cecil's pocket. "No need to have Fan here," he said, acting (rather well, he thought) the northerner embarrassed by being obliged to display feeling. "Father and son, you know." (This incoherence struck him as particularly effective.)

"Thank you, father," said Cecil with a pale smile.

Unable to resist the impulse, he drew out the cheque and opened it. At once his face became irradiated with bliss.

"Father," he began.

Luckily at this moment the flight to London was announced.

"Come along," said Morcar brusquely, touching his son's arm.

After a few agonising moments he was seated safely in the plane, with Cecil and Fan waving at him from the airport balcony, arm in arm.

Whether it was satisfaction in leaving Cecil, reminder of all his life's early miseries, behind, or satisfaction in leaving South Africa, with all its appalling problems, behind, or satisfaction in a generous act, or in elucidating the mystery of Fan's uneasiness which he had sensed throughout his stay, or pleasure in presenting the daughter of Francis Oldroyd, offhand, with a cheque for twice the large sum she had asked, or something else, he was not sure. Whatever it was, though soaked with sweat and emotionally exhausted, he smiled happily as the plane left the ground.

He enjoyed the flight, and as the plane was late in London he had a rush to catch the train to the north, and felt still in an active, bustling, cheerful mood when it crossed into Yorkshire. As he passed the pit-stocks and mill chimneys, he felt again that deep, half-playful, tenacious affection for his native county which he had always found so satisfying. In Annotsfield the sky was grey and the rain falling heavily, but that was only to be expected; a nice change, in fact, from the African blue.

Jonathan met him. A little confused by his recent sojourn in differing seasons, Morcar was surprised to find him at home for his Easter holidays.

"How are things in South Africa?" said Jonathan as they walked down the platform together.

"Bad," said Morcar. "This apartheid business is shocking."

Jonathan expressed eager agreement. "Are the native locations as bad as they're reported?"

"I didn't see one," said Morcar.

Jonathan looked at him in astonishment, and fell silent.

Morcar coloured. He perceived at once that his recent euphoria proceeded from a renewal of his self-confidence because he had felt himself infinitely more liberal and advanced than all the people he had recently met. His condemnation of apartheid was sincere, but also he had enjoyed being on the same side as Jonathan. Now that was over; he had fallen short, as usual, of the boy's standards. To visit Victoria Falls and not a native location, he now saw, betrayed an unawareness of, a callousness to, one of the great problems of the day. He ought to have conducted a thorough investigation of the colour problem. He had appeared, as usual, hidebound and out of date.

4. Gap

THESE UNCOMFORTABLE THOUGHTS persisted through the night, but fell away in the morning as he drove down through spring sunshine to Syke Mills. Syke Mills was his own sphere; nobody could criticise him there, he thought; in his own textile trade he was supreme. He smiled with pleasure as he drove under the great archway past the gleaming brass plate proclaiming his name—in spite of his absence the brass still gleamed, he noted with approval—and saw a couple of handsome lorries with *Henry Morcar Ltd* on their side, standing at the loading bay in the yard. The men nodded their heads sideways at him and grinned, which was as much acknowledgement as you could expect from a West Riding employee nowadays, thought Morcar. He parked accurately in the space reserved for him, and ran up the steps to the office. There was a general air of expectation and hanging-about-in-waiting in the outer office, and a new girl with smooth hair in the desk by the inner door, he noticed; then Nathan rushed up to him, excited and laughing, and he was involved in greetings. Nathan's grey quiff was retreating and diminishing, Morcar observed; had diminished indeed quite a bit while Morcar was away. Nathan without his quiff would be strange indeed! But then, he'd never got over losing his son in the war.

"Well, Nathan!" said Morcar heartily.

"It's good to have you back, Mr. Morcar," shouted Nathan.

Both men then felt slightly ashamed of this (as they considered)

34

ebullience; they calmed down and got themselves hastily through the door into the inner office. On Morcar's desk in neat piles stood masses of letters, some with scraps of cloth, and some with small swatches of yarn, attached.

"Good Lord!" groaned Morcar, throwing his hat on the stand. "Plenty of work for me, it seems."

He was really delighted by this prospect. Sitting down at his desk, he began at once to go through the papers. Some he threw into the waste-paper basket at once, others he divided according to their degree of urgency and difficulty.

"Miss Symonds!" he roared.

"Miss Symonds has left, Mr. Morcar," said Nathan apologetically, stepping back to signal through the doorway. "She got married."

"In a hurry, wasn't she?" said Morcar crossly, not, however taking much notice.

"Well—" began Nathan.

"Usual reason?"

"I'm afraid so."

"Well, they will do it."

"That is so. More than ever, nowadays."

"Who have you got for me, then? That smooth-haired piece by the door?"

"You don't miss much, Mr. Morcar."

"That's my aim, Nathan. Is she any good, then?"

"Seems so. She's young, but she was highly recommended by the Technical and Miss Symonds approved her. High speed. This is Miss Mellor, your new secretary, Mr. Morcar," said Nathan formally as the girl came in.

"How do you do?" said Morcar, shaking hands.

He eyed her shrewdly. Her hair, cut in a fringe, of an ordinary dark shade, curved smoothly over her cheeks towards her chin in a way Morcar particularly disliked, but her dark grey eyes were bright and even sparkling.

He proceeded to give rapid instructions for a number of easy letters, including a wedding present cheque for the once Miss Symonds. Miss Mellor, who had not spoken, though pencilling notes on each document with apparent comprehension, withdrew in silence.

"Now, Nathan," said Morcar, sitting back in his chair: "What's gone wrong while I've been away, eh? Sit down and let's have it."

Nathan at once dropped into the likeness of a small child caught with its fingers in the jampot.

"Well, there's one or two things, Mr. Morcar," he said hesitantly.

"Aye, I supposed there would be. Come on, let's hear the worst."

Slowly and with reluctance Nathan related the sad tale. Beginning with a few minor misfortunes, such as might well have happened had Morcar not been absent, he worked up gradually to major disasters. Some pieces had been milled when they ought not to have been milled, and this had led Nathan into a sharp tiff with the head of the finishing department, which was housed at Daisy Mill.

"They weren't fit to be sold," said Nathan.

Morcar said nothing, but his face was expressive.

Then somehow or other a thread of yarn with the wrong twist had—somehow or other—been woven into a series of pieces, making them, admitted Nathan, horribly "barry".

"I suppose the customer rejected those too."

"Aye, he did."

"Well, that's a few thousand pounds you've lost Syke Mills, with one thing and another."

"There's worse to come," said Nathan miserably.

"Worse?"

It seemed that a thread of yarn of wrong colour had been woven into a whole series of pieces, which—

"Wrong colour!" bellowed Morcar, colouring violently himself. "From Syke Mills! Nay, Nathan! How did it happen, for heaven's sake?"

"I don't rightly know."

"Whose order were they?"

Nathan named one of the huge ready-made clothing firms in England to whom Morcar sold direct—one of his largest customers.

"But that's serious, Nathan," said Morcar, staggered.

"I know."

"They weren't sent out, I hope."

"They were."

"But why on earth did you deliver them?"

"We didn't know what else to do with them. You weren't here," said Nathan.

"And they were all sent back, I suppose."

"They were."

"And what do they say about it, eh?"

"I haven't talked with them," said the wretched Nathan.

Morcar swore, and picked up the telephone.

"Hello, Robert!" he said cheerfully when he reached the appropriate official of the firm in question.

"Oh, is that you, Mr. Morcar?" came the reply in a very cold tone.

"Yes. I've just got back and heard about this frightful bloomer of ours with your pieces."

"Where've you been, then?"

"I had to go to South Africa to see my son," lied Morcar, lowering his voice to give the impression of confidential intimacy. "Difficult situation out there, you know."

"I can imagine," said the voice, slightly warmer. "Well, what are you going to do about this order of ours, then?"

Morcar, making a rapid calculation, gave in a few short, practical sentences a promise to send a completely fresh series of pieces by a set date.

"Well, we shall have to make that do, I suppose," said the voice, considerably mollified. "It's a tiresome delay, very tiresome, but we liked the pattern. I must tell you we were thinking of cutting it out altogether and going to somebody else. When I rang Syke Mills the other day you weren't there and I was told there was nobody who could speak to me."

"What?" shouted Morcar. "Never!"

The voice chuckled. "I'm glad you're back, Harry. Don't be late with your delivery date, now."

"Is this true, Nathan?" bellowed Morcar, almost before he had replaced the receiver. "Did you actually tell him there was nobody here could speak to him?"

"What else could I do? When you're not here, who do I turn to?" shrilled Nathan.

The two men glared at each other.

"Well, for heaven's sake don't let's waste any more time," said Morcar irritably at length. "Get down into the weaving shed and see when they can clear enough looms to get these pieces started. It'll mean overtime to finish to the date, for sure, and that'll cost us a pretty penny, on top of the original loss."

"*You* set the delivery date, Mr. Morcar," grumbled Nathan.

"I did and I shall keep it. But to tell him there was nobody could speak to him! Couldn't you have found a head of a department?"

"Aye, but which? Nobody would know the whole story, when we could deliver a fresh lot, I mean. And whichever I asked, the others would be mad. You weren't here, Mr. Morcar."

"All right, all right. Forget it. Let's get started with this lot. I'll inspect every stage personally," said Morcar. To himself he thought: "I blame myself for leaving Nathan in charge," but he decided this was too cruel to utter.

Having successfully convulsed the whole mill out of its routine in order to fulfil his promised delivery date, Morcar discovered that the hour was four o'clock. He had forgotten to have lunch, and, as he told himself with a certain grim satisfaction, Nathan and several other non-Trade-Union employees had had to forget it too. He sat down at his desk, and found a pile of cheques and letters awaiting his signature. Signing, he observed with pleasure that they were well and accurately typed.

"She seems to know her job," he remarked to Nathan, who was hovering round, beginning to recover his calm now that the storm of Morcar's anger had almost blown over.

"Oh, she does. She's a connection of those Mellors who were in Old Mill with Mr. David, you know," said Nathan. "That's why I took her, really, out of several with equal qualifications."

Nathan had always been fond of David, remembered Morcar with a pang. If only I had David here now! Well, there's Jonathan. If only he were older. He'll be leaving school this summer, after his A level; then he'll need three or four years of a textile course at Leeds. Then it'll be three or four years under me before he's able to be really in authority here. If only he were older! For Nathan's right; when I'm away there's nobody at the top.

As a natural consequence of these considerations he said to Jonathan, as they were sitting at coffee after dinner at Stanney Royd:

"I'd like you to come down with me to Old Mill one day this week, Jonathan. Say tomorrow. No, that's Bradford market day, say Friday."

"Of course, Uncle Harry," said Jonathan cheerfully.

Jennifer, however, made a slight movement as if to demur.

"Isn't it convenient, then, eh, Jenny?" said Morcar genially. "Next week will do."

"It's just that I feel Jonathan should work hard, not waste his time these holidays," said Jenny, stirred out of her usual tact.

Refraining from remarking that a visit to the mill which brought his living was not a waste of time for Jonathan, Morcar observed:

"Work? What at?"

"A-level's coming on," said Jonathan with a grimace.

"If he's to get a place at a university—at Oxford," said Jennifer, slightly breathless, "he must do well in his examinations."

"I'm taking two special papers," proffered Jonathan.

It was a severe blow. University! Oxford! Well, of course, Morcar told himself irritably: I ought to have thought of that before. Jennifer has an Oxford degree herself, she'd never be satisfied that her son should lack one. But this meant extra years before Jonathan could rule at Syke Mill.

"How long will you be at Oxford, then?" he asked.

"I don't know that I shall get there."

"Of course you will. One way or the other," said Morcar mildly —his fierce disappointment must, he knew, be controlled.

Jonathan did not brighten at this implied offer to pay for his university studies.

"Three or four years," he said.

Three or four years! And then a textile course! In spite of himself, Morcar sighed. This is going to be damned awkward, he thought. I really ought to get in somebody really good. But who? There's nobody good enough. And if I do, it will upset Nathan, and by the time Jonathan's ready there won't be room for him, the new fellow'll be all over the place. How would a merger be? With a board? He could see that Jonathan had enough shares to get him a seat. If there were anybody fit to merge with, he thought. There's nobody as good as me. I might look around, I suppose.

He picked up his home copy of *The Yorkshire Textile Industry* —he had another at Syke Mills, of course—from the stand beside his chair.

"Where are my reading glasses, I wonder?" he said irritably.

Jonathan bounded up and proffered them with a smile so kindly and agreeable that it tore Morcar's heart.

5. Young Ambition

"I'LL GO UP and work now, and then I shall be free to go to Old Mill on Friday," said Jonathan. He said goodnight politely to Morcar and his mother, and withdrew.

In his bedroom, he picked up a notebook from his work-table and threw it down violently on the bed. A trifle relieved by this release of temper, he restored the notebook to its proper place with loving care.

"They don't understand," he muttered fiercely to himself. "I'm not a boy any longer. I'm a man. Uncle Harry doesn't even know that you can't get into any University nowadays by paying. If I can't get a place at Oxford I'll get one somewhere else."

He sighed at this, however, for Oxford was his great desire.

"Well, if you want to get there, work, for heaven's sake!" he exclaimed.

He sat down and drew his books firmly towards him. Turning the pages of Hammond, however, he found time to glance over his shoulder at the insignia which represented his father.

"I hope you would have understood," he said aloud. "But if you wouldn't, then I can't help it."

He buried himself in the condition of the town labourer in the new civilisation 1760-1832.

6. Merger

MORCAR LOOKED AROUND for somebody really good in the textile sense, quite vigorously in the next few months, as far as he could do so without betraying his intention either within or without Syke Mill, but he did not find any person or firm suitable to his purpose, or any clue to such a firm or person, until the summer, when Jonathan was again at home. The boy had done extremely well in his A-level, as Morcar had expected, gaining distinction in both his papers. When these results arrived, he announced joyously that he meant to take a week's complete holiday from work, and for the week he went whistling about the house, or sat in the garden—the summer was hot—reading, with a look of relaxation.

"That's a nice jacket you're wearing, Jonathan," said Morcar, finding all three of his household sitting round the summerhouse when he came home from the mill one evening. They had actually contrived to carry old Mrs. Morcar downstairs, and she sat there in her padded chair, beaming. Morcar stretched out a hand towards the jacket, one of those loose tweedish sports affairs fashionable nowadays. Jonathan, to whom this textile gesture was familiar, put out his arm so that the cloth might be felt between the fingers. "Don't you think so, Mother? Colouring's good, eh?"

Mrs. Morcar, pleased to have her one-time skill in embroidery colours remembered, put out her thin shaky old hand; Jonathan, smiling, bent his arm in her direction.

"It's an A-level celebration present from mother, but I chose it," he said.

"Yes. The design's good, too," pronounced old Mrs. Morcar. "It might almost be one of yours, Harry."

"Where did you buy the coat, Jonathan?" asked Morcar quickly.

Jonathan took off the jacket and showed him its label, which was that of a multiple store which had many branches in the West Riding.

"Not a costly purchase," he said.

"It's not bad, it's not bad at all," said Morcar, turning the garment about in his hand to see the effect of the pattern on back and sleeve. "H'm. Well. Thanks."

He handed back the jacket without expressing what was in his mind, the wish to know who had made the cloth of which it was composed.

If there was anything Morcar disliked in the ordinary surface details of life, it was asking people questions, the answers to which would be of assistance to him. Perhaps this trait sprang from the customary West Riding dislike of incurring obligation, perhaps from something deeper and more individual to his nature. In such cases he really had to force himself to take up the telephone, to put the necessary question; he tried to approach the matter sideways, and had to make an effort to prevent his voice choking in his throat. Accordingly it was several weeks—though the matter kept nagging at him all the time—before he brought himself to enquire of the store the name of the manufacturer of the cloth in question. The manager of the local branch was quite shocked by the question, which seemed to him to indicate some suspicious intention, a complaint or a double-cross of some kind. He did not know the answer in any case, and was extremely reluctant to indicate the departmental head office address to which application could usefully be made. This obstruction of course roused Morcar's natural obstinacy, and he pursued the matter steadily, till at length he discovered that the cloth had been manufactured by Messrs. Hardaker and Sons of Ramsgill, a mill which lay in a valley between Annotsfield and Hudley. He was surprised. On the telephone that day to his friend Robert—the ruined cloths had now been replaced and relations were again excellent—he suddenly bethought himself to say casually:

"I saw a good bit of sports jacket tweed of Hardakers' the other day." He described it.

"Yes. I know the one you mean. We should have liked it. But we hadn't been doing any business with Hardakers' for some time, and Associated got it."

"I was agreeably surprised. I've thought Hardakers' designs a bit stuffy lately," said Morcar, carefully putting a hint of interrogation in his tone.

"Yes, so did we. But they've got a new young fellow there just lately. Very smart and up-and-coming."

"Oh. Well, about those greys due on Thursday," said Morcar affably. He longed to know the new young fellow's name, but would not ask for the world—if he did his interest would be known all over the West Riding by lunchtime, and its cause speculated upon.

Another few weeks passed while Morcar ruminated. He knew old J. L. Hardaker well, and respected him as an honest and hardheaded man of business, well versed in textiles but not particularly inspired. J. L.'s son, Luke, had been killed in the war—Dunkirk, he thought—like David, and this similarity in loss drew him to the man. There was a grandson whom Morcar thought he had seen here and there, a good-looking agreeable young man but not too bright. His age was in his favour, however, for he was in his late twenties or early thirties, Morcar had heard, so not too old to understand Jonathan. About the up-and-coming young fellow Morcar could learn little at first, except that his name was Edward

Oates, that he didn't belong to any of the well-known West Riding families, and that he had begun his career as a designer with a large Annotsfield firm. This firm, and Hardaker's, were of course Morcar's competitors, so he had to go warily, but he presently discovered that Oates had left Annotsfield of his own free will, to better himself with Hardakers', and had presently married J. L.'s grand-daughter. This was both good news and bad. To marry J. L.'s grand-daughter he must surely be accepted as a decent sort of chap, but the marriage tied him firmly to Hardakers', so there was clearly very little chance of tempting him away to Syke Mill.

"It would have been a low trick anyway," reflected Morcar philosophically, amused by his belatedly virtuous attitude.

He ruminated further, unready to make up his mind, until as autumn turned to winter two happenings brought him to a decision. On the one hand Jonathan, who had been to Oxford for a week to sit for a scholarship examination, on returning to school wrote home saying that the papers hadn't been too bad, and describing pleasant interviews with Merton tutors and even the Warden, in which though he did not say so he had clearly made a favourable impression. His chance of a place seemed good. On the other hand Morcar heard at the Bradford Wool Exchange one Thursday that J. L. Hardaker was ill. A severe coronary thrombosis, it was said.

"He'll need me as much as I need young Oates," thought Morcar at once, and he decided to go over to Ramsgill House as soon as he heard that J. L. was well enough to receive visitors.

When he was at length admitted into Hardaker's handsome old-fashioned bedroom by his daughter-in-law, a pretty but fluttery woman just at the turn of her looks, Morcar was shocked by his competitor's appearance. Hardaker had always looked a tough, sinewy man—a trifle craggy and lined, and limping from his first World War wound, of course, but with a healthy if dull complexion and a solid body. Now his face against the massed frilled pillows looked limp and yellow and his lips were leaden.

"He won't last long, I'd better get on with this merger business fast," thought Morcar. Aloud he said: "I wanted to have a word with you, John. It's this awkward gap in the generations left by the war. Here am I touching seventy, and David Oldroyd, my adopted niece's son, is seventeen. My own son's not with me, you know; couldn't settle after the last war; went out to South Africa to join his mother's brother."

There's two lies for you, thought Morcar grimly; why did I call Jonathan by his father's name? Wishful thinking, I suppose, as usual. Cecil didn't go out to join Hubert Shaw; heaven forbid. But never mind; it's a good Yorkshire motto, keep thysen to thysen; no need to tell Hardaker all the Morcar affairs.

"They're heading for a lot of trouble there," said Hardaker, guarded.

Morcar observed Hardaker's avoidance of comment on Morcar's family matters. He winced slightly. But he was used to this kind of tact. A divorced man with an adopted niece must expect it. For the thousandth time he steeled himself to show no wound, and went on in loud cheerful tones:

"They are indeed. But Cecil and Fan have a fine place. Tobacco." (He couldn't bring himself to admit to apples.) "I went out there last winter. However—to come to this merger idea of mine." Hardaker started, and his dull eyes lighted. "It's this way, who's to fill the gap at Syke Mill between David—Jonathan, I mean, David's son; Major David Oldroyd was my partner, you know—" Hardaker nodded appreciatively—"Who's to fill the gap between the boy and me? I make nothing of managers."

"Nor me."

"Now your two youngsters—what age are they?"

"Both just turned thirty."

"That young Oates of yours you've just made a director—a clever young fellow, by all accounts."

"Yes, he is."

"Married to your grand-daughter, so he's in the family."

"That's right. They've a son."

He's a shrewd, crafty old fox, thought Morcar; he won't come a step to meet me. However, that's all right with me, I don't want a fool in my business.

"Oates is a good designer."

"From you that's praise indeed."

"Capable on the managerial side too, I'm told."

"Aye, he is. But I'm bound to say it's Lucius, my grandson, that I'm most concerned about."

Of course you are, thought Morcar, just as it's Jonathan who's my first care. We've each got a bargaining point in the other's affection. I shan't give mine away.

"Well," he said, with a considering, slightly dissatisfied air. "I'm not an ungenerous man, John."

"I know that, Harry."

"I don't believe in dead wood on boards of directors, though. Your Lucius would have to take his chance."

"That's not a proposition to attract me."

"I can see it wouldn't be. But he'd have his shares, after all."

"He's very good with customers, Harry. They like him. He's very steady and reliable. Especially since he married."

"Oh? He's married? Children?"

"Two boys and a little girl," said Hardaker with satisfaction. "He must have a seat on the board."

Morcar's eagerness was slightly dimmed. Three boys already in the next generation! Nothing pulled a firm down so much as too many relatives drawing salaries from it. However, a gap in the generations was worse. He said carelessly:

"What's your grandson's best line, then? Does he know yarns?"

"He's not too bad there."

I don't believe a word of that, thought Morcar, feeling insincerity in the old man's emphatic tone. Still, if Oates is clever and Lucius is agreeable with customers, it's not a bad combination. Jonathan could learn from both.

"Well—I'll have to think what terms I can offer," he said.

"Aye, do. And let me know. Write to me here, not at the mill."

"I'll do that. No use shouting about the thing till we've got a bit further with it. If it doesn't come off, no one need know."

"No. I'd rather the lads didn't know yet. Might unsettle them," agreed Hardaker.

"He's afraid Oates would leave Ramsgill and come to me if he had the chance," thought Morcar. "Well, we'll see." Aloud he said:

"If we were merged instead of being competitors, we could effect a lot of economies."

"We could."

"And be a really big concern. It's the modern trend. Our cloths would fit in. Your quality's always been good, John."

Quality, yes: design, no, he thought.

"It has been and it is," said Hardaker staunchly.

His eyes gleamed, his cheek had coloured, he looked pounds better than when his visitor had come in, thought Morcar approvingly. All the same, he probably wouldn't last too long. Morcar of course would be chairman of the merged firm's board, because Syke was a much larger concern than Ramsgill; Hardaker could be vice-chairman and fade out quietly after a few years. Then Oates could succeed him and Lucius move up, leaving room for Jonathan.

"Of course, I should have to tie things up pretty tight on my side, you know," he said, thinking of these future developments.

"You'd be foolish if you didn't. But I know I can rely on you to be fair."

"You aren't all that far away from me at Syke Mill," said Morcar, changing the subject because embarrassed by this tribute.

"Not as the crow flies. But we aren't crows. There's a two-three Pennine hills on the way between Ramsgill and the Ire Valley, think on."

"They've improved that road down to the Valley from the moor road above you, considerably of late."

"Is that so?"

"Yes. I came that way this afternoon. You must have a look at it when you're about again."

Neither man was much interested in this matter. Easy inter-communication would, of course, be useful, but transport to Leeds and Bradford was of more importance to the trade of both. The interview was petering out; best cut it short.

"Well, goodbye, John. Take care of yourself."

"I will."

Morcar wondered whether he ought to shake hands but couldn't bring himself to such a display of sentiment, so he waved a farewell instead.

Driving back towards the Ire by the hilly road he had mentioned, Scape Scar Lane, he tried to achieve a dispassionate estimate of the interview just over. He had introduced the idea of a merger without too much fuss, and carried the negotiations sufficiently far to bring out what he and old Hardaker respectively wanted. They were each out to protect their own, naturally; Hardaker, his grandchildren; Morcar, Jonathan. As he topped the hill and turned towards the Ire Valley his mill chimney came into view. It struck Morcar with a sudden pang that he did not really wish in the least to surrender any slightest part of his rule over Syke Mills. He detested, he found, the thought of a merger. But he rebuked himself. For Jonathan's sake, it must be done. He must look to the future. Mergers were the modern trend. For Jonathan's sake, it must be done.

After a good deal of thought he drew up the terms on which he considered a Morcar-Hardaker merger might reasonably be effected, consulted his solicitor as to their legality and feasibility, cut down the legal verbiage in the solicitor's reply and wrote a letter, which he explicitly declared to be unofficial and off the record, to old J. L. Hardaker telephoned fairly promptly to say, of course, that there were several points which required modification but in general the scheme struck him as a basis for discussion. A meeting was arranged at Syke Mills for four o'clock on the following day.

Just before that hour a call was put through to Morcar from Mrs. Edward Oates, who announced in a rather breathless and blurry tone that she was Mr. Hardaker's grand-daughter and he had asked her to let Mr. Morcar know that he would be a few minutes late.

Morcar was annoyed. He had cleared his afternoon and his desk, and arranged to get Nathan out of the way, and postponed his cup of tea till Hardaker could share it with him; he had keyed himself up to the interview and prepared some necessary statistics; he detested unpunctuality, which he thought sloppy and un-businesslike. Moreover, he thought Mrs. Oates' accent languid and la-di-da. His voice was gruff, therefore, as he asked:

"And how long will a few minutes be?"

"He's just left me here, and is driving straight to you. I'm at Ram's Hey; it's an old house on the west flank of Ramsgill."

This precision was an improvement, though Morcar privately thought *flank* a rather highbrow word to use about a hill.

"I don't quite know where Syke Mill is, I'm afraid."

"I know the west side of Ramsgill all right. He'll be ten to fifteen minutes, I reckon."

"I'm exceedingly sorry, Mr. Morcar. I'm afraid the delay is my fault. I detained my grandfather."

"Oh, it's of no consequence," said Morcar, trying to be less gruff as he remembered that both the husband and the brother of this girl would be his partners if the merger went through.

"I'm sorry," came faintly over the telephone, which then clicked off.

"Sounds almost as though she were crying," thought Morcar, surprised and a little sorry.

47

The worst of this delay was that it gave time to recall all his regrets at having to merge Syke Mills. But he stamped these regrets firmly down; he had made up his mind to engage in a merger and he was not a man who changed his mind; he would engage in the merger and make a success of it; he always made a success of what he undertook. He signed a few letters and thought of giving Miss Mellor instructions to put no telephone calls through to him while Hardaker was with him, but decided against it, he did not wish to stress the importance of Hardaker's visit until the negotiations were much nearer completion. And here at last was Hardaker, flushed and breathless.

"Sorry I'm late."

"You shouldn't have hurried up those steps," said Morcar kindly, pushing him into a chair. (He was certainly getting old.) "Tea, Miss Mellor. Cigarette, John?"

"I'm not allowed them."

Tea came and was administered, and Miss Mellor withdrew. Hardaker sipped from his cup gratefully, and his breathing eased.

"I may as well be straight about it, Harry," he began, setting down the cup. "It's a habit of mine. I'm afraid the merger is off."

"Off? Why? Young men don't like it?"

"Nay, I haven't told them. But the one you're interested in— Edward Oates—I don't feel certain about him. My granddaughter and he are splitting up—she thinks he's a scoundrel."

"It may be just an ordinary matrimonial row," said Morcar, laughing a little. (She was crying, then, as I thought; they've had a blazing row and she was crying. Well, well!) "Young women— especially if they're in the family way—get hysterical ideas sometimes."

"She's not in the family way. Nor likely to be. They split rooms a couple of months ago."

"A couple of months? That sounds more serious," said Morcar. "Haven't they any children, then? I thought you said—"

"One. A wreckling, poor boy. Elizabeth says Edward only married her to get into Ramsgill."

Well, that's happened a two-three times before today, thought Morcar sardonically. Princes acquired kingdoms in that fashion, and their subjects followed their example on a lower scale. The marriages didn't turn out all that badly, either. "It would be more

48

convenient if all this were just a young couple's flare-up," said Morcar soothingly.

"It would. But I don't think it's that. Somehow—" Hardaker paused and ruminated. "Somehow I don't think I've ever been quite sure of Mr. Edward Oates. Of course if you want to offer him a big job here in Syke Mills, now's your chance. Take him and welcome."

"Thank you for nothing," said Morcar with a grimace. "I want somebody I can trust."

"Well, you may find yourself able to trust him."

"But *you* can't."

"No. Of course, I may be doing him an injustice. But when his own wife says he's dishonourable and wants you to throw him out—"

"It gives you to think."

"It does indeed."

"Still, women, you know," said Morcar, shaking his head. "They get these whims." He thought of his wife, Winnie, and her entirely false obsession about her brother's death. "And once they've got them, nothing on earth will make them change their mind."

"True."

"Does Oates hold any Ramsgill shares?"

"Yes, damn him," said Hardaker with a sigh. "I shall have to buy him out and that's going to cost a pretty penny. I wish I were misjudging him. He's such a clever lad—really very capable, and as you said yourself, a good designer."

"Pity."

"Would you like to come over and have a look at him? Elizabeth may be wrong, you know."

"I might at that," said Morcar thoughtfully.

He turned his shrewdest look on J. L. Hardaker. An honest, capable business man, not soft, not soft at all, in fact perhaps a trifle hard. What Jonathan would call lacking in imagination. It struck him—a horrid cynical blow—that Hardaker appeared to Morcar as Morcar appeared to Jonathan. It was just possible that Hardaker was being a trifle obtuse, a trifle elderly-prejudiced, about young Edward Oates. Was Morcar prepared to trust Hardaker's judgment in a matter of character? I'd rather trust my own, he thought. He remembered Elizabeth Oates' voice on the telephone. She may be a maungy piece, he reflected. How very convenient it would be if he could get Oates to Syke Mills without any merger! As for a man getting into disagreement with his wife, Morcar, divorced, had not the right to cavil at it. From these confused but relevant reflections, he came to a decision.

"I might at that," he repeated. "But only if he doesn't know what I've come for. Otherwise it's useless."

"How could he possibly guess? *I* shan't tell him, you may be sure."

"Have you mentioned anything at all about the merger to them?"

"Harry," said Hardaker soberly. "I give you my word I haven't said a word of a merger with Morcar's to a living soul. It crossed my mind this morning, when Lucius and Edward Oates both seemed a bit uneasy, that they might have heard a word of it from your side—"

"No!"

"—so I told them I was coming over to see you this afternoon. Just to see their reaction, how they took it, as it were."

"Well?"

"There wasn't any. They showed complete indifference. Didn't even ask me what I was coming to see you about. They dismissed it as just one of old grandfather's—"

"Ploys."

"That's right."

"All right, I'll come," said Morcar, who thought that Lucius Hardaker, Elizabeth's brother, and Edward Oates her husband, partners in the same firm, might well appear a trifle uneasy over a resounding row between Elizabeth and Edward. "Tomorrow, eh? Because if it's not to be a Ramsgill merger, it will have to be somebody else, you know. I want to get a good man settled here and working under me to learn my ways, as soon as possible."

"I understand. And I hope you'll think better of Oates than I do. Come about half-past three and we'll all have our cup of tea together."

"And no mention of a merger or anything of that kind, to a soul."

"You have my word," said old Hardaker stiffly.

Morcar escorted him to the steps. Halfway down he paused and turned.

"Harry, I remember now I mentioned the word merger to my grand-daughter, but not your name in connection with it."

"Tcha! She'll tell her husband and he'll put two and two together," said Morcar, vexed.

"If I'm right about her relations with Oates, she won't."

"And if you're wrong and it's just a married tiff, she will and it won't matter," said Morcar with a grin. "Tomorrow at three-thirty, anyway."

"Well, don't say I didn't warn you."

"I won't."

Like most modern middle-aged households, the Stanney Royd establishment kept no resident help. They would gladly have done so, but nobody nowadays was willing to submit to the curtailment of liberty consequent on residence in an employer's house, and for his part Morcar did not blame them. By employing two daily shifts they managed well enough and left Jennifer free for her cultural and sociological commitees, but these non-resident helps changed often and their free nights changed with them. Of these Morcar had long lost count. He was therefore not surprised when, the house doorbell ringing while they were at their meal that evening, Jennifer signed to Jonathan, who had come home for the Christmas holidays that afternoon, to answer it. He came back looking serious.

"It's the police. A detective inspector to see you. I've put him in the morning-room."

"Jonathan, is this another C.N.D.—" began Morcar, rising.

"'Prank'?" said Jonathan.

Morcar winced. Fancy the boy remembering Morcar's careless word for three or four years.

"No," continued Jonathan. "It's nothing to do with me, Uncle Harry. He wouldn't tell me the purpose of his visit."

Morcar with an impatient exclamation threw down his napkin and strode into the back room, which was generally known in the household as his den. Jonathan had not drawn the curtains, it was a clear night, through the windows the lights of the Ire Valley displayed their usual fine pattern of diamonds on black velvet, clusters on the lower slopes, long slender chains across the upper hills.

"Detective-Inspector Watkins, Annotsfield C.I.D." The fortyish man awaiting him presented his warrant card and gave his name. "Mr. Henry Morcar?"

Morcar grunted assent. "Don't tell me the mill gates have been left open?"

"No. I'm afraid I have some bad news for you. Not about Syke Mills," added the man hastily.

"Is it Nathan?" asked Morcar in alarm.

"No. It's Mr. John Luke Hardaker. I'm afraid he's dead."

"Dead? Well, poor old chap. He was talking to me only this afternoon."

"Yes, that's why I'm here, Mr. Morcar. We understand from his grand-daughter that he left Ram's Hey at three-fifty or so to come and see you at Syke Mills."

"That's correct. He arrived about ten past four."

"And when did he leave?"

"Four-thirty, or perhaps four-forty, four-fortyfive. I don't know exactly. The mill wasn't out. We didn't talk very long. Perhaps four-thirtyfive," said Morcar, wondering what effect old Hardaker's death would have on the proposed merger. Not be able to discuss it for long enough, he thought irritably. Hardaker was a warm man; his estate will be largeish and probate will take forever. Lucius and Elizabeth will inherit. For practical purposes that means Lucius and Oates. Will young men want a merger with me in the chair? Oates will have Elizabeth's shares under his control now, he won't want to leave Ramsgill. Tiresome. "Why does the time matter?" he asked.

"Mr. Hardaker apparently met with a fatal accident on his way home."

"Good God!"

"His car turned over and burned out in the rough ground beside the upper stretch of Scape Scar Lane." Morcar's eyes turned towards the distant hill where the very faint lights of this narrow roadway could be seen coming over the ridge in sharp descent. "The flames were seen by a passing lorry-driver and reported to us by phone about four-fifty."

"The time fits. Well, I'm very sorry," said Morcar soberly. "Sit down a minute, officer. This has staggered me a bit. How did it happen, I wonder?"

"That's what we are wondering too."

"He must have missed his gear change at the top of the Lane," said Morcar. "It's a steep turn there into the main road. You can see for yourself. Or—wait a minute—he might even have gone into reverse gear by accident. Some of the gears in these modern cars are very close together; it's easy to get into the wrong one."

"Mr. Hardaker's was a very good car, sir," said the detective, naming its make.

"True. But Mr. Hardaker's an old man and he's been very ill. The shock would kill him before the fire started, that's one thing to be thankful for. All the same, I wish I'd never mentioned Scape Scar Lane to him."

"You mentioned that route to Mr. Hardaker? May I ask when?"

"Oh, it'll be several weeks ago now, when I went to see him while he was in bed."

"Then anyone might have known he would travel by that route?"

"Anyone could have known in any case," said Morcar crossly. "The re-surfacing of Scape Scar Lane has been a good deal talked about, and discussed in the press, both before and since it was done. It's shortened the route between Ramsgill and Iredale, tremendously."

"Yes, that is so. Mr. Hardaker's body was thrown clear of his car, and sustained multiple injuries."

"I'm very sorry, very sorry indeed. What a way to end! Still, perhaps it's better than lingering a long time with heart trouble. But no, it isn't," said Morcar stoutly. "Everyone wants to live as long as he can."

"You and Mr. Hardaker had a business conference, I suppose."

"Yes."

"I wonder—would you mind telling me its purport?"

"Yes, I should mind very much. It's important to me that it shouldn't be publicly known."

There was a pause.

"Mr. Morcar," said the detective at last, "I hope you will treat what I have to say in complete confidence."

"Of course."

"The fact is, there's some suspicion of foul play about Mr. Hardaker's death."

"What? Foul play? What do you mean?" cried Morcar, horrified.

"The injuries aren't compatible—"

"Oh, come, Inspector, you know how rocky that rough patch of ground is."

"Yes. But it's not just that. The lorry driver thought he saw another car turning out of the lane a moment after Mr. Hardaker's car burst into flames. And besides—this is extremely confidential—"

"Go on, man!"

"A spanner and a jack lever, both blood-stained, have been discovered in the boot of the car of Mr. Hardaker's granddaughter, Mrs. Elizabeth Oates."

"You're not suspecting her, for heaven's sake?"

"No. It seems that her husband was driving her car about the time of Mr. Hardaker's crash—with her brother, Lucius Hardaker. After returning to Ramsgill Mills, Mr. Oates then drove the car home to Ram's Hey. Mrs. Oates then put a suit-case into the boot of the car and drove to her grandfather's house. The suitcase when taken out was found to be bloodstained. To find the cause of the stains, naturally the boot was investigated, and the two weapons were drawn out. They were heavily bloodstained. There was hair too," added the detective.

"Horrible!" said Morcar, feeling sick. "And did Mrs. Oates inform you of all this?"

"No, it was her mother, sir."

"A silly, fluttery woman."

"Mrs. Hardaker is apt, we have observed, to be a little emotional at times. But on this occasion all her statements proved accurate. The weapons are being tested for fingerprints. We are looking, of course," continued the detective after a pause, "for a motive."

"Well, I can't help you."

"But perhaps you can, Mr. Morcar. Perhaps your talk with Mr. Hardaker that afternoon might throw some light."

"I don't see how it can, because neither Mr. Hardaker's grandson nor Edward Oates knew its subject."

"How do you know that?"

"Mr. Hardaker gave me his assurance that he had not told them. However," said Morcar, swinging his foot irritably, "I can see I shall have to tell you."

"If you please, Mr. Morcar."

"We were discussing a proposed merger between our two firms. Mr. Hardaker had more or less decided against it, but we were to have further discussions."

"Did Mr. Hardaker say anything about the terms he was on with his grandson and Edward Oates?"

54

"Well," began Morcar, sighing heavily—"I don't see the use of this, Inspector. Hearsay is not evidence."

"No, but it might give us a line to work on."

"Mr. Hardaker told me that his grand-daughter Elizabeth had fallen out with her husband."

"Edward Oates?"

"Yes."

"Ah! I may say that Mrs. Oates' mother told us the same. And this might affect Oates' future at Ramsgill."

"Possibly. I thought it was just a young couple's tiff, myself. But if it was serious for Oates, that wouldn't account for Lucius Hardaker's attacking his grandfather, would it?"

"There were two bloodstained weapons."

"Well, you'll have to get a firm of accountants in and investigate the Ramsgill finances," exploded Morcar impatiently. "Embezzlement's the only answer, if this foul play story is true at all. I can't believe it, myself."

"It's true, Mr. Morcar," said the Inspector quietly. "It's murder all right. I may say that we've already had the idea about the finances. I'm much obliged to you for your information."

He took his leave, after arranging that Morcar should make a signed statement about the timing and purpose of Hardaker's visit to Syke Mills, at the Annotsfield Police Station, on the morrow.

Morcar returned to the cold room and sat on there, needing solitude in which to absorb the shock and arrange his thoughts. He felt wretched. Although he recognized that he was legally and even morally quite free from blame in J. L. Hardaker's death, he recognised also that his merger plan, which had brought Hardaker to Syke Mills, had at least taken the old man to Scape Scar Lane, where his murderers had had the chance to reach him. Even if the police were mistaken and the car crash was an accident, still Morcar's merger plan had taken Hardaker to Scape Scar Lane. Again, he had not told the Inspector about Hardaker's distrust of Edward Oates, and no doubt this was wrong; on the other hand, much as he now agreed with Hardaker's distrust of Oates, somehow he could not bring himself to hammer nails into Oates' coffin. His plan for a merger would leak out now, and the whole West Riding would wonder what Harry Morcar was up to. He shuddered to think what he had escaped. Suppose he had taken that scoundrel Edward Oates into Syke Mills! Landed Jonathan with him! No more mergers for him! And if no more mergers, what other solution could he find? Of course old Hardaker's death wasn't really Jonathan's fault either, but still ... Yes, he felt wretched.

7. Achievement

"WOULD YOU LIKE a confirmatory copy?" shrilled the telephone.

"Yes, please. When will it arrive?" asked Jonathan eagerly.

"Tomorrow morning."

"Mummy! Mummy!" shouted Jonathan, racing towards the stairs and falling into this childhood's mode of address in his excitement.

"What is it? What is the matter?" cried Jennifer, coming quickly out of old Mrs. Morcar's room with a look of alarm.

"I've got a telegram."

"A telegram?" said Jennifer. She turned pale. (A telegram had brought the news of David's death, all those years ago.)

"Yes. I've got a place, I've got a place. A telegram from Merton. I'm offered a place, I've got a place. In fact, I've got a Postmastership."

"Oh, how splendid, Jonathan, how splendid! I'm so delighted," cried Jennifer.

Colour flooded her face, she ran downstairs, seized her son in a loving hug, and kissed him.

"It's good, isn't it?" said Jonathan, excited out of his customary reserve. "It's more than a place, it's more than an exhibition even, it's a Postmastership! I hardly hoped for that. It doesn't make any financial difference nowadays, of course, but it's a Postmastership. The confirmatory copy will come tomorrow morning. I wish it were here now," he added wistfully.

All his noble dreams for the future, his ardent respect for the work of the scholar, his vision of a university as a place of light, liberty and learning, glowed in his face.

"Come and tell Mrs. Morcar," urged Jennifer. Jonathan bounded up the stairs. "Here's a postmaster of Merton come to see you, Mrs. Morcar."

"My dear boy! Congratulations!" said Mrs. Morcar, stretching out her arms.

The two women made much of him. But Jonathan felt restless; he wanted to be out in the open air, where he could express his excitement in swift steps, he wanted to be alone, where he could triumph in his success, gloat over it, without showing himself conceited or unmannerly.

"I think I'll walk down to Syke Mills and tell Uncle Harry," he said.

"Do, dear," agreed Jennifer.

Jonathan went off down the Ire Valley at a cracking pace, and burst into Syke Mills bright-cheeked and happy. Miss Mellor followed him into the inner office with Morcar's morning coffee.

Morcar had just returned from making his statement to the police. On his desk lay the north-country newspapers, large headlines proclaiming DEATH OF A HUDLEY MANUFACTURER and FATAL ACCIDENT TO MR. J. L. HARDAKER, while smaller print made the ominous announcement that two men had been at the Annotsfield Police Station all night, "helping the police." Morcar looked cross, sallow, and even a little untidy; he had caught cold the night before, sitting in his den without a fire, and felt uneasy in the grip of its incubation.

"I've got a scholarship to Merton, Uncle Harry!" cried Jonathan, suiting his word to Morcar's inexperience.

"Good. I congratulate you," said Morcar drily. "Have a cup of coffee, eh?"

"No, thanks," said Jonathan, to whom anything so mundane as coffee seemed vulgar sacrilege upon this moment of glory.

"Well. Your mother pleased?" said Morcar.

"Yes, very."

At this moment Nathan came in, his ingenuous brow wrinkled with worry, as usual, a letter with a small cutting of cloth pinned to it in his hand.

"Well, I won't interrupt your work, Uncle Harry," said Jonathan hastily. "I just thought you'd like to know."

"Yes. Thank you. Congratulations again," said Morcar, turning to Nathan.

Jonathan rushed out. The cold wintry air seemed marvellously fresh and bracing after the atmosphere of the Syke Mills office and the slight wet-woolly smell which in Jonathan's opinion always haunted textile establishments.

Really, it's a bit too bad, thought Jonathan. He doesn't care a button. Here I've achieved the great ambition of my life, and he doesn't say a word. Well, he did utter *congratulations* twice, as a matter of fact, admitted Jonathan, who prided himself on a scholar's truthfulness and accuracy. But in what a tone! His old bits of cloth are far more to him than my entrance to Oxford. Oxford! thought Jonathan, and winged away again into his radiant dream-world.

8. *Loss*

"I'VE ALL THE troubles of a merger and none of the benefits," grumbled Morcar.

Nathan, who had not forgiven him for having entertained the idea of a merger, looked at him reproachfully and said nothing, but agreed.

For the Hardaker affair went on and on, and Morcar seemed to become as much involved in it as if he had indeed been J. L.'s partner. The West Riding in general appeared to regard this as perfectly natural and took Morcar's participation in Hardaker affairs entirely for granted, while the three Hardaker women whom the tragedy had left without adult male support turned to him with increasing frequency. Laboratory tests established the presence of the fingerprints of Lucius Hardaker and Edward Oates on bloodstained lever and spanner respectively, and there was little doubt of their guilt even before Lucius broke down and confessed to their crime. To Morcar's relief the motive for the murder now appeared not as dislike of the merger but, as he had suggested to the police, in embezzlement of the firm's funds, though the sum concerned, which had been stolen jointly by the two young men—£1800—was ridiculously small, indeed quite pitiful.

"Murder for £1800! It's out of all reason," he said. He turned to Jonathan and added soberly: "Jonathan, I want you to promise me that if ever you get into money difficulties you will come to me before you attempt any remedies on your own behalf."

"I don't intend to get into any money difficulties," said Jonathan.

"None of us do," said Morcar grimly.

"You don't want to be murdered," said Jonathan, evading the subject by making a joke.

"I don't want anybody to be murdered. Jonathan, I'm asking you seriously for your word."

"I don't want to give it to you, Uncle Harry. I'd rather manage by myself."

"That's just why I want your promise. I think you owe it to me, Jonathan."

Jonathan hesitated. "If it can be understood between us," he said at length, "that in informing you of any money difficulties I am not asking for your help and would prefer not to have it, I promise to inform you."

Morcar coloured with annoyance. "You're a great stickler for your own terms, Jonathan," he said gruffly. "But I accept them." He shook out his newspaper and retired behind it, hurt.

"I don't expect it was only the embezzled money which provoked the murder, Uncle Harry," said Jonathan after a few moments' silence.

"What else, then?" said Morcar, emerging, interested in spite of himself.

"Old Mr. Hardaker bossed them too much. They couldn't call their souls their own."

"Oh, tcha!" exclaimed Morcar irritably. "That's child's talk. If people don't want to be bossed they shouldn't allow themselves to be bossed. They should take their own line and stick to it."

"True," said Jonathan thoughtfully. "But you see, he didn't even tell them about the merger. It was their lives he was arranging, and he didn't even tell them."

That Jonathan was probably right, Morcar discovered when at the three women's request he accompanied them to the gaol to see Lucius and Edward.

Lucius was already a broken man; his dark head was grizzled, his face had fallen, his eyes stared blankly, and his body was so emaciated that his clothes hung loose. He wept to his mother, whom Morcar had almost to drag away to give his wife access to him, that he had feared his grandfather's anger too much to confide in him. Between Lucius and his wife Carol there was obviously such a deep love that Morcar turned away to leave them

59

in privacy, and fixed his attention on the other pair. Edward Oates he detested on sight; one of these smooth, foxy, glib young men, completely self-assured and as clever as a load of monkeys, he was now engaged in exercising all his considerable personal charm in trying to win his wife over to his side—he seemed to regard his murder of her father as a mere unfortunate peccadillo for which everyone would find excuses. Under this appeal, to which she made no response, Elizabeth looked sick and exhausted. Morcar well understood why she had come to despise her husband. Not that Morcar cared much for Elizabeth; he thought her too thin and pale and melancholy, over-refined, one of these highbrow types, lacking in vitality, born to be a victim. He noticed, however, as the dreary period of waiting for the trial drew slowly along, that Jennifer liked Elizabeth; they grew quite friendly, and Elizabeth came fairly often to Stanney Royd.

Carol, on the other hand, Morcar liked enormously. If anybody could retrieve anything from the ruin of the Hardaker family, Carol would be the one. Carol was a bouncing, bright-cheeked, black-eyed girl with a thick mop of black hair. Morcar judged her upbringing to be working-class, and she showed all the straight-forward robust common sense natural to such a milieu. During consultations with solicitors she at first sat silent, taking it all in, but later adopted boldly the line that Edward Oates, who it appeared was her brother, was the instigator of the crime.

"He dragged Lucius into it. Lucius would never have thought of such a thing for himself."

"That is a very dangerous suggestion, *very* dangerous to your brother," said the solicitor, shocked.

"I don't care. It's the truth."

"If that is to be the pleading, the two accused must have separate counsel."

"Let's do that, then."

"It will be very costly."

"We all care more for Lucius than for brass."

"Yes, yes," said Lucius' mother eagerly.

"What is your opinion about this line of action, Mrs. Oates?"

Elizabeth turned her head away. "I agree," she said in almost inaudible tones. "Edward must have a separate defence, of course."

"Do you think there's a chance of getting Lucius off, Mr. Morcar?" said Carol as he was driving her home to Hill Rise, the

60

modern style bungalow, with picture windows and everything handsome about it, reflected Morcar sardonically, which old J. L. Hardaker had given his grandson as a wedding present.

"No. But he won't be—"

"Hanged? The worst of it is, Mr. Morcar," said Carol, turning to him in a sudden burst of tears, "He himself wants to be. He told me so."

"Never!"

"Yes, he does. He says it would be less bad for the children. Once he was dead, he says, people would forget."

"Not in the West Riding, they wouldn't."

"We can move," said Carol, undaunted. "But if, just as the children are growing up, their father comes out of prison, a convicted murderer, it will be awful for them."

"He should have thought of that before," said Morcar, grim.

"*I* don't want him dead, Mr. Morcar."

"No, I'm sure you don't," said Morcar with genuine sympathy.

"But what should we do about the mill? I ask you because you understand more about mills than that solicitor. Mrs. Hardaker has no more sense than a baby, and Elizabeth is no use at present. She's—"

"Stunned."

"She's defeated," said Carol bitterly. "Just when we need her, she's no use. But about the mill."

"You won't be too badly off, I think," said Morcar, for old Hardaker, shrewd business man that he was, had settled quite a nice lump of money on his grandchildren, and this, Morcar supposed, they were still eligible to inherit, though their fathers' crime debarred Lucius and Edward from profit.

"But about the mill?" pressed Carol. "Why don't you buy it as a going concern, Mr. Morcar? That's the expression, I believe."

"You learned that from your brother."

"Yes. I did. Why not? He's done me and mine enough harm. He owes me plenty. Why not buy it, Mr. Morcar?"

"It's impossible," said Morcar with a sigh.

"Don't tell me you couldn't find the money."

"Oh, I could find the money, or make my bank find it for me. But I've too much on my plate already, and nobody to share the responsibility with me for a long time yet."

"But, Mr. Morcar—"

"I'm only in the Hardaker affairs by accident," said Morcar irritably.

"Lucky for us that you are!"

This kind of painful scene—visits to the prison, consultations with solicitors, tears from Mrs. Hardaker senior, tortured silence from Elizabeth, forthright attacks from Carol—went on, it seemed to Morcar, for months. Each time he saw the prisoners, Edward Oates looked plumper and smoother, Lucius Hardaker thinner and more haggard. (Young Hardaker won't last long in prison; his spring's broken, thought Morcar.) The heads of departments at Ramsgill got into the habit of ringing him up for advice; at first they had orders to fulfil, and when these were concluded, questions of seeking for more, or paying off the men and closing down, were debated with Morcar by Hardaker's executors. (Luckily one of these was a bank, for Lucius, the other, would not be able to take part.) Morcar was wearied to death with the whole affair, and agreed perhaps rather more quickly than he ought to have done to the closing and auction of Ramsgill Mills.

For in the middle of all this Hardaker worry old Mrs. Morcar suddenly died. As she was now well turned ninety and very frail, this was neither surprising nor greatly lamentable, but Morcar felt vexed on her behalf that her death should have taken place when her son was so harried by other business that he could hardly pay it the full attention it deserved. He made handsome and appropriate funeral arrangements, of course, with his usual competence, but when he tried to think tenderly of his mother, his boyhood when she was really a mother to him seemed light-years away, and though he could recall affectionate incidents from those days, the feeling in them was gone. He sighed and turned perforce to his present problems.

At long last—but how very long it seemed—Edward Oates and Lucius Hardaker were tried at the Leeds Assizes, found guilty, and sentenced to life imprisonment. (Morcar gave evidence and felt that all the Oates and Hardakers stared at him in hatred.) At long last somebody bought Ramsgill House for a nursing home, and somebody else bought Hill Rise for an about-to-be-married daughter, and an art master at Hudley Technical College rented Ram's Hey. The Hardakers then moved away from the West Riding, Mrs. Hardaker with Elizabeth and her ailing child to the south coast—it must be crammed with retired persons; heaven keep me from ever living there, thought Morcar—Carol and her three children to a northern seaside resort; "I won't go away from Yorkshire," said Carol obstinately. Ramsgill Mills were put into appropriate hands for disposal; premises and contents were valued, suitable arrangements for renting made.

All this had taken so much time that it was not till the following December that the auction of Messrs. Hardaker's premises and equipment was advertised.

Jonathan was at home. He had now been a term at Oxford, and had certainly grown up in that time. Physically, though a little taller than before, he now looked more solid as to shoulder and hip; his voice was deeper, his mode of expression more assured; he was now, in fact, a young man, no longer a boy or a lad. Somehow or other he had learned to drive a car, and going off to Annotsfield on the day after his return, triumphantly passed his driving test, which it seemed he had sensibly applied for some weeks ahead. Morcar, pleased, hinted at buying him a bubble car or even a Mini, but Jonathan seemed to have a scruple against accepting such a present. However, Jessop being laid up with rheumatism—"he's getting old," thought Morcar of his ex-soldier chauffeur—Jonathan made himself useful driving Morcar about on business errands here and there, thus easing the parking problem. For really nowadays there were so many one-way streets and ring roads and *no-parking* areas that it was exceedingly difficult to get near one's destination, or at least to park near it; one had to leave one's car half a mile away and walk the intervening distance, which to Morcar's irritation proved apt to make him tired and a little short of breath.

The auction being fixed for a Tuesday, Ramsgill Mills were open for inspection on the Monday and some preceding days. Morcar being regarded as part of the Hardaker family was allowed to retain a set of the mill keys and he took the fancy to visit Ramsgill again, for a final look, on the Sunday morning. He invited Jonathan to accompany him, and the young man agreed.

They entered and made their way to the weaving shed. It was very quiet and very cold. The winter sun shone on the long rows of looms which stood in tragic stillness; they seemed as if yearning for movement, condemned inexorably to death. Here and there one had been covered with a stretch of old ragged cloth. Pools of moisture, condensation from the roof, lay about the uneven flagged floor. The silence, so unnatural in the presence of looms, could be felt. Somewhere a tap dripped very slowly.

"It's a terrible thing to see the place like this," said Morcar, leaning against the end of a loom.

Jonathan looked around but said nothing.

"We haven't acted rightly by this place. When the country needs exports so much, we shouldn't throw away a well-organised production unit like this." Morcar used this abstract description, which he disliked, instead of saying *a mill in full work*, in a conscious effort to adapt his terms to Jonathan's.

"There I agree. But who's *we*, Uncle Harry?"

"The West Riding. We should have formed a syndicate and bought J. L. Hardaker Ltd. as a going concern. If I'd been a bit younger or you'd been a bit older, Jonathan, I'd have bought the firm myself. But as it is, I've got almost more on my plate already than I can manage." He sighed.

There was a long pause.

"Uncle Harry," said Jonathan at length in a strained voice: "I don't want to go into textiles."

Morcar's mouth dropped open. He gazed at the boy, stupefied. "What do you mean?"

"I don't want to go into textiles. They're not my line. I'm not interested in them. I've tried, but I can't be interested."

"But Old Mill's all your mother's," said Morcar in a bewildered tone.

He could not help remembering for a moment his own generosity in this respect. David Oldroyd's Will, of which he and Edwin Harington, Jennifer's only brother, were executors, had bequeathed to David's wife Jennifer all of which he died possessed, which was mostly half the fabric and site of Old Mill and half the shares of Messrs. Oldroyd and Mellor, Ltd., who had carried on textile manufacture there. When G. B. Mellor perished in an air attack over Burma, Morcar bought from his widow, at a rather more than fair price, her husband's half of the fabric and shares, and put them into Jennifer's name, thus securing her, he thought, a reasonable income on which to bring up her infant son. So that Jennifer could feel independent, he did not tell her of his part in the transaction, and indeed nobody knew of it but Morcar and his solicitor. (Edwin Harington by reason of his naval profession—he had risen to some kind of admiral by now—was always off at sea on the other side of the world; with an aristocratic wife and a son at Osborne he concerned himself little with his sister's affairs, trusting them all to Morcar.) Morcar then proceeded to manage

64

Old Mill himself as one of his own properties, taking no director's fee, and had done so ever since.

"Yes, it's all your mother's," he said, thinking of this past history. Suppressing these self-righteous thoughts hastily, he went on: "And half Syke Mills will come to you from me. The other half will be Cecil's, of course, but he'll just draw the dividends on his shares; you'll have the management."

"I don't want it, Uncle Harry!"

"Do you really mean you want to throw away the chance of being at the head of a big textile organisation like mine?"

"Yes, I do. You said yourself that a man should make up his mind what he wants to do, and do it—not let himself be bossed into falling in with someone else's plans."

Morcar was silent. For a moment he saw nothing but his own life, his long hard road to success, the pleasure and pride he had taken in the thought that he could leave half his substantial achievement to David's son, Christina's grandson. Now the whole landscape of his life had collapsed into dust and ashes. Well, pull yourself together, he said to himself at last; don't give way. He made a painful effort and returned by force of will to the present. He saw the rows of motionless looms and the troubled face of the young man before him.

"The Oldroyds have been making cloth for nigh on two hundred years," he said with careful mildness. "And you want to break the tradition."

"I can't help it, Uncle Harry. One can't always be looking back at the past. The day of the family firm is over, anyway. Managerial competence is what counts, not family inheritance. And it's my life, after all. I've only one, and perhaps not much of that."

"What do you mean?"

"Since you and those like you won't ban the bomb."

"Oh, pooh," said Morcar impatiently. "I've been through two wars, and I don't feel so worried."

"The next one will be very different," said Jonathan, sombre.

"True. But I'm not bothered."

"I'm very sorry to disappoint you," said Jonathan stiffly.

"Oh, don't give that a thought. I'm glad it's all come out in good time, and I'm glad you told me of your intentions yourself," said Morcar, sardonic. (I can thank Hardakers' for that, he thought.)

"I haven't spoken of it to mother yet."

"She'll be upset. Your father cared for the textile trade."

Jonathan exclaimed impatiently.

"Jonathan, I've seen you reading books about the history of the industrial revolution. That's just books. Your ancestors *were* the industrial revolution. They made it."

"I can't help it. I'm looking to the future, not the past."

"And what does the future hold for you, if I may ask? What do you mean to work at?"

Jonathan hesitated. "Eventually, I expect, I should like to go into Parliament."

"Well, I hope you'll invent a new political party, then. I make nothing of the three we've got. Two of them are greedy and one's cissy."

Jonathan appeared surprised. "Aren't you a Tory, then, Uncle?"

"No!" roared Morcar. "Good heavens, boy! I was a Liberal before you were born."

"As Roebuck Ramsden said to Tanner in *Man and Superman*," said Jonathan, laughing.

"What does it matter whether Shaw said it or not?" said Morcar, irritated. "I'm saying it now."

"Tanner's answer was revealing," said Jonathan, irritated in his turn.

"Well, come on, let's hear it."

"He replied: 'I knew it was a long time ago,'" said Jonathan. After a moment he went on in a calmer tone: "I'm sorry, Uncle Harry. That was damned rude of me. I'm truly sorry. But the generations can't agree; their ideas are bound to differ. After all, if young people always agreed with their parents, we should all still be wearing woad."

"And who said that?" enquired Morcar, who flattered himself he could detect quotation marks in the voice as well as the next man.

"Anthony Trollope."

"I always thought he was a dyed-in-the-wool church-and-state man."

"He was a man of sense."

"I hope I'm that too," said Morcar. He put on a cheerful look and spoke in an everyday prosaic tone, partly to cover up the tragedy of his disappointment, for it was his Yorkshire nature so to do, but partly also, he admitted to himself, to dash the high

66

drama which Jonathan was evidently playing. "I shan't try to persuade you, Jonathan. I should think that wrong. If you change your mind, come and tell me. What are you going to do before you try for the House, eh?"

"Teach, I think."

Morcar groaned. "Teaching's an awful grind," he said.

"Everything's an awful grind unless you like it, Uncle Harry."

"And you like teaching better than textiles."

"I do," said Jonathan with fervour.

"Well, the best of British luck to you. Let's go home."

"Don't you want to see the rest of the mill?"

"What's the use?" I've earned this lad's living for him all his life, and this is what he gives me in return, thought Morcar. Of course, he admitted, he never asked me to do so. Still ... He felt as though some giant hand had dug out his heart with a sharp-pointed grapefruit spoon. He led the way out of the mill and locked the doors. "You can drive," he said, getting into the passenger seat of his car. "That's what you want, isn't it? To go your own way?"

Jonathan exclaimed, not enjoying this coals-of-fire generosity. He drove out of the yard, stretched out a hand for the mill keys, which Morcar dropped into his palm, and locked the mill gate. Returning to the car and handing back the Ramsgill keys, he did not immediately start the engine.

"Uncle Harry," he said, hesitating: "Nobody can take it from you, you know."

"Take what?"

"Your life's achievement. Your contribution to the textile trade."

"Oh, come off it!" cried Morcar impatiently. The words: *You've dealt me a mortal wound and now you're applying the best butter to it* sprang to his lips, but he managed to suppress them. "Don't worry, lad. I shall get over it, I daresay."

"Thank you, Uncle Harry," said Jonathan.

After this episode Morcar never called Jonathan by the name of David again.

9. Old Mill

THAT EVENING JENNIFER came into Morcar's den, looking pale and harassed.

"Have you a moment, Uncle Harry?"

"Of course. What's wrong? Is it about Jonathan not coming into textiles?"

"Yes. He told me this afternoon. It was the first I had heard of his feeling."

"Well, you don't care," said Morcar out of the soreness of his heart. "You're a Southerner. You don't care about textiles."

"David cared," said Jennifer quietly.

"Yes. But you don't. You'd just as soon see him a headmaster."

"Yes, I would," said Jennifer proudly, raising her head.

"Well, then," said Morcar, "what's wrong? What have you got to worry about?"

He thought he knew all too well what was wrong, namely that Jonathan had taken a decision affecting his whole life without consulting his mother, not even mentioning the matter to her until he had settled it with Morcar. It was her son's lack of confidence in her which distressed Jennifer. Morcar knew it, and knew his pretence not to do so was a lie, but he could not prevent himself from implying this lie, from indeed taking pleasure in doing so.

"I should like to sell my Old Mill shares, Uncle Harry," said Jennifer coldly.

"Good God!"

"To you, of course. I should be grateful if you would buy them."

"I can't do that, Jennifer," said Morcar irritably. "An executor is not allowed in law to purchase any trust property."

"Even if the estate was all settled long ago? It's twenty years since David—was killed."

"It might be legal after such a lapse of time, but I shouldn't like to do it—I should feel under a slur. A trustee isn't allowed to derive any advantage from his position. Wait a minute, though," exclaimed Morcar in sudden recollection. "I seem to remember—"

68

He drew out his keys, opened his wall-safe, and ruffling through the papers in his deed box, drew out his copy of David's Will.

"Yes, there's a clause," he said reluctantly. He read it aloud: *I authorise my trustee the said Henry Morcar notwithstanding that he shall be a trustee of this my will at any time to purchase by private contract all or any part of my shares in Messrs. Oldroyd and Mellor Company Limited if my wife at any time after my death desires to sell any of the said shares.*

The sight of David's clear, firm, highly individual handwriting in the Will's signature, the thought that David's hand had actually touched this paper which he now held, struck like a spear into Morcar's heart. He looked at Jennifer and saw tears in her eyes. There was a pause.

"So you see you *are* allowed to make the purchase," said Jennifer at last.

"Seems so. Why do you want to sell out of Old Mill, Jennifer? David trusted me. Don't you trust me to earn your living for you there?"

"Of course, Uncle Harry," said Jennifer impatiently.

"Why then?" As she hesitated, he burst out: "It's for Jonathan's sake, to free him from textiles. That's it, isn't it?"

"Yes," said Jennifer, weeping.

"To sell Old Mill would have cut David to the heart."

"I know. But it's Jonathan I have to think of now. I must look to his future."

"Leave it a few months, Jennifer," urged Morcar. "Jonathan may change his mind, you know. He's young yet. I won't deny this is a deep grief to me."

He felt he simply could not bring himself to make the loss of Jonathan irrevocable.

Jennifer sighed but acquiesced.

10. Admission

FOR THE NEXT few months Morcar was not only exceedingly unhappy, which might have been borne, but also exceedingly uneasy and uncertain. His life was cut away from under his feet, his aims had been thrown back in his face, he simply did not know what he should do with himself. Meanwhile somebody had to look after his large business, his income, Jennifer's, Jonathan's, and that of his customers and his five hundred employees; there was nobody to do it but Morcar, so he just had to do it. He therefore continued to work and to follow his established routine. Outwardly, he flattered himself, he behaved exactly as usual; he grinned, joked with fellow textile men, kept a sharp eye on everything that went on in Syke, Daisy and Old, made good purchases at the Bradford Wool Exchange, argued keenly about the Government's Beeching policy, drove across Yorkshire to look at the Fylingdales early warning station ("Early! Ha!" said Morcar) and snorted cynically about the House of Lords recommendation that a peer should be able to renounce his peerage for life. ("They want to have it both ways, do they?" he snorted.) But beneath this customary jovial shrewd personality-mask everything was at first hollow, then presently filled, in self-defence, with anger. If the younger generation, represented by Jonathan, rejected him, then by God he rejected them.

Accordingly, all those manifestations of contemporary life which he had hitherto observed with an amused but kindly eye, he now allowed himself to resent. The whole of the West Riding was being torn up to make new roads, so that, for instance, Morcar could now hardly find his way about Bradford. Before Jonathan's defection Morcar, though he felt a nostalgia for the nineteenth-century back streets, the solid Victorian warehouses, which he had known and respected since he was a boy, had admitted that their lighting was often poor, their facilities highly inconvenient, their exteriors dirty, their interiors drab. He had even been able to admire, up to a point, the new soaring, plain, many-windowed buildings. But now he allowed his nostalgia to drown his appreciation.

"The towns are going to become just a swirl of roads with a few buildings allowed to poke their noses in here and there," he said with disgust. "It's all nonsense anyway—in fifty years motor-cars will be out of date, everyone will use a helicopter."

"Well, we shan't be here to see it," said someone comfortingly.

"No, thank goodness," said Morcar.

There was the question, too, of fashion. Morcar was still by no means unsusceptible to the charms of women; he always, from professional habit, noted the clothes they wore, and was proud of

Jennifer's quiet elegance. He had been amused by the *haute couture* racket but knew well how to take advantage of it to his own textile profit. Now suddenly modern fashions seemed unendurably odious to him. These so-called "shifts" deprived women of most of that charming feminine outline which was one of the male pleasures in life, instead making them all look pregnant, so that his eyes almost fell out of his head when he met an elderly lady wearing one. If not in a shift, the younger ones covered themselves—you could hardly call it dressed—in huge roughly knitted clumsy woollen pullovers which hung almost to their knees and deprived them of any outline at all. They thickened their agreeable legs in black ribbed wool stockings, or when dressed up wore hideous shoes with pointed toes and thin heels, balancing on which made their calves swell. Their hair, streaming down in wisps, or piled up in frowsy tangles, looked as if it had not been brushed for a week or washed for a month; their faces were a painter's palette. As for the young men, while black leather jackets and tight jeans were rather agreeable in Morcar's opinion, this frightful fashion of long hair and fringes down to the eyebrows struck him as not only ugly and effeminate but also thoroughly unpractical. How could a man see what he was doing, for heaven's sake, through all that hair? (Even if it was clean.) He gave strict instructions that any employee of his who sported long hair must confine it in a net.

"They may not wish to accept those conditions, Mr. Morcar," said Nathan timidly.

"Then we'll do without them," barked Morcar. "It's a question of safety, Nathan."

Although this was true enough, he knew that to allege it as his main motive was a lie.

Things went on in this embittered, uneasy, not to say wretched manner for some months, with Morcar at his most caustic, until one spring morning when, looking through a rather long business letter which he had dictated the previous afternoon, he found a mistake in it. He summoned Miss Mellor and pointed out the wrong figure to her.

"You've left a nought out," he said. "That's ten times an ordinary mistake, you know. Why, and it's here too. And here. It's all over the letter. You'll have to do all three pages again."

He took up a soft pencil from his desk, and drew thick crosses over each page. He knew this was a cruel over-emphasis of the girl's mistake, but the action eased his overladen heart. As he drew the third cross, however, he read the last sentence of the letter, and instantly remembered having dictated it—he could hear his voice saying the words. This last sentence contained one of the wrong figures in question. He swung round at once to Miss Mellor, who was standing at his side with bent head.

"It was I who gave you that figure," he said. "The mistake isn't yours, it's mine." The girl remaining silent, Morcar exclaimed: "Why didn't you tell me, you silly girl?"

"I have too much respect for you, Mr. Morcar," returned Miss Mellor.

Her tone was quiet and sincere, but behind it defiance crackled.

"Well, well!" said Morcar, rather pleased. "Neither you nor I often make mistakes, Miss Mellor."

"No, sir," agreed Miss Mellor primly.

"And neither of us likes admitting them," said Morcar.

"No, sir." The girl raised her head. Her dark grey eyes sparkled with mingled fun and fury, and she was about to explode into angry comment when Morcar forestalled her.

"Especially when it isn't our mistake," he said.

The girl laughed. It was a joyous sound. For a moment Morcar felt irritated by her youthful mirth. Then his essential good nature, his belief in fair play, rose up in him. "If I can't laugh with her now I've become the kind of oldie young people think we all are," he thought. He laughed, and said: "Well, I apologise, Miss Mellor. What is your first name, by the way?"

"Ruth."

"Well, Ruth, let's go over this letter together and correct my errors. Two heads are better than one."

While the letter was being corrected Morcar felt more like himself than he had done for months. But when this was done and Ruth withdrew to retype it, he sank into gloom. If he had begun to make mistakes when dictating letters, he had indeed entered old age. For the first time he was obliged to admit that he had shown himself no wiser than the younger generation. Ruth, an adolescent with long curving hair, had seen his mistake before Morcar. You'd better show the young some indulgence, he thought, because you're going to need some yourself. He felt defeated, daunted.

But here his Yorkshire tenacity rose up sternly, saying: well, don't give in. You've always prided yourself on working hard and

72

trying to be fair; well, keep on working hard and trying to be fair. Don't give in!

"I won't," he said to himself. "But it's going to be a tough job," he added grimly.

His spirits went up and down from day to day according as he succeeded or failed in keeping this decision.

11. Jonathan's Mother

"MAY I COME in, Jonathan?" said Jennifer, tapping on her son's bedroom door.

"Come in!"

Jonathan was sitting up in bed, surrounded by an apparatus of textbooks, notebooks and writing materials.

"You're looking very dashing, Mum."

"I've been to a musical evening."

"For some charitable cause, no doubt."

"No doubt."

"I like that little black number you're wearing."

"Uncle Harry doesn't; he thinks it shows too much, I'm afraid."

"Oh, Uncle Harry!" said Jonathan, and they smiled kindly together.

"I came to ask you a question, Jonathan. Please answer truthfully. I want to consult you before I take a decision."

Jonathan coloured a little under the implied reproach in his mother's phrasing.

"I'm usually fairly truthful, I believe."

"Yes, you are. It's this. I received a proposal of marriage tonight."

"What!" said Jonathan, crimsoning.

"From Nat Armitage."

"I remember him vaguely. He's a sort of connection of the Oldroyds."

"Who isn't, in the West Riding? The connection's not near enough to matter."

"And are you thinking of accepting?" asked Jonathan drily.

"I'm asking your views on the matter, Jonathan."

"I'm rather surprised, Mother," said Jonathan in a choked tone.

"I shall never really love anyone but your father," said Jennifer, looking aside. "But one has a life to live. And you don't need me any more."

"Mother!"

"I should deceive myself if I thought you really needed me any more."

What was one to say? "Well, one grows up," muttered Jonathan.

"Exactly. If I thought it would hurt you—deeply," proceeded Jennifer, bringing out her words with difficulty, "of course I should decline."

"That's not fair," said Jonathan hotly. "To put the decision upon me, that's not fair. Of course I should be jealous," he went on, trying his utmost to be honest, "yes, I should be jealous in some degree. But I shouldn't consider I had any right to—obstruct—the match in any way. He's just the kind of man I dislike, as it happens," he burst out suddenly: "Very public school and Tory, and rich, shooting-box and territorials and a big mill and all that. And a widower. But if that's what you like ... At least he has the sense to appreciate you. You're very beautiful, Mummy," he concluded wistfully, gazing at her.

Jennifer smiled at him rather sadly.

"Thank you, dear."

"Why has it come to a head now? He's known you long enough."

"He has asked me before, but I declined. You don't need me now, Jonathan."

"I *do*, Mother. But don't let that deter you, of course."

"If I accept, and we marry, will you come and live with us?"

"No!" exploded Jonathan. He thought suddenly of the memorials of his father which hung above his head, and felt a burning jealousy on their account. But that's not the whole truth; I feel jealousy on my own account, he admitted honestly. "Mother, I shall soon not be living at home at all," he said in his most controlled and courteous tones. "When I've taken my degree I shall find a teaching post. So don't consult my—" He hesitated. Wishes? That implied he disliked the marriage. Convenience? Cold and untrue. He threw away the sentence unfinished—a habit he despised—and went on: "You must follow your own—" again he hesitated, but forced himself to find a word—"inclinations. Uncle Harry's going to be lonely. But of course you mustn't think of that."

"He wouldn't want me to think of that. He would wish me to lead my own life."

"That's true," said Jonathan, for the first time feeling some real remorse towards Morcar.

"But I don't believe I can bring myself to do it," said Jennifer with a sigh.

Jonathan found himself struggling not to feel an immense but he judged ignoble relief. Such Freudian jealousies, he had thought, belonged surely only to an older generation unaware of them.

II

CHUFF AND SUSIE

II: CHUFF AND SUSIE

12. Winnie is Still Winnie

MORCAR HAD BOUGHT some new machinery for dealing with cloth woven from man-made yarns. He hated man-made yarns as much as he loved wool, but he saw that the future might largely lie with them, so he conceived it his duty to participate in their promotion. In spite of his prejudices he became interested in their promise, and was standing in the shed across the yard looking at the machines one morning when Ruth Mellor, looking rather pale, approached him.

"There's a cable for you, Mr. Morcar," she said.

Morcar held out a hand for it.

"I left it in the office."

"Oh?"

"It's from South Africa."

"Cecil," thought Morcar. "Wanting money again, I expect."

Half exasperated, half pleased that his son should turn to him and he should have the power to help him, he strode across the yard, with Ruth Mellor keeping up pretty well at his side. When they reached the office she ran ahead, snatched up the cable from where it lay on his desk, and handed it to him, folded.

"I'm afraid it's bad news, Mr. Morcar," she said, and withdrew.

Morcar unfolded the slip of paper and read:

DEEP REGRET INFORM YOU CECIL FAN KILLED BANTU RIOT MORCAR AND I EXECUTORS CHILDREN SAILING ENGLAND END MONTH HUBERT SHAW.

Morcar sat down abruptly. Cecil dead! The good, kind, slow Cecil, his son whom he had never really known. His thoughts flew back to that day, so long ago now, it must be over forty years, when he, a young soldier returning from the First World War, held his baby son proudly in his arms and loved him. The very pattern of the woollen shawl in which Cecil was wrapped, the feel of the infant's slight warm weight against his body, came back to him. He grieved.

And Fan! That bright, undaunted little pussy. A pity. He must telegraph her mother. Ah! Cecil's mother! Winnie! It will break her heart. I shall have a bad time there.

He pressed the bell, and Miss Mellor came in, with a steaming cup of coffee in her hand. No wonder she had looked pale. Tactful of her to get him back to his office so that he was not in the public eye when he received the news.

"Miss Mellor," he said, his voice hoarse but in control. "Take this telegram." He dictated a longish message to be sent to Mrs. Oldroyd senior, embodying the news of Fan's death. "And telephone my wife, Mrs. Winifred Morcar—" he gave the address in Hurstholt Road and the telephone number—"and say I'm coming over to see her at once. It's very urgent. She must wait in for me. I'll compose obituary notices when I get back. Tell Jessopp to bring the car round."

"Yes, Mr. Morcar. Have a cup of coffee before you go."

"All right, Ruth. Get Jessopp. 'Phone my wife quickly. Don't mention the news."

As he drank the hot liquid—which was certainly steadying—he read the cable several times again. There was a kind of mean scantiness about it which was just what he would have expected from a Shaw. As he re-read, he became eventually aware of a rather odd construction in its phrasing. Why say *Morcar and I*, and not the more natural *you and I*? Oh, of course, thought Morcar sardonically; he's sent the same cable to Winnie—there's a cheaper rate for the same wording to two addresses, I daresay. Well, I shan't have to break the news to her, then, he thought, relieved. Children sailing *end month*. That's quick. They won't inherit much. And anything they inherit Hubert Shaw will grab if he can. Morcar drew the telephone towards him, rang up his solicitor and instructed him to employ the most reputable lawyer in Jo'burg to act for Morcar in the matter of Cecil's estate. Ruth Mellor came in to say that Jessopp and the car were waiting.

He was halfway to Hurstholt Road before he remembered that it was tactless of him to take Jessopp where Winnie could see him, but it was too late to do anything about that now. He wondered whether to tell Jessopp to put him down at the end of the road, but refrained, partly because Winnie would instantly detect the deception and partly because his native obstinacy would not allow him to attempt any concealment from her. As they drew up he noticed that the small flower-bed, which he remembered bright with red geraniums, was now planted with dreary bushes bearing speckled leaves, and that the curtains were all drawn at the windows. Though he was relieved to find his guess thus confirmed that his ex-wife already knew of her son's death, this outdated sign of mourning struck Morcar as the height of vulgarity, and he strode up the short asphalt path in a fury. The front door opened before he reached it, and Winnie stood there waiting for him.

As always, the sickness he had felt in anticipation of seeing her was doubled by her actual appearance. Now extremely thin and somewhat stooped, her hair frizzed to a kind of burned saffron, her once pert little features reduced to a predatory sallow sharpness, clad in an ill-fitting dress of shrill green with a great many strings of beads of varied colours round her withered neck, she resembled a witch in a television fairy tale; the sight of the wedding ring on her wrinkled hand, and the thought that he had once experienced copulation with her person, brought his nausea almost up into his mouth. Then he saw her red tear-filled eyes, pity rushed back and he regained his control.

"This is very bad news for both of us. I see you know it, Winnie."

"Hubert cabled. I haven't had time to change into my black," said Winnie, leading the way into the small front room.

"Never mind," said Morcar, wincing at this stale vulgarity, and at the awful bad taste—the clashing colours, the cheap materials, the hideous shapes—of the furnishings of the room, some objects of which had a horrible cheap would-be "with-it" smartness, and some he recognised as having formed part of their original ingenuous household nearly fifty years ago. What does she do with her alimony? wondered Morcar, furious; at the same time reflecting gratefully how much he owed to Christina, who had educated his taste, and to Jennifer, who managed his household so gracefully and well. In spite of himself his voice roughened.

"I've had my solicitor cable out to a good lawyer in Johannesburg, to look after Cecil's affairs," he said.

"Hubert will look after them," said Winnie sharply. "Sit down, Harry. Do you know anything about—how it happened?"

"No. Only what you do," said Morcar, who had observed a copy of the cable he had received from Hubert, lying on the table.

"Poor Cecil. My poor boy, he was always so good to me," said Winnie.

She wept. Morcar sat silent, respectful to her grief, waiting gravely till she should feel able to speak again. At length she dried her eyes, and without looking at him said in that peculiar tone which Morcar had learned to recognise as marking the onset of some chicanery:

"The children are sailing for England at the end of the month, I see."

"Yes. Hubert will notify us of the ship they're sailing on, I suppose, or if not—" if he's too mean to spare the shillings for the cable, thought Morcar—"I'll get my Jo'burg man to do so. I'll meet them in London." He forced his generosity, his sense of duty, to its utmost limit, and managed to utter: "Would you like to go with me?"

"No, I think I'll wait for them here," said Winnie. Morcar repressed a sigh of relief. "I shall be busy, getting their rooms ready, and that."

"Their rooms ready? What are you talking about, Winnie? Chuff and Susie will come to Stanney Royd, of course."

"My grandchildren will come to me!" shrilled Winnie, her small eyes suddenly blazing.

"Now listen to me, Winnie," said Morcar in a burst of rage. "You took my son, you took Cecil, from me. You're not going to take my grandson. He's coming to me. You made a mess of Cecil, you're not going to spoil Chuff's chances."

"I did *not* make a mess of Cecil!" shouted Winnie. "He's a good boy."

"You brought him up to be a dunderhead, an innocent, a dullard who can't write a decent letter or stand up for himself."

"He's your son as well as mine."

"It's a pity you didn't say that in the first place."

"I don't know what you're talking about."

"Oh yes, you do. When I came back from the war you told me Cecil wasn't my child. That's the cruellest thing a woman can do to a man."

"Oh no, it isn't. It might have been true," said Winnie with malice.

"I don't think adultery would have been as bad," said Morcar bitterly. "As it was, by a lie you deprived me of my own son's love all my life."

"No, I didn't. He always doted on you."

82

"But why on earth should he?" said Morcar, disgusted, remembering nevertheless that Fan had said the same.

"How should I know? He was obstinate, like you, that's all. Pig-headed. Oh, Cecil! My poor Cecil! What have they done to him? He was always such a good boy."

"Winnie, I know how you loved Cecil, and I respect your grief," said Morcar gravely. "But Chuff and Susie are coming to me."

"No!"

"By God, Winnie!" shouted Morcar. "If you take Chuff from me, I warn you I'll cut down your alimony to what was legally assigned to you."

"If you do, I'll take you to court."

"That'll cost you plenty."

"But you wouldn't do that to me."

"Oh, yes, I would. Now I'm warning you."

"You wouldn't do that when I've father to keep."

"I thought he was dead long ago," said Morcar roughly.

"He's lying in bed upstairs this minute. You'd best see him, he'll expect to see you."

Morcar had not the slightest desire to see Mr. Shaw, whom he had always detested, but he felt he could not refuse, and followed Winnie up the steep narrow stairs reluctantly.

Mr. Shaw, the arch-twister, lay, a crumpled mass of wrinkles, grey hair, tangled grey beard and repulsive purple and orange striped pyjamas, beneath a stained crimson quilt. Morcar, used to seeing his mother in the clean bed-linen and pastel shades of silk and lace which Jennifer provided, was shocked

"He's nearly ninety-two," said Winnie proudly, smoothing the coverlet.

"Well, Mr. Shaw," said Morcar, forcing himself to offer his hand.

"Well, Harry."

"Winnie and I have been talking about Chuff, Cecil's son."

"I heard what you were saying," said Mr. Shaw, his beady black eyes sparkling with malice.

"Well, I hope you're on my side, and mean to let your grandson have all the advantages I can give him."

"You've got the money, Harry," said Mr. Shaw with an air of virtue in defeat, "so I expect we shall have to do what you say."

Winnie burst into tears. For the first time, Morcar felt sorry for her.

"I'll just have little Susie, then," she sobbed.

"No, you won't. I'm not going to separate brother and sister."

"You are cruel, Harry. Cruel. Am I never to see my own grand-children, then?"

"Of course you are," said Morcar irritably. "They can come and see you every week. Every Sunday, say. And go holidays with you. But they'll live with me."

Winnie turned and led the way downstairs. Morcar perforce followed. Mr. Shaw's thin voice, demanding his morning cup of tea, pursued them.

"You're blackmailing me, Harry," said Winnie, turning on him at the foot of the staircase.

"I know I am." (It's the only way to deal with the Shaw family, he said to himself.) "I don't care. I mean to have my grand-children in my charge."

"I'd best put the kettle on," murmured Winnie.

She went into the tiny kitchen. Morcar followed and stood in the doorway, one hand on the wall.

"You've ruined my whole life, you know, Harry," said Winnie, turning to him.

"You've ruined mine."

"I don't think so. You wouldn't have gone so far up, so fast, with a wife and child hanging round your neck."

The awful sordidness of this wrangle beside a gas cooker while his son lay dead, his wife holding a spent match while the kettle began to sizzle, struck Morcar of a sudden as unbearable.

"There are more things in life than money, Winnie," he said.

"It's easy for you to say that when you've got plenty."

"I've had no wife, no child, no home, all my life," said Morcar, the words tumbling out fast: "You took all that from me. And for what? A silly mistaken obsession about your brother's death—"

"You left Charlie out to die."

"No, I did not!" shouted Morcar. "Listen to me, Winnie; for once in your life, listen to me. Charlie and I and Jessopp and two other chaps were out on patrol. We came under machine-gun fire. Charlie got a bullet in his head and Jessopp got one in his jaw."

"Why didn't *you* get a bullet?"

"God knows. It was just one of those things. I carried Charlie back to our trenches, and then I went back to help Jessopp."

"And got a medal for it."

"Charlie was dead the moment the bullet struck him."

"Who says so? If you'd stayed to look after him—"

"Captain Francis Oldroyd. I may say that when I met Colonel Oldroyd some twenty-five years later, he said that Charlie was dead when he reached the trench."

"He said that because you asked him."

"No! He said it to me at once. I've told you all this twice before, Winnie. This is the third time. I shan't tell it you again, and I expect you to believe me."

There was a pause.

"It was the medal I couldn't stand, Harry. I couldn't stand you getting a medal while Charlie was dead."

"Winnie, Charlie was my best friend; I've never had another."

"It's all very well, Harry, but there's that Jessopp sitting out there in a fine thick uniform in your fine handsome car, while Charlie's dead. And Cecil's dead," she broke out, wailing. "Was he happy in South Africa, Harry? I couldn't tell from his letters. And you never thought to come and tell me about him, after you'd been to see him."

Morcar coloured, ashamed.

"Yes. I think he was happy. He and Fan—it was still good between them, and he had two fine children."

"Of course I know you always hate to see me." Morcar was silent. "But you might have come and told me when you got back from South Africa. You might have done more for him, Harry."

"I bought him his farm and he had an allowance every year."

"They were always short of money, though."

"I didn't know that till recently," thought Morcar, but he did not speak the words. Winnie gave him a sharp glance.

"And what will your grand Oldroyds think of all this, then? Two more kiddies to inherit your wealth."

"They'll welcome them, of course."

"Are you sure of that, eh?"

"Quite. They're not your kind of people at all," said Morcar, unable to refrain from this insult.

"I'm glad of that," flared Winnie.

"So am I," said Morcar brutally.

"Is that Jennifer your child by Christina, then?"

"Don't be silly, Winnie. No."

"Everybody in Annotsfield thinks so, you know."

"They can think what they like. It isn't true. Jennifer was in her teens when I first met her mother," said Morcar, hating himself for stooping to an explanation.

"I reckon you wish she was your child, though."

"Yes, I do."

At this moment the kettle began to whistle its head off.

"I must go up to Father," said Winnie, turning to the cooker.

"I'll go. I'll keep in touch with you about the children, Winnie, notify you of the date of their arrival and so on."

"All right. Harry!"

"What now?"

"Don't be too hard on Hubert. You've got plenty and he hasn't, you know."

"It's not in me to let myself be cheated, Winnie."

"We've all noticed that," sneered Winnie.

With an exclamation of fury Morcar flung himself from the house. Winnie, in spite of the kettle's shrill message, followed him, and stood at the front door to watch him go.

She wore a strange smile. Morcar, throwing himself back against the car cushions, sweating and exhausted, suddenly found himself wondering whether all this sound and fury had not been a pre-arranged scene, planned by Winnie with her father to force upon him the entire care of their grandchildren. He was to think it a victory for him while she knew it was a victory for her. Winnie was capable of such a scheme. Yes, he inclined to think this was the truth. Yet, he could not but remember her real love for Cecil. Well, he would never know. Let her think what she liked. He would have the children.

When he reached Syke Mills he found Jonathan in the office. The young man rose as he entered and greeted him gravely.

"We've heard the news, Uncle Harry. Miss Mellor telephoned. I'm deeply sorry. I just come down to see—I don't suppose there's anything I can do?"

"No, thanks, Jonathan. I appreciate your sympathy," said Morcar, seating himself at his desk.

"Is there anything more known about how it happened?"

"Not yet. A Bantu riot, the cable says."

"A terrible end."

"Oh, I don't know. It would be quick, anyway," said Morcar wearily.

"Yes, but the fear! But what can they expect, out there?"

"Cecil wasn't a *baaskap* man in the slightest degree. He was very mild and kind and unprejudiced."

"The innocent suffer with the guilty."

"They do indeed. Cecil's two children will be coming to Stanney Royd."

"Oh, good!" said Jonathan, brightening.

13. Grandchildren

WITH HER CUSTOMARY tact Jennifer gave Chuff a bedroom of the same dimensions and view as Jonathan's, and allotted to Susie old Mrs. Morcar's large front room. When she requested Morcar's approval for these decisions, he thought the latter arrangement would have pleased his mother, but the room rather large for so young a girl. He said so.

"But she'll grow up. They grow up so quickly, Uncle Harry," said Jennifer.

"Too true," said Morcar grimly, remembering Jonathan's overnight transformation.

He stood now on the London dock and watched his grandchildren descending the ship's gangway. Chuff seemed to have grown rather large and tall, and his reddish hair had settled into a not unpleasing tawny. If he held himself better, developed better manners and (for heaven's sake! thought Morcar, looking with disgust at the lad's cheap striped suit) wore better clothes, he would be quite good-looking in a heavy way. Susie hung her head, so that her fair hair drooped about her face; Chuff, Morcar noticed, held her arm tightly. Stepping off the gangway, they stood looking round, uncertain, buffeted a little by other disembarking passengers. Morcar had cabled to the ship that he would meet them, and was a little disappointed, though he told himself that this was unreasonable, that they did not at once perceive him. He stepped forward and waved. Chuff's face at once lighted.

"Grandfather!" he exclaimed.

Morcar shook hands, and stooped to kiss Susie. She did not raise her head, and Morcar's lips touched her cheek only through a veil of hair. Even this slight contact, however, disconcerted him;

the cheek which Morcar remembered as warm, round, firm,
seemed now slack, pale and limp.

"Have you had a bad voyage? Rough, I mean? The English
Channel can be rough, I know."

"No," said Chuff. "Not rough. But long."

"It would have been better perhaps to come by air," said
Morcar.

"Uncle Hubert thought otherwise."

He spoke on a note of sarcasm which Morcar had never heard
in Cecil's voice. Morcar glanced at him sharply. The boy's face
was sullen with pain. Natural, of course.

"I'm very glad you've decided to come home to England, Chuff.
A bit surprised, perhaps. But glad."

"Well, it will be different," said Chuff, glum.

They piled into the taxi which Morcar had pre-engaged and
began their long drive west. Morcar pointed out objects of historic
interest: the Tower, St. Paul's, the various bridges. Chuff looked
at them with a certain sulky interest which however seemed to
increase, Susie did not move or speak.

"I thought you might want to stay out in Africa with your
Uncle Hubert, but I'm glad you didn't," resumed Morcar, trying
to ensure that the boy felt welcomed.

Chuff's face hardened. "Uncle Hubert didn't want me. He's
only my great-uncle, father's uncle, after all. I just call him
Uncle—"

"By courtesy. Yes."

"He's got plenty of children and grandchildren of his own to
look after. He doesn't want me. I don't want to go where I'm not
wanted."

"Quite right," agreed Morcar with emphasis, remembering a
time in his youth when he had felt just the same.

"I don't think much of the Shaws, Grandfather."

Morcar bit back his own strong agreement with this proposition.

"Of course," said Chuff slowly, "Father was different."

"Yes."

"He was only half a Shaw, he wasn't like them at all. Never
went after his own advantage. He was too good, really. I see that
now. Mom was a bit hard on him, I think."

"Your father and mother were very much attached to each
other."

"Yes, I think they were, really," said Chuff, a hint of question, however, in his tone.

"I know they were," said Morcar emphatically.

Chuff seemed reassured.

"Are we," he began slowly, "are we going to live with you or with Grandmother? You don't live together, I believe." He blushed in embarrassment.

"With me," said Morcar.

"Oh. Well," said Chuff, brightening. "You don't mind me asking?"

"Not at all."

"I just wondered. Susie wondered."

Susie, sitting between Morcar and her brother, made a very slight movement, the first sign of life she had shown. Morcar put his arm round her shoulders, which he found painfully thin.

"Your Aunt Jennifer is looking forward to seeing you, Susie. She really is your aunt, you know; she was married to your mother's brother—well, half-brother. But they were very close."

Susie said nothing.

They were just in time to catch the Pullman to the north. Chuff seemed decidedly cheered by the amenities of this train, and ate heartily of the luncheon, which fortunately happened to be of good quality. Susie had to be coaxed to choose the dish she wanted, said one word in a whisper, and ate almost nothing. Morcar, remembering her merry little face, her former gay laughter, was growing disturbed. When she was absent for a few minutes in the lavatory, he took the opportunity to ask Chuff quickly:

"What's the matter with Susie? She seems so different."

"She seems as though she can't get over it, you see," said Chuff. "She was very fond of father."

"I know."

"She saw him, you see. He was all—sliced up," said Chuff.

His voice held pain, and tears stood in his eyes.

"Oh, no!"

"Yes. Well, it was like this, you see. Susie and I had been to Uncle Hubert's for a week in the holidays, and Father and Mom were coming to fetch us back. They didn't come and they didn't come, and there was no reply on the 'phone, and finally Uncle Hubert got annoyed and said he'd drive us back himself. Well, he did, and we came to this village and there were police all about and they wouldn't let us through, and we got out and went into the police station, and Susie ran ahead, and they were lying there —Father and Mom, I mean. Susie was dreadfully upset, and she's hardly spoken a word since. It was a mistake, you know, letting her in, but she slipped by."

"Good heavens! It certainly was a mistake."

"They didn't mean it," said Chuff, frankly weeping. "They wouldn't let me go in. It was a mistake. Susie ran ahead. It upset Susie. A shock, you know. She's only young."

"You must have had a difficult time on the ship with her."

"Yes, I did really," said Chuff with a sniff.

"Well, that's over now. We'll look after her. Your Aunt Jennifer will know what to do. We'll have the doctor. We'll get her well."

"I think Susie was kind of hoping she would live with Grandmamma—being father's mother, see."

The thought of the pale, delicate Susie in Winnie's coarse hands made Morcar feel quite sick, and he was about to say firmly that it had been decided that Chuff and Susie should live with him, when he remembered Jonathan's comment on old Hardaker's arrangement of the younger generation's lives. Yet uncertainty, he felt sure, would be the worst possible thing at the moment for these two homeless children.

"*I* don't want to," put in Chuff.

He sounded anxious. Morcar said cheerfully:

"I want you and Susie to live with me, and it's been decided with your grandmother that you shall do so. But if after a year you or Susie want to change, you can do so. I hope you won't, but I shan't take it amiss if you do."

"Shall we see Grandmamma, then?"

"Yes. Next Sunday," said Morcar grimly.

Chuff relaxed and became quite talkative and friendly. He explained what Morcar had said, to Susie on her return. She gave a faint smile but said nothing.

"I didn't recognise you when we first came off the ship, Grandfather," said Chuff cheerfully. "With your hair being so much more grey in front now, you know. That's how it was."

Morcar sighed.

14. Susie and Jonathan

JONATHAN, RETURNING FROM voluntary personal service in Jugoslavia, in dirty khaki shorts and shirt, very brown and dusty, and tired with the weight of the heavy knapsack on his back, emerged from Annotsfield railway station and climbed thankfully into the Marthwaite bus. To be at home and in a hot bath was his great desire at the moment, and as the bus rolled along the Ire Valley, quiet and empty on this hot summer Sunday afternoon, he could think of little else, though he tried hard to direct his mind to nobler subjects.

The bus paused at one of its appointed stopping-places. An old man dismounted. Jonathan glancing out idly saw a child standing at the other side of the road; when the bus drew up she started forward as if perhaps she suddenly realised that that vehicle was the one for her purpose. Neither driver nor conductor saw her, and the bus moved on. The child returned to the pavement and stood there listlessly, with hanging head. Jonathan felt idly sorry for her. The bus complementary to his own, on its way back into Annotsfield, passed by and drew up beside the child; she exchanged a few words with the conductor, but did not mount, and the bus moved on. The child gazed yearningly after Jonathan's bus. The road was now empty, the old man who had left the bus had vanished. There was something so forlorn in the child's stance that compassion stirred uncomfortably in Jonathan's heart. She's lost, he thought; she doesn't know which bus to take. There's nobody for her to ask. Oh, *Lord*, what a nuisance, thought Jonathan crossly. I shall have to get out. All that way back in this heat! He rose.

"Next stop, please."

"It's a long way on," said the Jamaican conductor, grinning ruefully.

"Oh, Lord!"

"You'se missed your right stop?"

"Yes," said Jonathan with a sigh.

"Bus slow down round this curve, if you'se hop off while I not looking—"

"A good time will be had by all."

The conductor laughed, showing his fine white teeth, and hauled Jonathan's pack out from behind the steps by one strap.

"I best throw this out after you. Too heavy to jump with."

"Thanks," said Jonathan. "That's very kind of you."

The descent of man and pack was safely accomplished, and Jonathan trudged back along the hot road. The child was still standing exactly where the bus had left her; it struck Jonathan that she was perhaps a little older than he had imagined. He crossed the road to her.

"Can I help you?" he began politely.

The child leaped back and cowered against the wall. She actually trembled, and there was a look of such naked fear in her eyes that Jonathan was shocked.

"Don't be afraid," he urged. "I only want to help you. You're lost, aren't you?"

The child nodded, her very fair hair rippling in the sunshine as it swung.

"Where do you want to go?"

"Stanney Royd," whispered the child.

"Stanney Royd! Why, that's where I live. You must be Mr. Morcar's grand-daughter. Are you? Are you Susan Morcar?"

"Yes," whispered Susan.

"Well, that's very nice," said Jonathan heartily. "Very nice indeed. Because I'm your cousin, you see. Half-cousin if you want to be exact. Your mother and my father were stepbrother and sister. I'm Jonathan Oldroyd."

To his disappointment this statement did not seem to reassure Susie; indeed she turned on him a look of pale despair which was quite heart-breaking.

"We shall have to wait for the next Marthwaite bus," he said cheerfully. "I'm afraid it will be a long time. The service is poor on Sundays. It comes on the other side of the road. We'll go across."

As she made no attempt to stir he took her hand in his and led her across to the bus stop. Here he shed his pack with relief, but looking at his watch saw with dismay how long they would have to wait before the next bus came. She looks as though she would faint, thought Jonathan in alarm.

"Let's lean against the wall. Well, why don't we sit on it?" suggested Jonathan. Susie looked at the wall as though to mount it were quite beyond her powers. "Turn round and bend your arms and keep your elbows in," he commanded.

She did this with a prompt accuracy which showed Jonathan that she knew this method of lifting. He put his hands under her elbows and heaved. A sinewy young man, he had yet expected to be obliged to a considerable effort, but Susie's weight was so slight that she came off the ground with ease. She gave a wriggle and was comfortably seated on the wall. Jonathan heaved himself up beside her.

"Well, this is pleasant," he said, kicking his heels against the wall. "Don't you think so, Susie?"

She rewarded him with a faint smile.

"That's Syke Mills," said Jonathan, encouraged, pointing to the large block which lay between them and the beginnings of Annotsfield. "The mill your grandfather owns. My grandfather used to own it. That hill is Scape Scar."

He wondered whether to embark on the story of the Luddites, to pass the time. But no, he checked himself hurriedly; there was a murder in that story, and Susie had had enough of murders lately.

"Do you see that small mill chimney over there, in the distance, up valley?" he said. "Down by the river."

She turned her head, but was not looking in the right direction for Old Mill. He took her hand and pointed it; she made a faint sound which might have been the beginning of a laugh.

"That's my mill," said Jonathan with a sigh.

"Do you work there?" breathed Susie.

"No."

"Why not?"

"I don't want to."

Susie turned and gazed at him. Her eyes were such a deep, pure blue and their expression so astonished that Jonathan was glad to turn away his attention to a car which just rushed round the distant curve. What a piece of luck! It was the white Jag which belonged to Nat Armitage. Jonathan leaped across the pavement and flagged it down. Nat looked particularly bad-tempered, and spoke crisply as he rolled the window down.

"Well, Jonathan?"

"Would you be so awfully kind as to drive Susie and myself home? She's Mr. Morcar's grand-daughter from South Africa."

"I know."

"She's been lost and she seems rather—distressed."

"I know. They're all out looking for her. Get in."

Susie had slipped down from the wall but was cowering against it; large tears rolled slowly down her cheek. She pulled back when Jonathan tried to urge her towards the car.

"Don't be afraid, Susie, there's nothing to be afraid about. Nobody is cross with you, dear," he said. "This is Mr. Armitage, a friend of ours, who's going to drive us home, so we shan't have to wait for the bus. Come along."

"Poor kid," said Nat briefly, opening the rear door.

Trembling and quietly weeping, as if afraid to make a noise, Susie was coaxed into the car. Jonathan beside her put his arm round her and drew her down to his shoulder. The trembling of her slight body against his seemed to him the most harrowing experience he had ever undergone. Nat Armitage drew up at the gate of Stanney Royd and Jonathan dismounted.

"Won't you come in?"

"I think not," said Nat drily. "Look out! She's off again."

Swinging round, Jonathan saw that Susie was running away towards the summer-house in the corner of the garden. He slammed the door and raced after her. A shout behind him made him turn; Nat stood beside the car with Jonathan's pack in his hand. Jonathan waved dismissively; surely he can just drop it inside the gate, he thought with irritation. The notion passed through his mind that Nat had been proposing to his mother again and been again rejected; but this was only a fleeting thought, he had no time to give it consideration.

Susie was on her knees beside the garden seat, her face buried in her hands. Jonathan dragged her up to sit beside him and folded her in his arms. Out of the corner of his eye he saw Nat Armitage stamping up the drive with Jonathan's knapsack slung awkwardly over his shoulder, irritation in every movement.

"That's good," thought Jonathan, relieved. "He'll tell Mother that Susie and I are here. Now, Susie," he went on in a warm loving tone. "What's the matter, love? Tell me all about it."

In a wild burst of tears and incoherent words Susie brought out the whole story. She sobbed, she wailed, she even screamed; now that the barriers of her repression were broken, her emotions were quite out of control.

"Daddy is dead. They killed him. His face was cut in half."

"I'm terribly, terribly sorry, Susie," said Jonathan, rocking her against his breast. "But it wouldn't hurt him long, you know."

"Yes, it would."

"Well, he is at rest now, nothing can hurt him any more," said Jonathan, horrified to hear himself uttering the conventional clichés of consolation, but finding them on the whole the best things to say. "How unhappy it would make him if he could see you now!"

"Why?" shrilled Susie, raising her head to glare at him.

The sight of her small young face, now red and swollen with weeping, smote Jonathan like a blow across his heart.

"To see you so unhappy, Susie, to see his little daughter so unhappy. He was very fond of you."

"Yes."

"It would make him very unhappy to see you crying so."

"He can't see me. He's dead," wailed Susie, striking a clenched fist against Jonathan's chest.

Jonathan agreed with her but could not find enough brutality in himself to say so. He laid his cheek against hers and kissed her, instead.

"I wanted to live with Grannie Morcar," muttered Susie, muffled against his shoulder. "I thought she would be like Daddy."

"I'm sure your grandfather will allow you to do so if you wish," said Jonathan. He felt ready to fight for her rights in this respect, but knew he should feel deprived of something if this palpitating little creature left Stanney Royd.

"I don't wish! She isn't like Daddy!"

Jonathan, who had never seen Mrs. Morcar senior, or even a photograph of her, in his life, but had always in his heart blamed Morcar for their divorce and reproached him for it, did not know what to say.

"I hate her! She's horrid!"

"Susie!" said Jonathan, staggered.

"Chuff thinks so too. I know he does. But he doesn't mind as much as I do. We had dinner there for the first time today. Afterwards I was supposed to go to the bathroom, and I ran away."

"You shouldn't have done that, Susie."

"Yes, I should. She isn't like Daddy."

"What *was* your father like?" said Jonathan, trying to introduce a note of reason into the conversation.

"He was rather like Grandfather, really," admitted Susie, calming as Jonathan had hoped she would. "Only kinder and slower. He's dead," she broke out again, wailing. "I shall never see him any more."

"Yes, that's true. You must try not to look back any more. You must try to like living with us. We all love you, Susie," said Jonathan. "Your grandfather loves you very much indeed."

"How do you know?"

"I do know," replied Jonathan emphatically—he felt a particular need to be generous towards Morcar because he feared he had always been unjust to him about the divorce. Susie's feeling about her grandmother was in his opinion the best justification of Morcar's attitude to his wife that could be presented. "Your brother of course loves you. And my mother loves you." It occurred to him that it was a good thing his mother had decided not to marry Nat Armitage, as she would be needed to look after Susie, but this was only a fleeting thought and he did not put the two halves of it together. "And I love you."

"Do you, Jonathan?"

"Yes, very much," said Jonathan with complete sincerity.

"I daresay I can bear it living here, if you do," murmured Susie.

Her slight body relaxed in his arms. They remained in this position for some long minutes. Then Jonathan thought he heard a distant rattle of china.

"I suppose we'd better go and have some tea," he said reluctantly.

"I suppose so," agreed Susie.

Her tone, though sad, was normal, and Jonathan felt with relief that the crisis of her trauma was probably over. They untwined themselves and rose; Jonathan put back Susie's hair from her face and lent her his handkerchief; they dragged themselves back to the house and entered the drawing-room through the open French windows.

Morcar, Nat Armitage, Jennifer and Chuff were all sitting there around a tea trolley. They all appeared miserable, indeed the whole group looked as if they had just ceased from tears.

"Would you like to wash, Susie dear?" said Jennifer in a choked tone.

Susie sighed, but obediently left the room. There was a pause.

"It seems that Susie," began Jonathan with an effort.

"We all heard it, Jonathan," said Jennifer, looking aside.

"Chuff, this is Jonathan Oldroyd, your mother's nephew. Jonathan, my grandson Chuff," said Morcar gruffly.

The two young men forced a grin and cordially disliked each other.

15. A Mill Changes Hands

"YOU SEE NOW why I can't, Nat," said Jennifer when presently, tea over, they stood together at the gate. "The child is all in pieces. The doctor says she mustn't go to school for at least six months."

"And you will teach her at home, I suppose."

"Yes."

"Yes, I thought that would be the way of it. When it was Jonathan who kept you from me I accepted it, he's your son, though I don't see why he couldn't come and live with us."

"He wouldn't, Nat."

"But now it's different."

"I can't leave Susie in this condition. Who would Uncle Harry get to live here and look after her?"

"I know you owe a lot to Mr. Morcar, but I don't see why you should sacrifice your life to his convenience."

"It's the child's life, Nat."

"What about my life, then? I haven't had much, one way and the other, with the war, and Bee dying so soon. Look, Jenny," he went on, putting his hand on hers as it lay on the top bar of the gate, "all these reasons you give me are just external ones, they're not from your heart. You never say you don't like the idea of me as a husband, you don't want to marry me."

Jennifer tried to look at him objectively. He was tallish, darkish, lean-faced, with a firm chin, a flat stomach, a slight limp from the war, and strong, if square, hands. His eyes were brown and kind, and held some warmth which she felt she had long yearned for. The dark grey hairline suit he had donned to make his formal approach to her that afternoon was impeccable, as was only natural for the head of a textile firm even longer established than the Oldroyds' and of a family of more genteel origins. She turned her head away.

"I believe you do want to marry me," he persisted. Jennifer said nothing. "I'm not asking you to forget David."

"You are, you are!"

"No, I'm not. I'm not going to forget Bee, and I'm not asking you to forget David. But I don't see why we should go on being lonely and miserable all our lives. Jenny! Marry me."

"I can't leave the child, Nat," said Jennifer.

"On that principle no generation is ever happy. We sacrifice ourselves for our children, they sacrifice themselves for their children, and so on and so on. Unto the fifty-third and fifty-fourth generation," he concluded smiling.

"That's how life is."

"Well, it's nonsense."

"No woman would agree with you."

"Jenny," said Nat Armitage very soberly, "I shall ask you again at Christmas. That will give this Susie—"

"She's David's niece."

"—time to settle down. If you turn me down then, I shall go off and marry some little twit with a lot of bosom and birds' nest hair."

"Nat, Nat!" said Jennifer, smiling.

"I shall. You had better take me seriously, Jen, I warn you."

He got into his car, closed the door with that absence of bang which indicates an expensive model, gave her a last decidedly menacing look and drove off.

Jennifer smiled sadly as she returned up the drive to the house. Morcar was sitting with the telephone to his ear, listening with an air of disgust to a shrill voice uttering angry words which occasionally became audible.

"Can't think how ... but why ... no manners ... return at once."

Jonathan, now washed and dressed, stood by the empty hearth, looking very like his father, and Chuff was sitting hunched up in an armchair looking sulky; both wore the embarrassed air of unwilling hearers, uncertain whether manners required them to go or stay.

"Where's Susie?" asked Jennifer in a low tone.

"She's upstairs on her bed, asleep," said Chuff.

"Good."

"The child is mentally disturbed, Winnie," said Morcar into the 'phone. "No, I shall not send her back. Yes, Jonathan found her in Iredale Road. She was taking a bus along the valley. Chuff will come to see you alone next Sunday, as we arranged." Here Chuff gave a kind of groan. "No, alone. Because I say so, Winnie. No, he can't come now." Chuff looked relieved. "Possibly, when she's recovered, but I can't promise. I'm afraid you'll have to, Winnie."

He put down the receiver with some emphasis. They're willing enough for me to give the orders when it gets them out of trouble, he thought with resentment. His glance caught Jennifer's, and he saw trouble in her eyes. At once he took alarm. Something more about poor little Susie, he thought. Jennifer looked away. Yes! There was some fresh trouble.

"I'd like a word with you, Jennifer," he said.

The two lads fled gladly into the garden.

"Is there something—worse—about Susie?" asked Morcar.

"No. Why?" said Jennifer, surprised.

"You wouldn't hide anything from me, Jenny?"

"Susie will recover steadily now she's broken the barrier, I'm sure."

"Then what's the trouble?"

Jennifer hesitated. "It's only Nat Armitage asking me again to marry him," she said in a would-be careless tone.

She felt at once that this lightness towards a man's serious love was vulgar; and coloured, abashed.

Morcar was stunned. He saw his whole home life, so graciously and smoothly managed, so stable, collapsing round his feet. At once he reproached himself for this selfish thought, and bent his mind on Jennifer. He recalled her father, the brilliant barrister whom he had loathed, her beautiful mother who had been his mistress, their death in an air-raid, Jennifer's marriage to David, her widowhood, her son, her time at Stanney Royd, her good works, her kindness to old Mrs. Morcar.

"She's not had much of a life," he thought. Aloud he said, in as kind a tone as he could manage: "And you're thinking of accepting, are you?"

"I don't know, Uncle Harry," said Jennifer. Her uncertainty made her irritable. "He has asked me once or twice before, but I felt I could not leave Jonathan. Now Jonathan doesn't need me any more." She looked away, fighting tears.

Ah, there's the rub; *Jonathan doesn't need me any more,* thought Morcar.

"And it's right that he should not," said Jennifer. After a moment she went on: "But there's you—and now Susie."

"Don't worry about me," said Morcar instantly. "You have been as dear to me as a daughter all these years, Jennifer; I shall miss you when you go but I shall rejoice in my daughter's happiness."

"You wouldn't think it wrong then if I—"

"No."

"I don't know how I shall decide. I don't know! Nat said he would ask for his answer at Christmas."

"Well, that gives us time to look around," said Morcar cheerfully.

"You seem to take it for granted that I shall accept. I haven't made up my mind yet by any means."

"I think you have, Jenny," said Morcar quietly.

"I don't know. What will you do about Susie? You can't let her go to—her grandmother. Not after today."

"No. I shall think of something," said Morcar.

Jennifer rose and stood for a moment, uncertain. Then she crossed the room in the graceful, gliding gait which she had inherited from her mother, and stooping over Morcar, put a hand on his shoulder in affectionate caress.

She withdrew, and Morcar was left to assimilate this new disaster.

After a few moments he gave a long sigh and shook his head. The pain was beginning to diminish.

It was just at this moment that another extremely uncomfortable thought struck him. Through his own generous act, Jennifer owned the fabric of Old Mill and the shares of Messrs. Oldroyd and Mellor Ltd. She was in fact in a position to do what she liked with that firm. Living as an adopted niece, widowed, under Morcar's care, she had left her business affairs entirely to him. He did not for a moment doubt her integrity or her goodwill, but remarried—possible even with children by her second husband—she fell inevitably into an entirely different situation. Morcar felt as if Nat Armitage already held Old Mill in his hand.

Morcar loved Old Mill; partly because it had been David's, partly because it had been the original Oldroyd building, dating back to 1810 or so, partly because it had a textile speciality which he enjoyed. It made woollen cloths of incomparable softness, using for this purpose old-fashioned wooden fulling-stocks. Morcar felt towards these soft tissues as another man might have felt towards a kitten. To form a merger, and have Old Mill managed by some bright young man under his guidance, was one thing; to have Old Mill removed from his direct control, to have his empire diminished, was another.

He made up his mind, and went upstairs at once in search of Jennifer. She was just emerging from Susie's room.

"I checked to make sure. She's fast asleep," said Jennifer, closing the door quietly behind her.

"Good. Jennifer, do you remember suggesting that I should buy your Old Mill property and shares?"

"Yes," said Jennifer.

"Do you still want to sell?"

"Yes, yes!" said Jennifer eagerly.

"Very well. I'll buy."

"Oh, I'm so glad, Uncle Harry, I'm so glad!" cried Jennifer.

Her face was bright. Morcar looked at her with pity and love. He perceived that she was glad not only because this sale freed Jonathan from textiles, but because it freed her to marry Nat Armitage without hurting Morcar. She did not know this yet, perhaps, but it was so, had probably been so in her unconscious mind from the first.

"Well, well," thought Morcar sardonically, as he sat in his den considering how to provide the money for the purchase with the least possible inconvenience to his other affairs: "This has been a delightful Sunday, I must say. A real day of rest."

16. Textile

"I DON'T WANT to hurry you, Chuff, and if you feel you'd like a few months' holiday before you settle down I agree it's your due," said Morcar. They were sitting together in the den next morning. "But in this country courses and terms and so on start mostly in September, and I'm off next week for a month in Scandinavia, so if you could make up your mind soon it would be helpful. Now, what do you want to do? Do you want to go back to school?"

"School?" yelped Chuff in horror. "No! I'm nearly eighteen."

"If you want to go to university you'll have to work up for exams."

"I don't want to go to university," mumbled Chuff.

"Jonathan is at Oxford," said Morcar, determined not to make the mistake he had made with Jonathan.

"I'm not Jonathan. Universities aren't in my line."

"Have you any idea what your line is, then? Farming here would be very different from in South Africa, I'm afraid."

There was a pause.

"I don't want to hurry you," repeated Morcar. He was in fact throbbing with impatience, for he had a great deal to arrange before he could leave for his regular "designing" trip to Copenhagen and points north, but after his mistakes with Jonathan he meant to be as calm, impartial and helpful as he possibly could.

There was another pause, but Morcar, eyeing Chuff, thought he saw signs that the boy was struggling to utter.

"Come along. Let's have it," he said encouragingly.

Chuff coloured, looked aside and twisted his fingers.

"Father used to talk about cloth," he muttered.

It was a lightning stroke under which Morcar reeled. I ought to be thankful, he thought, I ought to be delighted; but the contrast between the agreeable, highly intelligent, sophisticated and pleasing Jonathan he had hoped for, and this lout of a grandson he had received, was almost more than he could bear. Still! On second thoughts perhaps he was delighted. Yes, perhaps he was. At any rate, make the best of what you can get. I'm not going to pressure him into it, though.

"If you're going in for textiles," he said in a loud rough bullying tone, "you'll have to take a three-year course at Leeds University."

"I don't want to go to any University. I'll go to Annotsfield Technical College."

"How do you know about Annotsfield Technical College?" enquired Morcar, astonished.

"I read about it in the newspaper advertisements."

"You haven't wasted much time."

"Why should I?" said Chuff. He gave a sudden grin, and for the first time Morcar felt his heart warm to the boy.

"If you and I are going to work together, Chuff," he began—and paused, for he had already expressed the thought which filled

102

his mind—"We must take each other as we are," he concluded lamely.

"Yes, of course," agreed Chuff, not understanding but beginning to look very cheerful. "Is it a business trip to Scandinavia, Grandfather?"

"Yes."

"Can I go with you?"

"Not this time, Chuff. You don't know enough about cloth to learn anything from it." Chuff looked disappointed, and to soothe this feeling Morcar explained: "Norway, Sweden, Denmark—they're some of my biggest markets. I go over twice a year, and see my agents there, and we design my next season's ranges together, as it were. Men's suitings, chiefly. Checks, all-overs, stripes, you know. Well, you don't know. Of course for Scandinavia they have to be quiet, sober, not too much contrast. Then I come back, and we weave section ranges on the pattern looms and send them over, and then we have to send over lengths as well, so that they can make suits out of them to see how they look—it costs the earth. But nowadays it's not enough to make good cloth, you have to sell it as well. Then twice a year I make a selling trip. But August-September, that's a time for design."

Start me on textiles and I go on for ever, he thought, and stopped abruptly.

"And do you go to other countries as well?" asked Chuff.

"Oh yes. Germany, Austria. Not France much. Canada. U.S.A. Some firms go to Greece and Iran and even Hong Kong. I have agents there, but I don't go myself. I ought to, I know, but one man can't do everything."

"It must be very interesting, seeing all those countries," said Chuff wistfully.

"You don't see much of 'em. You just sit in an office and work. Very hard work," said Morcar grimly.

"But who do you sell to exactly? Merchants?" queried Chuff, shyly producing what to him was obviously a technical term.

"No, no. Merchants don't count for much nowadays—not more than ten per cent, I should say. No; it's the big manufacturers of ready-made clothing, both in this country and overseas, who are my main customers today."

At this point Jonathan in the garden, carrying books and papers as usual, passed by the open windows.

"Jonathan!" called Morcar in a commanding tone.

Jonathan returned.

"If I give you two lads a small car between you, can you share it without quarrelling?"

"Sure!" cried Chuff eagerly.

"Yes, certainly," said Jonathan coolly after a pause.

"Well, go out and buy one," commanded Morcar. He named the firm where the purchase should be made, together with the make and appropriate price of the car. "Show some sense, now. Sober colours and not too many gadgets."

"It's very kind of you, Uncle Harry," said Jonathan as before.

"Yes, indeed it is," echoed Chuff.

The conversation seemed over, but none of the three quite knew how to get away.

"Is Jessopp there, Jonathan?"

"Not yet. There's a leader in the *Times* this morning about the need for increasing our exports," offered Jonathan.

"Tell me something I don't know," said Morcar roughly, vexed.

"How much do you export every year, Grandfather?"

"Getting on for a million."

"Yards? Pounds?" said Chuff, awestruck.

"Aye, sterling."

"That's a lot."

"I know firms who do plenty more. One I know has a turnover of six million—but that includes yarn, of course."

"Here's Jessopp now, Uncle Harry."

"I must be off. Go and buy that car, and, Jonathan, get some L plates and take Chuff to put his name down for a driving test."

"I can drive, Grandfather."

"You'll have to take a test. And show him where the Technical College is. If it's open, get a prospectus about textile classes. I shan't be in to lunch," said Morcar, stepping out of the window and walking briskly along to where Jessopp waited with the car.

"You're going into textiles, then? I'm glad for Uncle Harry's sake," said Jonathan.

"Thank you for nothing. If you don't want to share a car with me, why don't you say so instead of just looking down your nose?"

"My reluctance about the car has nothing to do with you," said Jonathan. The truth was that he had agreed to accept a half-share in a car entirely for Chuff's sake, but he thought it would be low to say so.

"What has it to do with, then?"

"I don't wish to be indebted to Mr. Morcar more than I can help. He's not *my* grandfather," said Jonathan

"You're an odd fellow, Jonathan. I can't read you," said Chuff in a more friendly tone.

"Well, I'm not in the curriculum."

"There you go again. I don't know what that means."

"I mean that we can behave in a civilised way to each other without especially liking or understanding each other."

"Pretty grim. Still, I agree to those terms," said Chuff with a grin.

How like his grandfather he is, thought Jonathan, amused. Aloud he said: "I could find a book or two for you in the municipal library, to put you in the picture about the textile processes, if you like."

"Books?" said Chuff, suspicious. Always books and fine words from Jonathan, he thought with disgust. "Well, thanks," he said ungraciously.

17. Jessopp and the Past

"I'M VERY SORRY, very sorry indeed, Mrs. Jessopp," said Morcar soberly to the widow. "To lose Jessopp leaves a great hole in my life. We've been together for so long."

Mrs. Jessopp, a fresh-complexioned buxom woman in her early sixties, with her light hair, scarcely at all grey, drawn tightly back from her face in an old-fashioned knot, rocked herself slowly back and forth in an old-fashioned rocking-chair covered in black horsehair. Her hands, roughened with the honest toil of a lifetime, lay clasped slackly in her lap, and her eyes were red with weeping.

"He had a good life, Mr. Morcar," she said. "The children have turned out well, you know. And it was all due to you. We don't forget that, Mr. Morcar." She looked up to where, over one end of the mantelpiece, hung a small faded photograph in a rather ornate silver frame. "You're all there," she concluded, nodding towards it.

Morcar got up and inspected the photograph. With a shock he saw himself, Charlie Shaw, and Jessopp, in 1914 uniforms, those short ill-fitting jackets, those huge clumsy boots, those nuisances of puttees. Jessopp and Morcar stood stiffly side by side, solid and solemn; Charlie sat on a table-edge, swinging his foot, insouciant, lively, bright-eyed, laughing, as always. What a simple, ingenuous, ignorant donkey of a lad I was in those days, thought Morcar; Charlie was always worth two of me. The past rose out of its dusty bed and stabbed his heart full of pain. He grieved.

"You saved his life, Mr. Morcar," said Mrs. Jessopp.

Yes, it's true, I did, thought Morcar. I went back towards the shell crater and dragged Jessopp to the trench. And suppose I hadn't? Suppose I had left him out there in no-man's land and stayed in the trench by Charlie? Jessopp's children wouldn't exist. I should be still married to Winnie. As Winnie says, with a wife and child round my neck I shouldn't have risen so far, so fast. I should have stayed in old Mr. Shaw's firm. He wouldn't have plagiarised my cloths. I shouldn't have needed a counsel's opinion, shouldn't have met Harington or Christina. David wouldn't have met Jennifer, Jonathan wouldn't exist. He mused sombrely on the strangely interwoven patterns of life.

"I shall miss Jessopp terribly," he said.

"But you've often driven yourself, Mr. Morcar."

"Well, naturally. Sometimes it's best so. Depends what your errand is. But Jessopp's always been in the background, and lately I've relied on him more and more."

"Yes, I've noticed that. None of us get any younger, Mr. Morcar."

"No, indeed," said Morcar, wincing. "It's a real grief to me that I was away in Norway when Alfred died, Mrs. Jessopp."

"It came rather sudden at the end," said Mrs. Jessopp, and for the third or fourth time since Morcar's arrival she narrated the sudden onset of the rheumatic fever which had brought her husband to death. Morcar listened patiently, with respect; he knew from long experience that these narrations brought comfort to the bereaved.

"We were very sorry you couldn't be at the funeral," concluded Mrs. Jessopp.

"So was I. But I was up country and didn't hear about it till it was all over," said Morcar sincerely.

"It was good of Mrs. Morcar to send a wreath," said Mrs. Jessopp doubtfully. "We appreciated it."

Blast Winnie, thought Morcar in a fury. Seeing how she hated Jessopp, she can only have sent a wreath to vex me. Or was it perhaps a genuine expression of a lately conceived regret? Try to be fair to her. I can't, said Morcar savagely. I can *not* be fair to Winnie.

"Were all your family able to be present at the funeral?" he enquired politely.

"All but Fred's wife. She's having her third, and the doctor thought it was safer not."

"Yes, I'm sure he was right. And what about your lads, then, Mrs. Jessopp?" said Morcar. "I've one with me, I think, at Daisy?"

"That's right, he's in the press-room at Daisy. That's the eldest, Fred. And Alf, he's a policeman in Wakefield."

"Really!"

"Yes. He's a sergeant, doing well. And Clarice, she's married, of course. Down South they've gone. They're all married; I have eight grandchildren, Mr. Morcar."

"Splendid," said Morcar heartily. "You won't be lonely, then."

Mrs. Jessopp's fresh face clouded. "None of them are very near," she said. "Clarice wants me to go live with them, but I don't think I shall. Near London, it is. I shouldn't feel at home down there. But I don't know what I shall do, yet."

"Mrs. Jessopp," said Morcar on an impulse. "Come and keep house for me."

"I don't think I should be equal to it, Mr. Morcar," said Mrs. Jessopp shyly.

"Mrs. Jessopp, you kept house for me for years, at one time."

"But that's a long time ago. You've grander ideas now. Mrs. Oldroyd, she's from the South and that."

"I must tell you in confidence," said Morcar, "that Mrs. Oldroyd may be leaving us. She may marry again. I think she will. She thinks she hasn't made up her mind yet, but I think she has."

"Ah. It's Nat Armitage, isn't it," agreed Mrs. Jessopp, nodding.

There was no reason, Morcar told himself, why he should feel vexed that Armitage's feeling for Jennifer should be common knowledge, but all the same he had that feeling. He did not intend, however, to show it.

"So you've heard rumours," he said pleasantly.

"Well, yes. Alfred noticed it sometimes when he drove Mrs. Oldroyd to concerts and such. Mr. Armitage seemed often to be there, you know."

"Yes. Well, she's been a real daughter to me, and deserves all the happiness she can find. But it's my grand-daughter who's worrying me, you see. She needs care."

"Little Susie. A sweet little thing, Alfred said, but frosted, like, by losing her father."

"You're very fond of children, and good with them," said Morcar.

"My own have grown up well, and that's a fact," said Mrs. Jessopp. A more cheerful note had come into her voice, she smiled slightly and unclasped her hands.

"Well, think it over, and talk it over with Clarice and your sons," said Morcar. "I'll let you have a note about wages in a day or two."

"It wouldn't be the wages that'd worry me, Mr. Morcar," said Mrs. Jessopp with dignity. "I know I can rely on you to do what's right, and Alfred has left quite a tidy bit, you know, being in good work all these years, and there's his insurance, and the children are all doing well. But something useful for me to do, that—" She paused and looked at Morcar; but knowing the West Riding character, he knew better than to try to push her, and simply smiled encouragement. "That might be different. That might be different," concluded Mrs. Jessopp, slightly tossing her head.

18. Susie

ATTACKING HIS BOILED breakfast egg with the appropriate spoon one autumn morning, Morcar gave a violent start—a portion had broken off and now flew vigorously through the air. Susie broke into a merry laugh. It was the first time since she came to England that Morcar had heard her laugh, and he was delighted by the sound.

"What's the joke?" he said.

Susie continued to laugh, and Chuff also grinned widely.

"It's not a real egg, Grandfather," he said.

Morcar looked down at the egg, and perceived that it was in fact completely hollow, and composed of thick pottery, suitably coloured.

"Why, you naughty little pussy, Susie," he said, laughing. "You young scamp! Poor grandfather! No egg for breakfast!"

"It was Chuff's idea," said Susie, laughing again. "We saw it in Woolworth's."

"Run along and get grandfather's real egg from Mrs. Jessopp, dear," said Jennifer.

It was clear that all three—it was term-time and Jonathan of course was in Oxford—had shared the secret of the artificial egg, but Jennifer's smile struck Morcar as rather faint. It occurred to him that whereas in previous years the occupants of Stanney Royd had been one-and-a-half Morcars and two Oldroyds (counting old Mrs. Morcar as a half), at present there were three Morcars and only one Oldroyd. Jennifer might well feel outnumbered—and an imitation egg was rather too childish a joke to appeal to Edward Harington's daughter. She smiled kindly, but did not really find it funny, whereas the three Morcars certainly did.

A few days later—it was evening, and Morcar sat in his den checking some figures—Susie came in; she sidled up to him and laid a hand on the arm of his chair.

"Well, Susie," said Morcar encouragingly.

"Pussy," said Susie, laughing. "That's what you called me, Grandfather. Pussy."

"Very well," agreed Morcar good-humouredly. "Pussy. That's a nice name for a little girl."

"Just between ourselves. A kind of secret."

"Certainly," agreed Morcar, touched. He put his arm round the child and hugged her to him. "What do you want, Pussy, eh?"

Susie swayed back and forth within the circle of his arm for a few moments in hesitation, then looking down got out with some difficulty:

"Did you think it was unkind of me on Wednesday, Grandfather? About the egg?"

"No, good gracious me, no," said Morcar, laughing. "I enjoyed the joke."

"Jonathan thinks it was rather unkind, he thinks you might have been hurt."

"Jonathan?"

"I told him about it in a letter, and he thinks you might have been hurt."

"Oh, so you and Jonathan write letters to each other, do you?" said Morcar, surprised.

"Yes. He writes to me, so I write back. Chuff addressed the envelope for me the first time, but I can do it myself now."

"I see. Well, it was kind of Jonathan to mind about me being hurt, Pussy," said Morcar, not without irony, "but I wasn't hurt at all."

"He *is* a very kind boy," said Susie earnestly.

19. Chuff

"NATHAN!" CALLED CHUFF from the yard.

"He shouts for me just like you do, Mr. Morcar," said Nathan, smiling.

"Don't be a sentimental old ass," growled Morcar, nevertheless unable to suppress a grin. "Call him up, will you? I must give him a serious talking-to."

"He won't like that, Mr. Morcar."

"I don't expect him to."

"Will you come up, please, Mr. Chuff? Mr. Morcar wants to speak to you," said Nathan decorously from the window.

He withdrew with his hands full of letters and patterns as Chuff came with his slow slouching stride into the room.

"Close the door," said Morcar in an ominous tone.

Chuff's face clouded, he closed the door and returned to the desk with a look of sulky defiance, once frequent on his face but of late rarely seen.

"Now, Chuff, what's all this," said Morcar, picking up Chuff's term report from the Annotsfield Technical College, which lay on his desk. "Your textile subjects are all good. In fact one or two of them are very good. I've no complaint there."

"Thanks," said Chuff, intending sarcasm.

"But your English is poor and your mathematics almost as bad. *Inattentive. Careless work. Could do better. Shows no interest.* What does that mean, eh?"

"It means I'm not interested," said Chuff, insolent.

"Do you want to run a successful firm, or don't you?"

"English and Maths haven't anything to do with textiles," said Chuff.

"Oh yes, they have. How many times have I to tell you that it isn't enough nowadays to make good stuff? You've got to sell it as well."

"It oughtn't to be like that."

"Well, it is. Your handwriting, too, that's appalling."

"You don't write letters nowadays. You dictate them."

"You couldn't dictate a readable letter to Miss Mellor to save your life."

Chuff coloured, and was silent.

"Maths, too. A business man has to be good at maths."

"You have an accountant," mumbled Chuff.

"What's the use of an accountant in Annotsfield when you're in Berlin and customers are trying to knock down your price? You must be able to calculate quickly, in your head mind, no paperwork, what a ha'penny a yard off is going to cost you for the whole order and whether it's worth it."

"I wish we had a decimal coinage," muttered Chuff.

"There I agree with you."

"I've no head for maths."

"You'd better grow one, then. Besides, that's not true. Your design work is good—yes it says here: *Good and promising*," said Morcar. "And that means good graph work." Mollified, he went on in a kinder tone: "Now don't go and spoil everything by a fit of sulks, Chuff."

"I'm not having a fit of sulks," shouted Chuff suddenly, furious.

"You've got to learn to write good English, and speak it too."

"Like Jonathan, I suppose," said Chuff.

"Aye! Like Jonathan. He's got English and no textiles, you've got textiles and no English. If I could mix you, the result might be some good to me. Now Susie, now she's come to herself, is much more fluent than you are, Chuff. How is that, eh?"

"It's just the way she is," muttered Chuff, in, however, a less hostile tone. He was fond and proud of his sister, Morcar had observed, though he concealed it as much as possible.

"Well, come now, Chuff," said Morcar, descending gradually with each speech from the heights of anger towards ordinary relationship level: "Have another try. *Careless, inattentive, could do better;* I don't like to see that, you know. It sounds a bit spine-less."

"No!" objected Chuff. "I'm not spineless."

"No, I don't think you are. I'm pleased with your work in the mill, you know. Yes, you've made quite a good start. You don't get on too badly with the men, either."

"I don't stand any nonsense from them," said Chuff, flushing.

"That's all right so long as you realise they won't stand any nonsense from you."

Chuff sniffed. "They're working up for a row in the far weaving shed," he said. "Those Pakistanis, you know."

"What's the matter with them?" said Morcar sharply.

"Well, nothing, really. Just that black and white don't get on together."

"Now, Chuff, you've got to forget all that prejudice—we've all got to forget all our prejudices, or we're going to blow the world up between us."

"I can't forget my father and mother," said Chuff, scowling.

"No, and black folk can't forget the slave trade, I daresay."

"Jonathan's all wrong about it."

"Well, I don't know," said Morcar carefully, uncertain whether or not to feel pleased. "He's young and full of big ideas."

"And I'm young and not full of big ideas, is that it?"

"I don't know what your ideas are, Chuff; you don't express them."

Chuff swung away with such violence that he stamped his foot on the floor.

"Now, Chuff," said Morcar in his kindest tone: "I shan't say any more about it, but I look forward to seeing a different report next term."

Chuff made a sound between a snort and a groan, and flung out of the office.

20. *Night Off*

"ARE YOU WANTING the car tonight, Jonathan?"

"No. I should like it tomorrow night, though, if it's all right to you. I have to go to a U.N.A. meeting in Annotsfield. Would you care to come with me?" added Jonathan as a polite afterthought.

Chuff stood silent for a moment, hesitating. Eventually he grinned, and said: "I'll come with you tomorrow if you'll come with me tonight."

"It's a deal," said Jonathan cheerfully, throwing aside the *New Statesman*. "Where are you you for tonight, then?"

"Bowls."

"Bowls?" said Jonathan, dismayed. He had not the least desire to go a-bowling, but was too kind-hearted to say so. "That should be interesting," he said.

"Don't you ever do anything because you enjoy it, Jonathan?"

"Well, of course!"

"No, you don't. You do it because you think it may be socio-logically—" Chuff got this word out in separate syllables, with a derisive effect—"useful or interesting."

"You have a point there, Chuff," said Jonathan. "But then, you see, that's what I enjoy."

"Oh, hell, man!" said Chuff impatiently.

The two young men got out their car and went down the Ire Valley towards Annotsfield, Chuff driving. He drove well, insist-ing on his rights more perhaps than Jonathan would have done, but extricating himself capably from awkward situations which arose from others' ineptitude. They parked satisfactorily, went up the broad steps to the large building, and pushed open the heavy glass doors. A continuous rolling thunder greeted them. While Chuff shed his black leather jerkin (he found the winter tempera-ture of Yorkshire trying) Jonathan strolled about and became interested—in the shelves full of rubber-soled shoes, the chart of scoring rules, the display of bowls, huge handsome heavy-looking affairs, some coloured in dark blue and red, with thumb and finger holes. I'd like to hold one, he thought. A middle-aged lady came along, put a bowl into a neat small machine which stood by the wall and inserted a threepenny piece in the slot provided. A whirring sound resulted.

"What is this machine for, Chuff?" shouted Jonathan through the thunder.

"Just to polish the bowls," said Chuff impatiently. "Come along."

"What is used to polish them?"

"Wire brushes. Come *along*."

"Are you going to play now, Chuff?"

"No."

"How many sets of—er—skittles? Ninepins?—are there?"

"Twenty-eight lanes," said Chuff shortly. "You're interested, are you?"

"Yes. Why not? When are you going to play?" said Jonathan eagerly, watching the bowlers of both sexes and all ages who with a skilful swing of the arm sent the bowls rolling down the long wooden lanes towards the tall white ninepins. ("Though why ninepins when there are ten of them?" wondered Jonathan.)

A mechanism of some kind picked up any ninepins remaining on their feet after the roll and swept the fallen ones away, then replaced those which had not been knocked down. The attitudes of the bowlers were often graceful, and it was exciting to see the ninepins fall. The long wooden lanes gleamed in the light, which was brilliant but not garish. Bowls, returned presumably from the far end of the lane on under-floor tracks, popped up smoothly into troughs at the near end, ready to the players' hands. Everything was fresh, clean, gleaming. At small tables at the head of the lanes sat girl scorers, recording the number of skittles knocked down; as they wrote, the figures, with their pens and sometimes hands, appeared in shadow on screens above their head, easily visible to the spectators and players. It was all neat, skilfully mechanised, extremely contemporary. Jonathan was enthralled.

"Do they always record their scores? What are those red lights for at the end of the lanes?"

"Your leader has just rolled a score of two hundred and twenty-eight," announced a loud-speaker.

"They're playing a league game at the far end," said Chuff. "Come along."

He dragged Jonathan up a few steps on to a long platform; a soft-drinks bar lined one side and seats in pairs and singles stood overlooking the lanes, on the other side.

"There's room here,' said Jonathan, making for a free pair.

Chuff gave him a sharp push and Jonathan stumbled on to the next group, a threesome. The object of the exercise, as Jonathan told himself, immediately became visible, for Ruth Mellor sat there, her handbag beside her on the velvet seat

"Good evening, Ruth," said Chuff in a rather defiant tone.

"Good evening," said Ruth Mellor coolly.

"You know my cousin, Jonathan Oldroyd, don't you."

"I believe I have seen you sometimes at Syke Mills."

Her tone, reflected Jonathan, was perfect; cool and calm. She offered her hand, and he took it; this too was cool and calm.

"Coffee, Ruth?" said Chuff.

"Thank you."

Chuff moved away, and Jonathan sat down opposite to the girl.

"It all looks very respectable," said Jonathan jokingly, glancing round the scene.

"Did you think you were coming to a den of vice?"

Rather taken aback, Jonathan began: "Well—"

"Or perhaps you only hoped so?"

"I didn't know I was to have the pleasure of meeting you here, or I would have revised my ideas," said Jonathan, pulling himself together.

"It's a family game, as you can see," said Ruth, relenting slightly. "That is my brother, G.B. playing down there. He's just going to roll."

The bearded young man indicated, who appeared strongly to resemble his sister, being slender, darkish and bright-eyed, was confronted by a difficult task, for the two ninepins left upright stood very far apart. He paused, considered, rolled; the bowl struck one ninepin a glancing blow which knocked it into the other ninepin; both fell. The team applauded; Jonathan, delighted by the neat, graceful, unexaggerated action, applauded too. Chuff returned with three coffee cups.

"You're looking glum this evening, Chuff," said Ruth.

"And well I might. Such a row I got from Grandfather this morning, you never heard."

Judging from her previous responses, Jonathan expected a sharp reply, but Ruth said: "Hard luck!" with sympathy in her tone.

And that tells the whole story, thought Jonathan.

"He seems to think everybody is made for him and his old mill," went on Chuff, petulant. "'If I could mix you and Jonathan together, I might have somebody of some use to me,' he said. As though all that mattered for Jonathan and me was being useful to him!"

"He's very kind really. I don't expect he meant it that way, he might have been only joking," suggested Ruth

"Joking!" said Chuff in a tone of deep incredulity. "Ha! You should have heard him."

"Is your brother in textiles, Ruth?" asked Jonathan, feeling a disloyalty in listening to this conversation about Morcar.

"No. Electronics."

"I think I'll just have another look at that polishing machine," said Jonathan presently, rising with the intention of leaving the couple alone.

"O.K. Be seeing you."

Jonathan gave the polishing machine a close inspection, looked into the children's playroom and patted the rocking-horse on the head, watched a few non-league games which were being played at some distance from Chuff, and studied the scoring sheet on the wall until he had mastered its principles. He was just turning away from this when he was picked up by a neat, crisp, friendly man in middle life, who proved to be the manager of the establishment. This man, evidently a bowling enthusiast, showed him every available detail of its workings, introduced him to orange-coated instructors, dropped bowls of varying weights into Jonathan's hands—they were very heavy—and finally asked him if he would like to go behind the scenes and see the machinery. Jonathan, amused and entertained but feeling he was perhaps being told rather more about bowling alleys than he wanted to know, hesitated and looked towards Chuff and Ruth.

Their heads were very close together, Ruth's eyes sparkled and she talked earnestly.

Chuff had now acquired clothes which he thought suitable to the English scene. Tonight he was wearing a thick black sweater agreeably ornamented across the chest and back with white and red patterns, which showed his broad shoulders to advantage. His African tan had quickly vanished under the weathering of a cold, wet, windy West Riding autumn, and his very blonde complexion had emerged. At present he was wearing the half-shy, half-pleased, wholly ingenuous smirk of a young man who is being shown favour by a woman for the first time. He smiled; his white even teeth were quite delightful.

"A fine animal," thought Jonathan. Aloud he said: "Yes, I should very much like to see the mechanism," for he by no means wished to disturb Chuff's courtship.

The manager, following the direction of his glance, enquired: "Would your friends like to come too?"

"I think not," said Jonathan, and they smiled together understandingly.

116

Jonathan was not fond of machinery, which seemed to him to make a frightful fuss about doing something which human hands did better; there was a gain of speed, but little else. However, he found a childish pleasure in the extreme skill of these complicated machines, which rolled the bowls round a huge upright circle and despatched them back immediately to the players, picked up the skittles by the scruff of their necks, shot them around, dropped them into curved holders, and when the last pin fell through its cone, placed them all—"gently but firmly," thought Jonathan with amusement—in their exact position, without a wobble, on the floor of the lane. He was urged to clamber up, to clamber down; he talked to the young mechanic, he strained his voice bellowing through the terrific backstage noise, far heavier than that of a loom-shed. He remembered how Morcar and his weavers prided themselves on never raising their voices amid the looms, and noticed that here the same pride obtained. At last he had seen all, and was led thankfully back to the public portion of the building. He gave the manager a grateful goodnight and approached Chuff and Ruth. They were sitting in exactly the same positions, wearing the same expressions, as when he had left them half an hour before.

"I think I'll push off now, Chuff," he said.

"Oh, no. The match isn't anything like over yet," said Chuff, throwing the lanes a cursory glance.

"No need for you to come. I'll catch a bus," said Jonathan.

"Oh, no. That's not fair. It's your car as well as mine," said Chuff, frowning. "Stay a bit, Jonathan."

"No, you go with your cousin," said Ruth in a sensible tone. "It's late. I'll wait for G.B."

"He'll be ages," said Chuff.

"Why don't we run Ruth home?" suggested Jonathan. "And go on to Stanney Royd from there?"

This was accepted with relief. Jonathan and Ruth stood together by the glass doors while Chuff reclaimed his jerkin.

"Chuff told me what you said about behaving in a civilised way to each other, Mr. Oldroyd," said Ruth severely.

"My name is Jonathan. I hope you'll use it."

"Jonathan, then. It was rather a cold welcome, I thought."

"It seems to have worked, however. We are becoming quite friendly now—at least, I am."

"Oh, Chuff is too. But it was difficult for him at first, you know, coming to a strange country. And in such sad circumstances."

"I realise that," said Jonathan with sympathy.

"And he was so troubled about Susie."

"Susie is all right now," said Jonathan quickly.

"I'm very glad to hear you say so. She seems to be a very sweet little girl," said Ruth, turning her eyes full upon him.

They were very fine eyes, dark grey with, Jonathan thought but did not like to look too closely, a dark blue iris; their gaze was penetrating.

"Yes," he said, returning her look steadily. He felt that they had communicated, that Ruth now knew the special feeling he had for Susie.

Chuff came up, they retrieved the car and drove off, sitting very close together, three in the small front seat. Jonathan observed with quiet amusement that Chuff knew well the route to the new block of flats where Ruth lived on the fifth floor, but did not expect to be asked up to her home. They parted without an embrace.

"You didn't know Ruth much before tonight, did you?" said Chuff as they drove up the valley.

"Scarcely at all. I like her," said Jonathan sincerely.

Chuff gave a grunt which seemed designed to express satisfaction.

"It's silly being called Chuff, really, now I'm not a kid any more," he said presently. "But I don't see what else I can do. I don't want to be called after any Shaw, so that rules out Charles. I can't be called Henry or Harry while Grandfather's around. Mom wanted me to be called Francis, but I don't fancy it. I'm not a Francis."

"No. Hal might have suited you," said Jonathan thoughtfully. "But it's too late now. Anyhow, Chuff is O.K. by me. I like it."

Chuff snorted.

21. Chuff and Ruth

"COME IN AND close the door, Chuff," said Morcar.

Chuff put his tongue in his cheek and chuckled to himself. On facing his grandfather across the desk, however, he saw him looking so extremely grim that he perceived he had been mistaken in thinking he had seen the height of Morcar's anger previously.

"Now, Chuff, understand me, I will not have any hanky-panky in the office," said Morcar sternly.

"I don't know what you mean, Grandfather."

"Oh, yes, you do. I saw you bending over Ruth Mellor's desk just now."

"Well, what's wrong with that?"

"I am not going to have you playing about with girls in the office."

"I'm not playing about with her," said Chuff angrily. "She's a friend of mine, that's all."

"All? It looked like a pretty close friendship."

"Well, why not?"

"Ruth Mellor is a good girl, she works in my employ, she's under my protection, and I'm not going to have you fooling round with her."

"I'm not fooling round with her! Don't you trust me, Grandfather?"

"With money, yes. With women, no."

In spite of himself Chuff gave a snort half-anger, half-amusement.

"And you'd do well not to trust yourself overmuch. We've had an example of the mess it can cause, in high places, recently."

"I think you're being disgusting," shouted Chuff, crimsoning. "I don't think of Ruth in that way at all."

"Not at all?"

"I respect her," muttered Chuff, hanging his head in acute embarrassment.

"Are you going to tell me this is a serious attachment?"

"Why not? If you object, that's just British snobbery. Anyway, Jonathan told me Ruth's father was Uncle David's partner once. They were cousins."

"That's right. I bought Mrs. Mellor's shares off her after her husband was killed, to make Old Mill all Jonathan's."

"And then Jonathan didn't want it," sneered Chuff.

"True," said Morcar, stiffening so as not to wince.

"Ruth's as good as we are, then, even by your old-fashioned standards. I don't see why you object to me and Ruth going together."

"I don't object in the least. Ruth's a clever girl, nice-looking and well mannered and quick in the uptake. In fact, I think she's probably just the kind you need, she'd be good for you. Sharpen you up." (Chuff ground his teeth.) "But you're too young to tie yourself up yet. You'll hover round half a dozen girls before you settle down. However, if you're feeling as determined as that about it, Ruth'll have to leave Syke Mills."

"No!"

"It's a nuisance, because she's the best secretary I've ever had, but I can't have this sort of thing going on."

"It's not that sort of thing."

"Think how it looks in the office."

"I don't care how it looks, in the office or anywhere else."

"Nat Armitage'll give her a job, I dare say. I'll see she gets a good one. She deserves it."

"The way you manage other people's lives!" burst out Chuff. "It's unbearable."

"I'm doing what I think right, for her as well as for you."

"It's not fair! The only bit of happiness I have, seeing Ruth every day, and you take it away from me!"

"That's better than a hasty, shotgun marriage," said Morcar very soberly.

"I shall go on seeing her at night," said Chuff with defiance.

"That's up to you to decide. I'll get your Aunt Jennifer to give a young people's party before Jonathan goes back, and invite Ruth. Would you like that?"

"Er—yes," muttered Chuff, rather taken aback.

"Now make up your mind, Chuff. That's the test. Do you want Ruth to come to Stanney Royd and meet Susie, or don't you? If you don't, then just drop meeting her—gradually, of course."

"Ruth would be good for Susie," said Chuff eagerly.

There was a pause.

"Very well," said Morcar at length. "We'll play it that way. But listen, Chuff. I married very young, and in a hurry."

Chuff looked the insolent enquiry he dared not utter.

"No, not for that reason," said Morcar sadly. "It was the War, and—well, never mind. I was away for several months. Then, since my return home in 1919, every minute of my life I've regretted my marriage. I don't want you to do the same. Wait a bit before you commit yourself. And don't make the girl fall in love with you while you're making up your mind, for that's not fair."

Chuff reflected, with some pleasure, that this advice was probably too late. The reflection showed in his face. Morcar sighed, and his face looked less grim.

"Don't send Ruth away, Grandfather," pleaded Chuff.

"Will you give me your word of honour to behave to her in the mill as though you have no special interest in her?"

"Well—I don't know if I can manage it. Can I tell her you say I must?" said Chuff.

"Yes. Make me out as much of an ogre as you like. She'll understand. She's got more sense than you."

"I know," admitted Chuff, nevertheless thinking to himself: We'll see about that. "Well, all right, then. If you always regret your marriage," he broke out suddenly: "I suppose you regret Father and me?"

"I did at one time," said Morcar. "But I'm getting rather fond of you now, Chuff. Heaven knows why."

"Tcha!" said Chuff, flinging out of the office.

He did not, however, slam the door.

22. *Christmas*

CHRISTMAS WAS AT hand. Morcar as a determined agnostic of fifty years' standing disliked the Christmas hullabaloo. He saw no evidence whatever for a benevolent and powerful God, for no such God would allow humanity to endure the suffering imposed upon it by its own nature, which He had created. Judged by His behaviour, God could be one but not both: either benevolent but often powerless, or all-powerful but often malignant. (The third possibility appealed more to Morcar: He was simply non-existent.) Morcar gave Him the benefit of the doubt, and declined to be convinced either way without more evidence. As for the Jewish preacher Jesus Christ, Morcar admired and respected his teachings, but sometimes felt that their excessive self-sacrifice, their almost masochism, was more than could be expected from human nature as at present constituted, and thus led to much lying and hypocrisy. However, Christianity was probably the best religion evolved so far, he thought, so for the children's sake Morcar lent himself to its celebration.

It struck him with sad amusement that everyone at Stanney Royd was pretending for the sake of everyone else. Jonathan, he guessed, was at the agnostic stage, Chuff never gave a serious thought to religion, Mrs. Jessopp since her husband's death took a sardonic view though she did not throw off her beliefs intellectually; Jennifer was, he feared, tormented by painful doubts. In spite of this, Christmas preparations went on apace—the old-fashioned word suited them. Mrs. Jessopp made mince pies and plum puddings, Jennifer tied up parcels in brilliant-coloured wrapping papers, Chuff who was good with his hands put up strings to hold Christmas cards and festoons of holly and mistletoe, under Susie's direction, while Jonathan stood by in a detached but complacent attitude, occasionally passing the hammer. What Susie thought was obscure; perhaps all this was for the benefit of her childish faith. Though she was hardly a child now, reflected Morcar; she had begun to attend the Annotsfield Girls' High School and had come along wonderfully of late; she was now a girl, a quiet but really very pretty girl with a low sweet voice. More than pretty, really; she had a pure, grave beauty, with her small but clear aquiline features, her dark blue eyes, her fair complexion, her curtain of smooth pale hair. Her school report was excellent; on showing it to Chuff, Morcar rather thought of pointing out the commendation she received for English, but the lad's smile was so candidly delighted with his sister's progress that he had not the heart to do so.

It was arranged that Christmas presents were to be exchanged at the breakfast table after the meal was over. Mrs. Jessopp drew the cloth and the unwrapping began. Morcar enjoyed this ceremony; he loved to give, and to give well-chosen gifts, exactly suited to the taste of the recipient.

Mountains of scarves, ties, waistcoats, cardigans, blouses, handkerchiefs, gloves, brooches, necklets, cheques, changed hands and were well received. A square white box, a small cube, stood in front of Morcar's place, lavishly tied up in silver ribbon. The attached card announced that it was *For Grandfather from Susie*. Morcar observed that Susie eyed this parcel, which stood about four inches high, with impatient excitement, and accordingly he made a good deal of fuss over dealing with it, removing the ribbon without cutting it, unfolding the paper carefully and so on, in order that the attention of all should be on the present when it emerged. He delved into the nest of tissue paper within, and drew out a china figure.

It was a sitting lamb, very modernistically rendered; creamy in colour, with the short woolly neck, the up-pointed, black-tipped ears, the tucked-in forelegs, the black anklets, the look of in-eradicable innocence, which Morcar knew so well, all slightly exaggerated into a contemporary stylishness. (It was always a pleasure to Morcar that no lamb, no sheep, had ever lost its life to serve the textile trade; it gave its coat, but that was all.) Morcar stroked its back; the china was smooth to the touch but the modeller's skill in some strange way presented to the sight the rather harsh tight curls of a real lamb's fleece.

"That's the essence of a lamb!" exclaimed Jonathan, beaming.

"The fleece is all right," said Chuff doubtfully.

"But that's a really good piece. Where did you find it, Susie?" asked Jennifer.

"It was in that art exhibition the school took us to. It's very modern," said Susie anxiously. "Do you like it, Grandfather?"

"I love it," said Morcar emphatically, stroking the lamb's head.

He felt deeply touched and pleased, and kissed Susie—who, he now for the first time noticed, always sat at his right hand—with very real love.

Colleagues of Morcar's whom he met in business and at his Club had sometimes hinted to him, laughing sardonically, that the Christmas assemblies of their families sometimes proved un-comfortable occasions—their sons' wives snapped and the grand-children quarrelled. Morcar, who had hitherto only experienced decorous gatherings of himself, Jennifer and Jonathan and was apt to idealise the family life he had lacked, had been a trifle incredulous of these revelations, but he now found that Christmas disagreements were all too probable. Jennifer announced her in-tention of attending church, and invited all to accompany her; this nobody seemed to wish to do.

"I've promised to go and see Grandmother," said Chuff.

"Quite right," approved Morcar.

"Will you come with me, Susie? I think you should."

"No, Aunt Jennifer," said Susie, frowning. "I'm going to the mill with Grandfather."

"The mill won't be open today, Susie," said Chuff, aghast.

"Grandfather has the keys."

There was an uncomfortable silence, and glances were exchanged expressing regret at this apparent recession to Susie's earlier *délabrement*.

"I'll drive you down," offered Jonathan.

As Morcar had not yet found a chauffeur to replace Jessopp, and the December roads were icy, he agreed. Jennifer coloured.

"I hoped you were coming with me, Jonathan," she said.

"I can't, Mother! I can't give public support to something I don't believe in," exclaimed Jonathan angrily.

"That's a piece of luck for Nat Armitage," thought Morcar, as he saw the tears spring to Jennifer's eyes. Aloud he said: "Agnosticism is a phase intelligent young men often pass through."

"Did you pass through it?" said Jonathan, looking daggers.

"I'm not through yet," said Morcar mildly.

Jennifer with an exclamation rose and left the table.

"I'm going to the Mellors' for midday Christmas dinner, if that's all right to you, Grandfather," said Chuff in a defiant tone.

"Oh, certainly."

"I'll be back for our evening Christmas dinner here, of course," said Chuff.

"See that you're not late."

"I won't be late," cried Chuff cheerfully, bounding away.

"Well, this is a nice how-d'ye-do, us all going off in different directions," thought Morcar, as he sat with his arm along the back of the car seat, round Susie's shoulders, while Jonathan drove rather faster than Morcar liked, down the valley. He could not make himself refrain from saying: "It's an awkward turn here, be careful, Jonathan."

"Yes," said Jonathan curtly.

Morcar unlocked the mill gates, and the various necessary doors; they arrived in his office, which felt wretched, both cold and stuffy.

"Now, where shall we place it?" said Susie in an extremely sensible and practical tone. She produced the white box, which Morcar had been uneasily aware she was clutching, and extracted the lamb. "I think here," she said, placing it at an angle on Morcar's desk.

In this position it looked extremely well. Morcar and Jonathan exchanged glances, relieved but astonished.

"I didn't know you meant me to keep it here, Susie," said Morcar.

"This is the place you like best, Grandfather, isn't it?"

"Yes, Susie, it is. I feel rather sorry to leave the lamb alone here today, though," said Morcar.

"We can take it home and you can bring it here when the holidays are over," suggested Susie, stretching out her hand towards the lamb.

"No, no. Leave it where you placed it. I prefer that," said Morcar hastily, giving the animal a settling pat. "It's cold here. We'd best go home."

As they approached Stanney Royd they saw Nat Armitage's white Jaguar standing by the gate.

"Well, that's settled, choose how," thought Morcar.

He sighed, and glanced at Jonathan. The young man gazed straight ahead, silent and sombre.

III

THREE TOGETHER

III: THREE TOGETHER

23. Susie and Jonathan

IT WAS NEW YEAR'S EVE; Morcar sat reading the *Wool Record* in his den.

"Grandfather?"

"Well, what is it, Pussy?" said Morcar, looking fondly at her.

"When Aunt Jennie gets married, will Jonathan stay here or go to live with her?"

"I don't know, Pussy," said Morcar, to whom this was a question bringing pain.

"I should like him to stay here."

"So should I."

"He won't stay unless somebody asks him to stay."

"Well, you ask him."

"He won't stay unless *you* ask him, Grandfather."

"How do you women know these things?" joked Morcar, for of course she was right.

"I know," said Susie gravely.

"Well, I'll see what I can do," said Morcar, sighing. "Of course, when he finishes at Oxford, he'll take a job somewhere and go and live there, you know."

"He could come home for holidays."

"He could. But I don't know if he will."

"Ask him, Grandfather."

Her voice held pain. Morcar had hardly recovered from this when Jonathan himself entered the room.

"We ought to start in ten minutes, Pussy," he said.

That this pet name, a cherished secret between himself and Susie, never used by them in public, never heard from Jennifer or even Chuff, and hitherto supposed by Morcar to be unknown to all, should spring thus naturally from the lips of Jonathan, was a thunderstroke. And Susie did not start or exclaim; to her it was a customary usage. She merely smiled, detached herself from Morcar's chair, and left the study saying she would fetch her coat. But the smile was a revelation. Good God, thought Morcar, those two are in love. Don't be absurd, she's only fourteen. But everybody says that young people nowadays are years older than they were in my time. He looked at Jonathan, whose fine lips were also curved into a smile—a tender, protective smile, thought Morcar; he doesn't know he's in love with her, but Susie knows. Morcar felt a strange anguish and a strange pleasure, in conflict throughout his body. He said hoarsely:

"Where are you off to with Susie? Theatre, eh?"

"Yes."

"Something highbrow, I suppose?"

"Brecht," said Jonathan, laughing.

Morcar made a *moue*. However, this was a good opportunity to broach the subject of Jonathan's future residence. He nerved himself and began.

"Jonathan, your mother tells me she plans to marry in the spring."

"March or April," said Jonathan stiffly, ceasing to smile.

"Now I hope you'll continue to regard Stanney Royd as your home," said Morcar. "There's no need for you to go rushing off to Nat Armitage, now is there?"

"No," said Jonathan in a choked tone.

"Well, stay here then."

"By the autumn I hope to be in a teaching post somewhere."

"But you can come to Stanney Royd in the holidays."

Jonathan stood silent, gazing into the fire.

"Jonathan," said Morcar very soberly—heaven knows whether I'm doing right or not, he thought, but the boy ought to know what he's letting himself in for—"Ought you perhaps to stay at Stanney Royd for Susie's sake?"

Jonathan shifted restlessly and looked aside.

"I don't want to be tied down to Stanney Royd. I want to be on my own, I want to have a home of my own," he said at length.

"Quite right," approved Morcar. "But come here sometimes in the holidays. You're an Annotsfield man after all, Jonathan. Don't you care at all for your native town? For the West Riding?"

"I do, very much."

"Well, come here sometimes. Stanney Royd will always be your home whenever you want it."

"You're very kind, Uncle Harry. But—"

"I'm very kind but I'm too old to understand. Is that it?" demanded Morcar angrily, losing patience and temper in the same moment.

"Well—"

At this moment a motor-cycle near-by started its raucous roar.

"That'll be Chuff, I expect," growled Morcar.

"Well, his classes haven't started again yet, Uncle Harry."

"What he wants a motor-bike for, I don't know."

"He wants to be independent, I expect. If he's saved up for it out of his allowance—or his Syke Mills wages, I don't know his affairs—it's his own affair."

"*He* won't be going to anything highbrow."

"Why should he, if he doesn't wish to?" said Jonathan. He was leaning over backwards in an effort to be fair in saying this, for he had found Chuff's open boredom and derision at a United Nations Association meeting to which he had taken him, rather trying. But he spoke in the reasonable tone Morcar always found irritating.

"Black leather coats, bowling alleys, a motor-bike and a girl on the pillion," said Morcar distastefully. "He'll be sporting a Beatle haircut soon."

"He only wants to be a man of his time," said Jonathan as before. "It's natural."

24. Wedding

JENNIFER'S WEDDING, POSTPONED for a few weeks owing to the death of Nat Armitage's old father—"everyone keeps dying nowadays," said Morcar peevishly—took place on a day of warm spring sunshine.

It was not, of course, a "white" wedding, but everything else was conducted on a ceremonial level. Jennifer looked beautiful in silvery grey; Susie, her single bridesmaid, looked beautiful in white; Morcar had insisted that Jonathan and Chuff should wear morning coats—at his expense, naturally—and though they joked about this old-fashioned notion, they became them well. The buttonholes, bouquets, church decorations, organ voluntaries, choral singing, flowers in the house, champagne, buffet, cars and all other bridal details were arranged on the most handsome and lavish scale which Morcar could command. Everything therefore seemed set for an agreeable occasion, and now that the weather too proved favourable, it seemed that nothing more could be desired.

But Morcar was aware that beneath this glossy and cheerful surface lay several extremely uncomfortable sets of feelings. True, Jennifer's Oldroyd-and-Mellor shares had long since been impartially valued and legally purchased, and now lay in Morcar's hands, so that he had nothing to fear or dislike on that score; the purchase money had been most judicially and advantageously invested, half for Jennifer and half for Jonathan on Jennifer's insistence, with the approval of Nat Armitage and the participation of his broker and solicitor, so there were no resentments or dissatisfactions on that side, though Jonathan had shown some bad temper over the transaction. But though Morcar was deeply glad to be safely in charge of the mill he always felt to be David's, the thought of having to take Jennifer on his arm up a church aisle—Jennifer attended the Anglican church in Marthwaite at the head of the Ire Valley—and hand her over to a man not David, churned him up to such an extent, made him so angrily wretched, that he really did not know how he should manage it. Of course he would manage it perfectly; he was a Yorkshireman and not a man to show his feelings, he would keep a smooth brow and a bland smile, but he found he could not eat his breakfast, and secretly threw it into the fire while (he hoped) nobody was looking.

And if he felt like this, what must Jonathan be feeling? Jonathan's behaviour was impeccable; he smiled affably, ran about the house answering the telephone, receiving telegrams, settling points about cars, having useful chats with waiters. But his face was white and looked hollow and beaky, and his eyes were burning.

Chuff on the other hand, who now stood with Susie by the hearth in Morcar's den—all other Stanney Royd rooms being now invaded by caterers, displays of presents and so on—looked solid and satisfied. He had asked Jonathan, who had asked his mother, who had agreed cordially and asked Morcar, whether Ruth Mellor and her mother and brother could receive invitations; the invitations had been sent and accepted, so Chuff was no doubt looking forward to some happy hours in his love's company. But Susie at his side wore a rather uncertain expression, Morcar thought. Her flowing white frock, exquisitely cut, showed off her charming young body to perfection; the tiny nest of white flowers and lace which perched on her smooth hair was perhaps rather less suitable to her personality. Jennifer, who now swept into the room in her shimmering silk, seemed to think so too perhaps, for she touched it with one finger, seemed to urge it from its place, and said:

"Could you wear it a little further forward, do you think, Susie?"

"Of course, Aunt Jennifer," said Susie sweetly.

Jennifer swept out, on her way, she said, to a last word with Mrs. Jessopp. Susie promptly snatched the lace from her head and threw it to the ground.

"Susie!" gasped Morcar, astounded.

Chuff, however, did not seem dismayed. He laid aside his grey wedding topper with care, picked up the fragile morsel, and offered it to his sister, saying mildly:

"Come on, now. You know you've got to wear it, Susie."

Susie made a slight grimace and tossed her head—her pale hair rippling in the sun was charming—and snatching the hat from Chuff's hand, ran out, murmuring something about getting "the woman" to arrange it for her.

"She means the milliner. It'll be all right," said Chuff soothingly.

"But what was all that about?" asked the bewildered Morcar.

"They never have got on. They both try but they can't manage it," said Chuff as before.

"Jennifer and Susie? But why?"

"Jealousy, I suppose," said Chuff with a shrug.

The words "Of Jonathan?" came to Morcar's lips, but he managed not to utter them. Chuff, however, appeared to understand them unspoken, for he nodded slightly.

Almost immediately Jonathan came in to announce that the groomsmen's car was waiting. Susie came in with the position of her headdress much improved. Jennifer came in, now wearing an agreeable grey hat and carrying a bouquet of freesias. Chuff picked up his hat and gloves. Morcar was so eager for the whole affair to be over that these actions seemed to him to take place in slow motion.

133

"We must be going, I think," said Jonathan.

He went to his mother, laid his hands on her shoulders, and kissed her very tenderly.

"Next time he does that she'll be the wife of another man," thought Morcar.

The young people went to the waiting car, and Morcar and Jennifer were left alone. They sat in silence for a while.

"I have tried to repay you for all your great kindness to me, Uncle Harry," said Jennifer at length.

Her voice shook, her eyes looked moist. Morcar perceived that—as usual, he reflected sardonically—the oldest member of the party would have to provide the courage and tenacity required by the occasion.

"My dear, you have repaid me a thousandfold," he said firmly. "I'm delighted that this happiness should come to you. It is your duty to be happy now," he added, congratulating himself on the shrewdness of this utterance, for he knew his Jennifer and her belief in the calls of duty. He smiled at her reassuringly, and concluded: "That's a delicious hat."

"Rather gay, perhaps?"

"Not in my opinion," said Morcar, laughing.

At long last the car came and they drove up the valley to the church. A small crowd had collected round the church gate, and when he entered the building and saw the congregation, Morcar was not surprised. They've had their money's worth, he reflected. For the number of mink stoles, petal hats, bright new suits, pale suède gloves, strings of real pearls, grey toppers and morning coats, was quite phenomenal; the textile aristocracy of the West Riding was assembled there.

"I wish Edwin could have come," said Jennifer, alluding to her brother, as they stood in the porch.

"The demands of the service," Morcar reminded her mechanically, hoping that he was using the right phrase—Edwin was at sea off Malaysia.

The ceremony was carried through in excellent style. The groomsmen had sorted the guests efficiently, Susie had recovered her temper and smiled sweetly (Jonathan had perhaps said a word, reflected Morcar); the organ notes rolled, the choir's trebles soared, admirably through the air; the sacred words were pronounced with proper dignity, the inaudible address to the married pair was brief; there was an uncomfortable moment in the vestry, when

Jennifer's hand, signing *Oldroyd* for the last time, shook, but this was soon over; the wedding march sounded in triumph, Nat Armitage appeared as happy as a dog with two tails as he limped down the aisle with his wife on his arm, and Jennifer all of a sudden, to Morcar's relief, began to look very young and very happy.

Involved at Stanney Royd with Armitage sisters and cousins and aunts, Morcar played the genial host with verve—it was a performance, but one he acted well, taking pleasure in his own virtuosity. Speeches were made, toasts drunk; voices grew shrill and loud; the bridal pair went off to change, and Morcar suddenly felt a hundred years old and totally exhausted. He sank down into the deep settee in his den; he badly needed a drink, and Jonathan was near, leaning against the mantelpiece engaged in earnest talk with a thin bearded young man so like Ruth Mellor that he must be her brother. But it was no use asking Jonathan for a drink, Morcar thought; Jonathan would bring him tomato juice, or perhaps, conceding a point, a very pale whisky, with a disapproving air. Above the heads of milling guests, he caught sight of Chuff and held up a finger; Chuff replied with a gesture indicating a glass and Morcar nodded. A waiter almost immediately came smiling to him with a double whisky, neat, alone on a tray; Morcar drank and felt better. But now, unfortunately, Chuff loomed in front of him with an unknown female in tow; she was in middle life, tall, thin, rather sallow, rather sharp in feature but not unhandsome, with dark grey eyes, and mid-brown hair going grey.

"This is my grandfather, Mrs. Mellor," began Chuff.

Morcar heaved himself up reluctantly from his corner in the settee.

"Pray don't rise. I'm G. B. Mellor's widow, Mr. Morcar."

"Ruth's mother," confirmed Chuff.

"Ah. I'm very glad to meet you," lied Morcar, eyeing her shrewdly. She was clad austerely in a navy blue suit of poor cloth, with navy blue gloves—"a good match but made of fabric," observed Morcar—a very plain hat and a very small brooch. "Can't afford real pearls and won't stoop to artificial ones. No beads, thank goodness."

"You treated me very honourably after my husband's death, Mr. Morcar."

"I hope I always behave honourably, Mrs. Mellor," said Morcar, annoyed.

"I am referring to your purchase of my husband's interests in Old Syke Mill."

"It was at the market price."

"Slightly above, I think."

Unable to deny this, Morcar slightly bowed. "The value has risen since," he said.

"But of course the pound has dropped."

"Unfortunately."

"You hold all the shares now."

"Did Chuff tell you that?" said Morcar, vexed.

"No, indeed. He would think it improper to discuss your affairs, and so, I assure you, would I. It's just common talk in Annotsfield, you know. Grape-vine."

"A tongue like a needle," thought Morcar, and it occurred to him that Chuff's slow speech, even his slow sulks, might be welcome to a girl whose mother had a tongue of such sharpness. Mrs. Mellor was certainly, however, a woman of intelligence, who expressed herself with lucidity.

"Won't you sit down?" he said, trying not to sound reluctant.

Mrs. Mellor had clearly been expecting this, and the two sat down together.

"Run away, Chuff," said Mrs. Mellor pleasantly, waving him off. "I want to talk to your grandfather."

Chuff and Morcar exchanged a glance of sympathy, which revealed that their opinions of Mrs. Mellor coincided; Mrs. Mellor regarded them with a smile which revealed that she was aware of this.

"I've taken an afternoon off work so as to have this opportunity of a talk with you, Mr. Morcar."

"Very kind of you," said Morcar sardonically.

"I teach domestic science at the Annotsfield Technical College," said Mrs. Mellor briskly. "I have taught all my adult life. Except for the few months when my children were born, naturally."

"Naturally," murmured Morcar as before.

"I expect you knew at once I was a teacher," said Mrs. Mellor. "One's profession marks one, I am told."

"Well," said Morcar, torn between respect for the widow who had brought her children up successfully on her earnings—even with the help of the Welfare State and the money from the sale of Old Mill—and dislike for her type: "I must confess I thought you were a do-gooder of some kind."

Mrs. Mellor looked at him sharply. Morcar gave her a kind if teasing smile. After a pause she smiled in turn. Her smile was agreeable.

"I can see that you are genuinely formidable, Mr. Morcar," said she.

"I was thinking just the same of you."

They laughed together amicably.

"Well now, what about my Ruth and your Chuff."

"Ah," said Morcar non-committally.

"I'm sure you're just as disappointed about the attachment as I am."

"Why are you disappointed, Mrs. Mellor?"

"I don't think Chuff is Ruth's mental equal, Mr. Morcar. Ruth is a serious, intelligent girl. I hoped she would become a teacher, and she could easily have found a place in a training college—her examination results were excellent. But she declined. It was a severe disappointment to me."

"She wanted to see a bit more life, I expect," said Morcar comfortably.

"No life is nobler than a teacher's," said Mrs. Morcar.

"Theoretically I agree with you," began Morcar, "but—"

"And now Chuff," went on Mrs. Mellor. "That too, Mr. Morcar, is a disappointment."

Morcar observed with amusement and pleasure that Mrs. Mellor's lack of interest in Chuff's extremely favourable financial prospects was genuine. He began to like the woman. But he must defend Chuff, yet avoid committing him.

"If only it had been his cousin, now," Mrs. Mellor was saying.

Morcar, startled, grunted interrogatively.

"Young Mr. Oldroyd. A really serious young man. With such admirable political ambitions, I understand. It was my husband's great ambition to stand for Parliament, Mr. Morcar."

"Yes, I remember your husband's political views," said Morcar. "I don't share them. He was Labour. I am a Liberal."

"Chuff, I'm afraid, is a born Tory."

"Well, in this country we can live together without cutting each other's throats."

"That is for the next generation to decide," said Mrs. Mellor with decision. "Mr. Morcar, I came here this afternoon in order to ask you a plain question."

"Then pray ask it," snapped Morcar. He thought of the use-

ful phrase: "I have other guests," but for Chuff's sake bit it back.
"Do you disapprove of an attachment between Chuff and Ruth?"

"No. Why should I? But I'm not going to guarantee that it will last. That's entirely up to the young people. I have my grandson's word that there will be no courtship in office hours, but if you think Ruth ought to leave Syke Mill—"

"Oh, no!" said Mrs. Mellor in a tone of surprise. "She likes working there."

"She's a good secretary," said Morcar, taken aback but rather touched by the innocence of Mrs. Mellor's tone.

At this moment he became aware that Ruth herself was standing in front of him, smiling. In a very neat suit of (an odd but good) deep rose, which showed off her admirable figure well but not too much, she stood as straight as a poker, with her feet well together; her eyes danced; her smile was mischievous and provoking. Morcar felt that she was well aware of being the subject of the conversation on the settee, disapproved of her mother's approach but did not care a damn for that or for anybody else's opinion.

"She's enough spirit to sink a three-decker," he thought with a grin of appreciation. "Chuff hasn't a chance to resist her."

"Well, Ruth," he said aloud. "We were talking of you. I was telling your mother that you are a good secretary."

"Thank you, Mr. Morcar," said Ruth demurely.

"We'd best go into the garden and line up for the bridal departure," said Morcar, hauling himself up by the arm of the settee.

Ruth with a look of affectionate derision made to put a hand beneath her mother's elbow.

"I can manage myself, thank you," said Mrs. Mellor sharply. "You had better help Mr. Morcar."

Ruth had fortunately far too much good sense to act on this (to Morcar) preposterous suggestion.

In a few moments the bride and bridegroom duly departed, amid the customary ceremonies. Jennifer again looked young and happy; it seemed to Morcar as he took her farewell kiss that her years of widowhood had rolled like a burdensome weight from her shoulders.

The guests promptly left; the house, at first a shambles, was soon restored to its normal neatness by the caterers under the superintendence of Mrs. Jessopp, but felt empty and suddenly cold. A snack meal from the remnants of the buffet was served by Mrs. Jessopp, and the five young people—for Ruth and her brother stayed to share it—ate heartily and with apparent enjoyment. In spite of this they managed to talk a great deal.

"Do you iron your hair, Ruth?" enquired Susie in her sweet clear tones. "To keep it so straight and smooth, I mean?"

"Well, no," said Ruth. "It sounds rather risky to me."

"At school it's the latest," said Susie. "Some girls iron it every night."

Morcar and Jonathan listened to this with indulgent smiles. Chuff laughed. G.B. (as they seemed to call him, like his father, observed Morcar) said disapprovingly:

"What a silly idea."

"It's not sillier than anything else, really," said Susie in a thoughtful tone. "If you want straight hair, ironing will do it for you, at very small cost."

"Don't try it, Susie," said Jonathan quickly. "You might burn yourself—your neck or your ears."

"Oh, I don't think so," said Susie. "You just spread it out on the table, like this." She suited the action to the word, laying her head sideways so that half the silky golden mass spread out horizontally. "You can damp your hair a bit if you like, and don't have the iron too hot. Then you do the other side the same way."

"You don't need to do *anything* to your hair, Susie," said Ruth with emphasis. "It's perfect as it is."

Susie laughed with surprised pleasure, and looked at Jonathan to see if he approved. He smiled and Susie was satisfied.

"I suppose human hair could be woven into a fabric," remarked Chuff. The association was natural, for his sister's extended chevelure resembled a carpet.

"You think of nothing but fabric, Chuff," said G.B. impatiently.

"It's my job."

"There are more important questions. Woollen textiles are a dying trade, anyhow."

"Oh, thank you very much!" exclaimed Morcar, furious.

"I'm sorry, Mr. Morcar, but you know it's true."

"People will always have to wear clothes, in this climate at any rate."

"The fabrics of the future will be man-made," pronounced G.B.

"Look, my boy," said Morcar, making an effort to speak

mildly: "You know nothing about textiles, so let's not discuss them."

"As you please," rejoined G.B., not at all discomposed. "But you can't ignore the trek to the south, Mr. Morcar."

"I ignore nothing," said Morcar gruffly. "If the fools want to go, let them go. Since you're so well-informed," he went on, conscious of a desire to strike back at the young man and not resisting it, "I should like to hear what you think about these riots of Mods and Rockers or whatever they call themselves, at the seaside resorts this spring."

"Not enough amenities are provided nowadays for the young to engage their minds," said G.B. gravely.

"In fact, it's everybody's fault but their own," said Morcar.

"That's not quite what I said," said G.B., colouring. "Society is responsible—"

"The time! Look at the time! We must be off!" exclaimed Jonathan suddenly. (And tactfully, as usual, thought Morcar.)

In a sudden scramble the five rushed away from the table to pile into the boys' car; it seemed they were off somewhere to some theatrical celebration of the four-hundredth anniversary of Shakespeare's birth. Morcar, relieved by the cessation of noise and bustle, found himself unable to eat further; retiring to his den, he sank thankfully on the settee. Jonathan, running past the window, caught sight of him and waved farewell, but presently returned.

"Would you like to come with us, Uncle Harry?" he said diffidently. "Yes, do come! I'm sure we can easily get you a ticket. I'll telephone now."

"No, no," said Morcar. In truth, he would quite liked to have attended the celebration in question, but not, he reflected, with those five youngsters frothing round his feet. Jennifer had been at once bridge and bulwark between himself and this rising generation; he was going to miss her badly. "No. Kind of you to think of it, but I'm a bit tired," he said. This was true, but not quite for the reasons implied. "I've some reading to do. You go off and enjoy yourselves."

Jonathan smiled and danced away, obviously relieved.

"I bore them as much as they bore me," reflected Morcar.

He put his feet up on the settee and lighted a cigar, feeling old and lonely.

25. *Summer*

Looking back on it from gloomier days, Morcar thought the summer of that year passed off rather well.

For strangely enough—but perhaps after all not so strange; in his ardent young creative days Morcar had often found his best inspirations arising after a bout of depression—the morning after the wedding he woke with a first-class design almost fully formed in his mind. It was a tweed for ladies' wear, the colours mainly a deep rose and a pale lemon. He was aware that these strangely assorted tints came from Ruth's suit in shadow and Susie's hair in sunshine, and chuckled to himself over the knowledge. The cloth would be just the thing for Old Mill, which specialised in woollens; a kind of large, broken check. He rose early, gulped down a cup of hot coffee brought by Mrs. Jessopp in a state of fluster, and rushed off down to the mill. At first, as had so often happened before, he met only doubt from Nathan and hesitation from his head designer, but this time he swept them fiercely along, this time he knew he was right. When the design was fully developed they both agreed; patterns were hastily woven and despatched to his agents all over the world; though it was a bit late for the ordinary season, orders poured in; Old Mill was simply "pulled out" with work. Put into other colour ranges, the design was less successful, but this was often the case and did not matter. The West Riding became aware, with admiring envy, that old Harry Morcar had brought it off again.

"There's life in the old dog yet," thought Morcar, and he felt happy.

Shortly after the wedding, the first set of Chuff's Technical College examinations approached and the lad was plunged into deep gloom. He was actually to be seen about the house with books under his arm, looking worried, and he even at times employed Susie to ask him questions on chapters he had memorised. Indeed he was so unlike the normal self-satisfied Chuff that Morcar decided to interview the head of the textile department of the College and ask his advice.

He was amazed when he dismounted at the College to see how greatly it had changed since his young days: three times the size, as plain as a mill, no scrolls or pillars, enough plate-glass to furnish a pair of multiple stores. He was directed to the basement (admirably lighted by fluorescent bars) and found the man he sought in a long hall amid several types of looms. It was morning and they were hushed and unattended.

"He's not an academic type, Mr. Morcar. He doesn't learn easily from books. And he doesn't express himself in examination style, if you follow me."

Morcar groaned.

"But he's not too bad at his textiles. He'll get through those all right. It's a great help to him being so much with you."

"Really?" said Morcar, surprised.

"Yes, indeed, Mr. Morcar. But he must finish the course, he must take all three years, he must go through to the end."

"Well, of course."

"He's talking about giving it up. But you must keep him at it, Mr. Morcar. You must indeed."

"Trust me," said Morcar grimly.

"Why not take him through every department of Syke Mills, Mr. Morcar, and put him a set of questions on each? As you walk along, you know. If he was weak on any point, you could explain it on the spot. He learns best that way. And after all, nobody is better qualified than yourself."

So low had Morcar's spirits been in the last year or two, through his conflicts with youth, that he felt actually surprised and pleased by this tribute. He did not quite know what to reply, so gave a non-committal murmur. Turning away, he found himself face to face with the Principal of the Technical College, a large firm solid man with a wide smile which Morcar perceived covered an iron will.

"I heard you were here, Mr. Morcar," said he.

Morcar gave another suitable murmur.

"It occurred to me to wonder whether you would care to distribute our certificates this year," said the Principal, as they paced away together. "And give us a short address."

"A prize-giving?" said Morcar, alarmed.

"No, no. We have no prizes. Just awards and certificates. And a short address."

"Well," began Morcar doubtfully.

"As a former student, you know. I've been looking you up in our records. It would encourage our students. I can give you the date now," said the Principal firmly. "Just a short address is all that's needed."

Before they reached the entrance hall Morcar found he had promised to do what the Principal asked. He felt in fact agreeably flattered; he had never been asked to do anything of this kind before and rather looked forward to it.

A day or two before Chuff's examinations began, Morcar took him on the proposed interrogatory tour of Syke Mills. Chuff, who started the tour jauntily enough, not knowing what was in store for him, soon wilted; he sweated with anguish, and gasped hoarsely from time to time that he hadn't learned anything about that particular item yet. At the end he gazed imploringly at his grandfather.

"Well, you're not too bad," conceded Morcar. "I should think you'll just scrape through."

Chuff, who was well aware that textiles were his best subject, groaned.

However, he managed, as Morcar had predicted, to scrape through, and would be amongst the students to receive a certificate from Morcar's hand.

A week before the prize-giving, as Morcar continued to call it, he suddenly discovered that he had not the slightest idea what to say in his address or how to say it. Enquiring among his business associates, he gained little help; most of them, accustomed only to after-dinner speeches, told him to be funny; the more experienced, town councillors and the like, wagged their heads solemnly and said that prize-givings were always difficult because there were present two age-groups, students and their parents; besides, something ethical and at the same time practical was expected. Morcar blenched. He sat at his desk in his den one or two evenings, trying to put a few words together, with little success. On a day when the affair was looming close, he gave a despairing sigh, and Susie, who according to custom was doing her homework as usual at a table on the other side of the room, rose and came over to him.

"Why don't you ask Jonathan what to say, Grandfather?" she suggested.

Morcar winced. This was only an infatuated child's idea, of course, but all the same he felt bitterly ashamed and cast down. Was he so old, so out of touch, so useless, that he must consult a young man nearly fifty years his junior? He brooded on the matter all night without coming to a decision, but next morning as he drove himself down to Syke Mills—he had not yet replaced Jessopp—he suddenly drew up, with a squeal of brakes, in front of the Irebridge Post Office, and going in wrote and despatched a telegram to Jonathan: *Grateful your hints prizegiving speech Annotsfield Technical College Friday Morcar.* He came out chuckling, pleased with himself for facing the facts of modern life; the pain and soreness beneath remained, however.

Next evening when he returned to Stanney Royd an envelope addressed in Jonathan's neat firm hand awaited him. *Dear Uncle Harry*, wrote Jonathan, *a few suggestions herewith.* On a separate sheet Morcar read the following notes:

1. *I am pleased to be here because I was a student in this College from (give dates). Of course the College has changed a good deal since those days. (If anything amusing about old buildings, tell it.) Compliments about its fine modern buildings. In those three (or five) years I took the following courses. (Give their names.) I was lucky enough to win a ?medal in the (title of whatever it was.) Nobody was prouder than I when I received that medal, which I still value; and therefore it gives me particular pleasure—and I mean real pleasure—to hand over medals and awards and certificates to the students of today.*

2. *It wasn't all easy, of course. Anecdote here of something you did wrong in those days. But life of course is never easy. Anecdote here of something Nathan grumbled about lately, or trouble with a customer.*

3. *The only way to achieve anything in life is to devote yourself to it. After family life, your trade or profession should come next in your interest. Total committal. Always be ready to learn something about your work. Anecdotes here about how you are always looking at colours, shapes etc, and about the invention of one or two of your best designs in this way. Very rarely off duty.*

4. *To add something fine to the life of the community is surely the ambition of all. A fine craftsman or woman constantly enriches life in this way. Examples: cloth, machines, housewifery, etc.*

"Why, that's easy," said Morcar, delighted. "I can do that standing on my head. There's that bother I had when I was in South Africa, about the wrong thread of yarn getting woven in. And there's my rose and lemon." He did not even have to remind himself about his City and Guilds medal; that youthful achievement was too greatly prized ever to be forgotten. "Why couldn't I have thought of that myself?" he grumbled, and felt a pang. "He's a clever boy, is Jonathan." He sighed to think how good it would have been to have Jonathan at his side in Syke Mills instead of Chuff. "I mustn't be unfair to Chuff, though," he told himself staunchly. "It's not his fault. Let's see. An anecdote of something I did wrong at the Tech as a lad." He cast his mind back, back over the years to the days when he was twenty, a fresh-faced, eager, ingenuous, trusting lad, the only son of a widow in poor circumstances, fond of cricket, walking to work and back every day because tram-fares were quite out of the question, and regarding a sixpenny bottle of ginger-pop as a great treat.

"Lord, what a simpleton I was!" thought Morcar. "And what have I got out of life through these fifty years of struggle?"

Money? Oh, yes, lashings of money. A couple of tragedies—Charlie, Winnie—and a lot of unhappiness; a brief poignant ecstasy with Christina; friendship with David, affection for Jennifer, and now these children, Jonathan, Chuff, Susie, who all turned out different from what he had hoped. The best thing in his life was his cloth; some of the finest cloths in the West Riding, after all, he reminded himself, feeling cheered.

Please forgive these very brief notes, but time presses this term, concluded Jonathan.

"Working his head off, as usual," snorted Morcar.

The Technical College speech was a great success; indeed Morcar was most agreeably surprised by the applause it received. He enjoyed handing out awards and certificates, and grinned pleasurably when Chuff, crimson with embarrassment, took the small scroll from him with a moist hand.

"I expect I looked much the same at that age," thought Morcar kindly. "His complexion's fairer, more gingery, than mine ever was, though. That's the Oldroyd streak in him, I expect."

The Principal's thanks struck Morcar as surprisingly warm.

"We don't often hear such ideas voiced nowadays," he said.

"They're not out of date, for all that," said Morcar sharply.

"I was certainly not implying anything of the kind," returned the Principal.

"Well, then, what about some more English courses for my Pakistanis?" said Morcar.

"We're doing our best, Mr. Morcar."

"Well, you've got to do better, then."

"And where do I get the money?"

"Shall I give you some?" said Morcar.

"No, no. That would rend the whole educational system from top to toe," said the Principal, sighing. "I'll see what I can do."

Now that this affair was over, Morcar realised that he had been worrying over it; he relaxed. A very happy custom had grown up between himself and Susie, that on Sunday afternoons they should drive over to Nat Armitage's house for tea, to see Jennifer. Chuff of course was out for the day; he went faithfully every Sunday to his grandmother's for a midday dinner, and then escaped joyously to the Mellors' for the evening. ("I hate going to Grandma's," he confided to Jonathan, "but I can't help feeling sorry for the old bag. She doted on my father. That was what was wrong with him really, you know. He never got free till too late. I expect that's why he went to South Africa—to get free, I mean." "Perhaps it was so," agreed Jonathan gravely.) Morcar respected his grandson's faithfulness in this matter, and asked him no questions about his Sundays. Morcar and Susie therefore lunched alone together on Mrs. Jessopp's choicest delicacies; Morcar then fell asleep over the Sunday newspapers while Susie, he guessed, wrote to Jonathan; then they set out together to drive slowly over the hill by a very stony unpaved lane, open to every wind that blew, to Emsley Hall, the huge square mansion under the brow, built in mid-Victorian days when large families were the fashion, where Nat Armitage obstinately still chose to live because it was near the Armitage mills.

Jennifer's marriage was obviously a success. Nat glowed with happiness; Jennifer at first wore the bemused, subdued, timorously delighted air of a young girl on the morning after her first night of marriage, thought Morcar, but after a while seemed to recover herself and settle into contentment. She improved the appearance of the house and wandering hillside garden no end, gave up some of her committees and at Nat's wish entertained a good deal. Her manner, to everyone but especially to Susie, was much softer than of old; she planned treats for the child, took her to social occasions and to shops, and saw that she was plentifully provided with everything a teenager required. Accordingly the relationship between the two seemed easier, and this gave Morcar pleasure. It appeared to him that while Nat and Jennifer could not really wish to have their Sunday afternoons intruded upon, yet the goodness of their hearts was such that they took pleasure in performing what they regarded as an affectionate duty, and thus gave Morcar and Susie a sincere welcome, feeling set free to enjoy themselves in their own way when this duty had been performed. Grandfather and grand-daughter always left the Hall before six o'clock, for either guests would drop in—though it was a severe climb rather than a drop—for drinks in the next hour or Nat and Jennifer would be due for them elsewhere themselves.

When they drove away down the long slightly moss-grown drive Susie always bore with her the letter Jennifer had written earlier that afternoon to Jonathan, which she now handed to Susie with a smile, to be posted at the Annotsfield General Post Office, whence it would travel to Oxford more speedily than if deposited in the single Emsley pillar-box. An agreeable fiction was maintained that Morcar was obliged to drive down to Annotsfield to post his own Sunday-written letters; Morcar, who never wrote a letter in his own hand nowadays if he could avoid it, usually brought a bill or two and their appropriate cheques home from the mill, to sustain this useful myth. Drawing up at the G.P.O., he took these from his pocket and handed them to Susie, who inserted Jennifer's letter and her own into the pile and put them together through the appropriate slot. There was no reason why the fact of Susie's correspondence with Jonathan should be concealed except that Susie evidently wished it so; when she returned to the car her cheek was always very faintly flushed and she wore a secret smile; Morcar would not for anything in the world have roughly brushed this delicate bloom of youth.

The death of old Mr. Shaw in early June did not bring any real grief to Morcar; he had always detested the old rascal, and felt glad on Winnie's account that she should be free from the care of him. Moreover, he was pleased with the way Chuff handled the affair. Chuff suddenly appeared before him in the mill one morning and said that his grandmother had telephoned him to say that her old father had just died, and would Chuff go at once and attend to the funeral arrangements.

"Surely one of her own brothers will look after that," said Morcar.

"There aren't any left here," said Chuff.

"There were four. Two were killed in the 1914 war," said

Morcar—Charlie's death came up before him at once; again he dragged Charlie up the side of that slimy shell-hole; Charlie, Charlie! "One went to South Africa."

"Two," corrected Chuff.

"Oh, well, if two went out there, then of course there aren't any left here," said Morcar gruffly. "But I'll attend to the matter."

"No—I'll do it if you'll tell me what's to be done," said Chuff.

Morcar informed him, and Chuff carried out his instructions faithfully and well. The undertaker, the conduct and place of the service and interment, the notices to the press, flowers from Chuff and Susie with a card suitably inscribed, the printing and despatch of thank-you notices, the wearing of a black tie and so on—all the conventions were well and punctually upheld. Chuff insisted that Sue should accompany him to the funeral.

"How do you feel about that, Susie?" enquired Morcar.

"She'll be quite all right," said Chuff roughly.

"I'm asking Susie."

Susie gave Chuff a cold look, and said: "I intend to go, of course," in a tone of careful indifference, as if her brother had not spoken.

"There is more in that young woman than meets the eye," said Morcar afterwards to Chuff.

"Well, she's mother's daughter, she's got some Oldroyd in her," said Chuff.

In the event Susie behaved, her brother reported, admirably at the funeral, supporting her grandmother when it was needed, but holding her off, as it were, by the perfection of her manners and the coolness of her demeanour.

"I think Grandma was rather afraid of her," said Chuff, laughing.

Morcar instructed his solicitors to write an official letter of condolence to Winnie on his behalf, and to enquire whether the change in her circumstances required any alteration in her alimony. They received from her in reply one of her customary ill-written notes, on cheap lined paper, saying: *If Harry Morcar wants to lower my allowance, he can.* At this Morcar naturally fumed and instructed his solicitors to tell Winnie that he had not, and never had had, any intention of decreasing her alimony. Winnie did not bother to reply. She moved, however, into a smaller house, telling Chuff that the housework of Hurstcote was too much for her nowadays. She found a small Victorian house on the main Annotsfield to Hudley road, not far indeed from the address to which Morcar and his mother had moved during his father's last illness. Although he had not thought of the house in Hurst Road for years, Morcar was vexed by this nearness; he did not want Winnie to be anywhere near anything which had ever belonged to him. At Chuff's request Morcar's solicitors conducted the purchase and sale for Winnie; she made them such a scene about paying their fees for the transactions that the junior partner was quite shaken, and in the event Morcar paid the fees.

"You'd better tell your grandmother than one of these days she'll come to the end of my patience and I shall put my foot down," he told Chuff grimly, and after the following Sunday enquired: "Did you tell your grandmother what I said?"

"Yes. I told her."

"Did she seem to take it in? What did she say?"

"She just grinned," said Chuff, grinning himself.

"Aye! She would!" said Morcar.

"It's a nice little house, Number 23," said Chuff consolingly.

Being now free of evening classes for a month or two, he spent a good deal of time in the evening at this house, helping his grandmother by hanging pictures, putting up shelves, moving furniture and so on. Morcar was pleased by this ready and good-humoured acceptance of a tiresome responsibility. It was not in Morcar's nature—or indeed, as he reflected, in the Yorkshire nature at all—to express his approbation directly, but he conveyed it, he thought, in his tone.

"We had a rare dust-up at Number 23 tonight," said Chuff cheerfully to him, coming in late one evening.

"Oh?" said Morcar, secretly pleased. "How was that, eh?"

"I took Ruth. She and Grandma didn't hit it off."

"They never do," said Morcar wisely.

Chuff perfectly understood this obscure remark, as relating to daughters-in-law (or grand-daughters-in-law) elect, and the two men laughed comfortably together.

Two other agreeable events occurred that summer.

Everybody expected that Jonathan would do well in his Finals, and of course he did. He returned from Oxford looking rather drawn and wan, and muttered remarks cryptic to Morcar about his *viva;* but one morning in August as they all sat at the Stanney Royd breakfast table opening letters, Jonathan suddenly choked, crimsoned and offered Morcar a document, saying in an odd tone:

"Read it, Uncle Harry."

"Read it to me," countered Morcar rather peevishly—he hated to be reminded of his need of spectacles: "I haven't my reading-glasses here."

"Well—I've got a First," said Jonathan, shy.

At this the family exploded into joy. Chuff said: "I say!" in an admiring tone; Susie rushed round the table and kissed Jonathan's cheek; Mrs. Jessop suddenly appeared in the doorway beaming, and cried: "Congratulations!" Morcar said very seriously:

"Well done, my boy."

He offered his hand, and Jonathan took it with some emotion.

It was indeed a solemn moment for Morcar, and he spent the day in a state of euphoria. He had kept his word to David Oldroyd, brought up David's son carefully and well to the point where he could stand on his own feet and earn his own living. Morcar felt the satisfaction of a good unselfish action, honourably and not without toil completed. Jonathan was Christina's grandson, too. While Jonathan rapturously telephoned his mother, Morcar went out into the garden and walked about alone, imagining for a few sweet secret moments that Christina was at his side and they were rejoicing together over her grandson's success.

Naturally Morcar told the good news to everyone he encountered at Syke Mills—Nathan was enraptured; "He was always a clever boy, was Mr. Jonathan," he said, smiling all across his face—and to all the business acquaintances he met on the Bradford Exchange and at lunch. They were suitably impressed, so that when Morcar on his return to Stanney Royd that evening found the floor of his garage covered with stretches of dark green waterproof material intermingled with short metal rods, he was in far too good a temper to utter a murmur to Chuff, who came running out of the house and began to bundle them all together in a hurry.

"What's all this, then?" asked Morcar jovially, dismounting from his car.

"It's our camping stuff," said Chuff. "For our holdiay. We told you, Grandfather."

"In the Lakes," added Susie, who had joined them and was struggling to fold up one of the odd-shaped objects.

150

"Oh, yes, of course. I'd forgotten. When are you off, then?" enquired Morcar.

At this Chuff seemed to scowl at him, and a shade of unhappiness blurred the brightness of Susie's face. Morcar therefore, though ignorant of what this signified, quickly changed the subject.

"What's that you're folding, Susie?" he enquired mildly.

"It's a washbowl," said Susie, setting the object on its feet.

"Very neat," approved Morcar. The things they think of nowadays, he reflected, it's amazing.

The small mystery of the date of their departure was cleared up a few days later, when Susie's examination results arrived and to Morcar's joy and amazement it turned out that she had acquired an astonishing number of O-levels. (Eight, counting one for Music.) It seemed that the holiday party had arranged to wait for the rather uncertain date of arrival of this pair of results, so important to Jonathan and Susie that they could not bear to risk being absent when the announcements arrived

When the news was announced Chuff, laughing, threw his arms round his sister and hugged her.

"You can do it if I can't!" he cried proudly.

Morcar was admiring the total lack of jealousy in this remark when he found that Susie had thrown herself into his own arms and was laughing and crying into his waistcoat.

"I thought I could do it but I didn't like to say so," she wailed in a muffled tone.

"My darling," said Morcar fondly—but not audibly. He stroked her hair. Aloud he said: "I'm very proud of you. We're all proud of you." To himself he thought: "Here's another for a university."

"We might set off tomorrow," suggested Jonathan happily from the background.

"Why not today?" cried Susie, raising her flushed cheeks.

"Yes, why not?" echoed Jonathan, laughing.

"We should have to warn Ruth and G.B.," said Chuff.

"They can come on Saturday as arranged."

Chuff looked sulky.

"I want to take Ruth in the car. She can't carry all her stuff."

"Well, you'll be seeing her this morning at the mill. She can come with us this afternoon."

"Should you mind, Grandfather?" asked Chuff.

"Oh, not at all," said Morcar sardonically. The cool way they ran off with his secretary! Still, he supposed one of the other girls in the office could cope in her place. "I can't give Ruth extra days' holiday with pay, Chuff," he said. "It wouldn't be fair to the other girls. Ruth's holidays are like everybody else's, for a fortnight. I suppose she fixed her fortnight to date from Saturday. It's the Annotsfield Wakes. I daresay I've seen the list, I don't remember."

"We'd better go up on Friday night," said Jonathan.

"Yes," agreed Chuff, still sulky.

Later, Morcar said to Jonathan:

"I'm sorry you're taking G.B. on this trip."

"Why?"

"I don't like him very much."

"He's an earnest, conscientious young man, eager to work for the good of the community," said Jonathan hotly.

"He's brash, self-opinionated, ignorant outside his own specialty and full of resentment."

"His views may be a trifle extreme. But their general tendency is sound."

"I don't suppose he likes me any better than I like him," began Morcar, making a great effort to be fair. "But—"

"On the contrary, he admires you as an interesting specimen of Victorian *entrepreneur*—a typical man of your time."

"Victorian! *Entrepreneur!*" exploded Morcar. "I was seven years old when Queen Victoria died. And I'm not an *entrepreneur*. I make things."

"You cause things to be made."

"And what does *he* make or cause to be made, eh?"

"He's busy with electronics research, Uncle Harry," said Jonathan reproachfully.

"Very contemporary. Well, we won't quarrel about him, Jonathan."

"No, indeed," said Jonathan warmly. "I don't want to quarrel with you about anything, Uncle Harry. I'm too sensible of all you have done for me."

Morcar made a deprecating sound (whose general tendency, as Jonathan would say, he reflected, was "Pooh!") and turned away. "I hope you all have a good holiday," he said.

"Thanks, Uncle Harry. We shan't see much of G.B. anyway, because he's a rock-climber and we aren't. He'll be joining a climbing party most of the time."

For the next two days the house was in a turmoil. Tents and groundsheets and washbowls, sleeping-bags and tins of food, lay everywhere underfoot; Mrs. Jessopp baked busily; trial packings took place on the lawn. At last on Friday evening the car was loaded; Susie sat in the rear surrounded by bags and tins; Chuff and Jonathan were in the front; Chuff drove; the spare seat was reserved for Ruth, whom they were to pick up at the Mellors' flat; G.B. was to make the journey tomorrow on his motor-cycle. The car left.

Morcar ate a peaceful meal alone. It was pleasant to eat in quiet and at one's own speed, to be surrounded by silence, not to have to try to keep up with swift youthful conversation in the obscure modern idiom. After dinner he lay on the settee in his den, lighted a cigar and began to read *The Journal* of the Bradford Textile Society. Mrs. Jessopp brought him coffee.

"I hope you're not too tired by all these preparations, Mrs. Jessopp."

"Well, I am a bit. But it's nice to see them all so happy," said Mrs. Jessopp.

"You're quite right," said Morcar comfortably. Like Mrs. Jessopp, he felt conscious of duty nobly done.

Yes, the summer of that year had gone off well.

26. *Jonathan's Future*

"I THINK HE could do with some advice. I'd be most grateful if you'd let him come and talk to you."

"By all means send him along. But he doesn't need any advice, you know. He needn't worry about training. With a degree like that, he can go straight into a minor public school. Or even a major one. What was his old school?"

Morcar, who had sighted the headmaster of the Annotsfield Grammar School in the restaurant car of the London train, and taken the opportunity to sit opposite him and introduce the problem of Jonathan's future, gave him the name of Jonathan's sufficiently well known public school.

"Well! There he is. They'd be glad to have him. Just tell him to write to the Head. And to his housemaster too, perhaps. Old Starkey'll jump at him."

"He wants to go into a comprehensive school."

"What! He must be mad!" exclaimed the headmaster.

"He's an earnest, conscientious young man, eager to work for the good of the community," said Morcar sardonically, for it seemed to him that the words Jonathan had used to praise G.B. really represented what the young man wished to be himself.

The headmaster stared. There was a pause.

"Well, if that's the case, of course it's very commendable," he said drily. "If that sort of thing is what he wants to make his career, he'd better go to the Department of Education at Leeds University. He may be too late to get in this year—he should have applied earlier. If he has any difficulty, I'd be glad to take him for a few terms myself. It would be useful teaching experience for him; he'd realise what he didn't know and needed to learn. We're terribly short of staff. Yes," he concluded, obviously turning his time-table over in his mind: "I could fit him in very well. But after a term or two in Annotsfield he must go away, you know, Mr. Morcar. It's a great mistake for a young schoolmaster to stay too close to home."

"I suppose so," said Morcar.

"Tell him to write to the Annotsfield Director of Education."

"I'll lay it before him," said Morcar with irony.

"Ah," said the headmaster, laughing, "that's what we have to do nowadays with these young people. Lay it before them and let them choose. I'm all for it myself."

"Quite," said Morcar with a sigh.

27. First Day

JONATHAN COULD HARDLY keep the smile of happiness from his face as he decorously followed the long line of masters into Assembly at the Annotsfield Boys' Grammar School on the first morning of the autumn term. All were wearing their gowns; Jonathan, wearing his for the first time in his native county, was very conscious of its freshness but could not help enjoying it and at the same time looking forward eagerly to the day when it would be old and shabby after say a quarter of a century's long and faithful service. Service was the operative word; after all these long years of feeding his own mind he was now at last going to do something for somebody else. He could hardly restrain his eagerness to begin.

A few minutes later the door of the classroom closed behind him and he was shut in with the thirty-five "twelve plus" year-olds of "his" form, IIA. (Ironically enough, he thought, on one of the walls of the room hung a large diagram illustrating the development of the woollen trade. However, let that pass.) He had met his form briefly before prayers, when the headmaster had introduced him as coming from "a very famous school," and explained what to do about the register. After his departure Jonathan had experienced a little tentative badinage about dinner-money. Jonathan had taken this correctly, he thought, quelling affably certain mystifying remarks which flew about the room—"Will it be Tuesday this term, Mr. Oldroyd?" "It's always Tuesday." "How do *you* know?" "Is it the same money this term, sir?" "It should be more for you, Smithy." "My mother says it should be less," and so on—by saying with a pleasant smile: "Now not too much noise, please," and asking a chubby fresh-faced boy named, it seemed, Grimshaw who sat in the third row and was active in the conversation, for enlightenment on the subject of dinner-money.

"Don't you know about dinner-money, Mr. Oldroyd?" demanded Grimshaw in a tone which Jonathan was forced to admit held a certain contemptuous incredulity. He coloured, but kept his irritation out of his voice and replied mildly: "No. Please inform me."

"Some of us stay to dinner at school," began Grimshaw.

At this moment a bell sounded; there was a general rush to line up at the door, and form IIA departed for Assembly with fair decorum.

Now they were all back again in class. Jonathan drew out from his desk the folder of material which he had carefully prepared for this lesson. Tudors and Stuarts formed the syllabus for form IIA, he had been told, and he looked forward immensely to presenting a rich, glowing picture of the world of the Renaissance to these boys, a picture they would never forget.

"Don't you want to hear about dinner-money, Mr. Oldroyd?" enquired Grimshaw, standing.

"Not now," said Jonathan. Grimshaw scowled and sat down with a flop. Fearing he had hurt the boy's feelings, Jonathan added hastily: "Later. Now we must begin our lesson." Suddenly experiencing a slight nervousness, he paused to collect his thoughts, and turned over the pictures in the folder, deploying them on his desk.

"Are those pictures, sir?" enquired a thin boy in spectacles, who sat in the front row.

"Yes—Shackleton," replied Jonathan, congratulating himself on remembering the boy's name.

"Can we see them?" pursued Shackleton with some eagerness.

"Later," said Jonathan, smiling.

"Latah, latah," chanted Grimshaw. "Everything's latah."

Jonathan, astonished, gazed at him reproachfully. Grimshaw stared back, undismayed.

"Will you put this map up, please, Shackleton?"

"Can we have some drawing-pins, sir?"

Jonathan, who had remembered this detail, produced a box of these at once.

"Ooh, they're *green*. Fancy, *green* drawing-pins," said Grimshaw in a mock-heroic tone.

The map, however, being large and very clear, attracted and held attention, and the slight shuffling and surreptitious conversation which had hitherto formed a background, died away. Jonathan began his lesson, explaining how, beginning from the period they were about to study, the extent of the known world had increased. In developing this theme Jonathan mentioned the spice routes from the East.

"Ooh! Gob-stoppers!" cried Grimshaw.

The class laughed.

"What are gob-stoppers, Grimshaw?" enquired Jonathan, who was not familiar with this (perhaps Yorkshire, he thought) expression.

"They're very large sweets, sir," explained Shackleton kindly.

"Sweets! But spices are not sweets," said Jonathan, laughing.

"Oh, yes, they are! Toffees! Chocolate almonds! Humbugs! That's spice," cried various members of the class.

"Pomfret cakes," added a boy in the back row.

"Pomfret cakes; well now, that's rather interesting," said Jonathan eagerly. "*Pomfret,* that is short for Pontefract. Liquorice used to grow round Pontefract, you know, and so Pomfret cakes were made there."

"They're still made there!" cried a boy. "My uncle says—"

"Yes, you're right, they are," said Jonathan, pleased to be able to agree. "But nowadays all the liquorice comes from Turkey."

For some reason the class seemed to find this rather disheartening, and fell silent.

"Well, that's what you said, sir," said Shackleton reasonably after a pause. "Spice comes from the east."

"But it's not that kind of spice I was talking about," cried Jonathan, horrified to find how far he had been led from his subject. "Spices are nutmeg, cloves, cinnamon—all pungent in taste, not sweet."

"Pungent?" said somebody in a questioning tone.

"Savoury," explained Jonathan.

"Spicy," said somebody else.

There was a titter.

"Well, that's where we get the word from," said Jonathan. "Nutmeg, cinnamon—"

"What do they use spices for, sir?" put in Shackleton.

"To flavour food when cooking, give it a savoury taste."

"Stew? Would they flavour stew with spice?"

"Stew—and—gravies," said Jonathan, somewhat at a loss.

"I don't like stew," came from the right.

"Oh, you should taste my grandma's stew," said Grimshaw, smacking his lips.

"Nutmeg, cinnamon, cloves," resumed Jonathan in a summarising tone: "were brought—"

"He clove her in twain," observed Grimshaw.

At this Jonathan looked very grave. For a moment he was silent, debating whether to notice the remark or not. To his surprise, he found that the class had fallen silent too, and was eyeing him with some anxiety. He decided to disregard Grimshaw's (perhaps ignorantly lewd) comment, because he really could not think of anything suitable to say in reply.

"Let us trace the spice routes," he said in a cold tone, turning to the map and beginning to talk about Venice.

For a few moments all went reasonably well. A picture of Venice, and one of a doge with fur-edged coat, were passed round the class with reasonable expedition, and favourably received.

"Where do furs come from, sir?" enquired Shackleton.

157

Jonathan hesitated, framing his reply.

"He doesn't know," said Grimshaw scornfully.

"At the beginning of the period we're talking about," began Jonathan. ("Who's talking?" enquired Grimshaw.) "Furs came chiefly from the East—"

"Everything seems to come from the East."

"But when towards the end of the century America was discovered by Columbus, after that furs—"

"Do kittens have fur?" broke in a rather plump boy named Smith.

"Of course they do," said Grimshaw scornfully.

"Certainly," said Jonathan. "Now—"

"Do all animals have fur, sir?"

"Either fur or hair," replied Jonathan, considering. "Fur-bearing animals—"

"Which have which?"

"Cows have fur," declared Grimshaw.

"No, they don't. Horses and cows and dogs have hair," said Smith.

"Kittens have fur."

"Fur-bearing animals have fur, and hairy animals have hair," pronounced Grimshaw. "So now you know."

"Let us get back to our subject, boys," said Jonathan in an artificially mild tone. ("What on earth am I talking about America for?" he thought amid the whirl. "That's the next but one lesson in the course, not this one.")

"Kittens. That's what we were talking about, Mr. Oldroyd."

"Could you make a fur coat from kitten's fur?"

"If you had enough, you could, but they're very small," said Shackleton, peace-making.

"Enough! There are too many kittens, always. You have to drown some."

"No, you don't! That's cruel!" cried the class.

"Yes, you do. My auntie's cat had two lots of kittens last year."

"She couldn't have had."

"Yes, she *could*. She *did*."

"My grandma's cat had seventy kittens in eight years," shrilled Grimshaw.

A roar of laughter greeted this contribution.

"It's true! My grandma told me," cried Grimshaw.

Jonathan lost his temper.

"Be quiet!" he shouted, crimsoning.

Instantly silence fell. Jonathan tried hastily to find his way back to his prepared script for the lesson. He could not remember a word of it. Something must be said, however. He pointed to the Hudson Bay area on the map, controlled his voice and said quietly: "All over this vast forested region with its great mountains and rivers, trappers were at work."

"What sort of animals did they trap, sir?" enquired Shackleton, who, as usual, really wanted to know.

"Fur-bearing animals," said Grimshaw *sotto voce*.

"Beaver," said Jonathan, hastily racking his brains, from which the name of every Canadian animal seemed to have fled. "Fox. Squirrel. Skunk."

"Ugh! Skunk!" said Grimshaw, wrinkling his nose.

At this all the class wrinkled their noses.

"Bob cat perhaps," said Jonathan hurriedly.

"Are bob cats like our cats?"

"Larger, and with yellow fur," said someone at the back.

"I think some have spots. I've seen them on the telly."

"Yes. so have I."

"My grandma's cat has four white boots," said Grimshaw.

"Oh, Grimmy's grandma's cat!" cried several voices in joyous derision.

"Leave my grandma alone!" shouted Grimshaw.

At this moment the bell rang and the lesson terminated.

Flushed, astounded, defeated and altogether wretched—how on earth had he been decoyed from history to zoology, and two centuries forward in time?—Jonathan hastily threw his papers together. "My pictures of Venice, please!" he cried repeatedly. At first he was not heard above the din, then at last Shackleton made a dash and rescued the pictures—creased and dirty—from the floor, and placed them in his hand. Thankfully Jonathan turned to leave the room.

In the doorway he met a long lean grey-haired master of commanding appearance who gave him a kindly smile. It was so obvious that this man had heard the uproar coming from Jonathan's attempt at teaching that the young man felt obliged in mere honesty to make a reference to his lack of success.

"I'm afraid I didn't do that very well," he said, forcing a rueful grin.

"Never mind. You'll learn," said the elderly master. "Let me give you a tip—beware the side-tracking question. Never answer it."

"Yes, indeed," agreed Jonathan fervently, seeing in a flash his errors in this respect. "I've learned that already, I think."

"Where are you going now?"

"Iᴀ English. I'm to help out with English here and there."

"Give them a bit of dictation to keep them quiet, and then let them read."

"But what?" said Jonathan, flustered, and thinking regretfully of the lesson he had earnestly prepared.

"*The Wind in the Willows* is the thing. There'll be copies in the form cupboard. Dictate a piece with no dialogue," said his mentor, disappearing into Jonathan's form room, which instantly fell still.

Jonathan thankfully accepted this advice, and things went fairly well until some of the forty-strong class began to repeat under their breath what he had said. At first Jonathan could not see the point of this, but he was already sufficiently alerted to judging the mood of a class to recognise that its intention was hostile. Genuinely perplexed, he looked enquiringly into the faces of those thus repeating, not always accurately, what he had dictated; they giggled and turned aside. It came to him (slowly) that their speech had a curious twang, not wholly native. Suddenly he remembered Grimshaw's "latah, latah," and it struck him with the force of a blow that these eleven-plussers were deriding, by imitating, his accent.

It had never occurred to Jonathan to listen to his own speech. He had taken for granted, without a single conscious thought, that he and his mother and Susie spoke the ordinary English of educated persons, and that Morcar had a hearty Yorkshire inflexion which Jonathan enjoyed. (To his affectionate amusement, Chuff's slight South African twang had recently shown signs of developing a Yorkshire note.) But that his own speech might be considered— obviously was being so considered by these children—"south-country" and "la-di-da" was a personal reflection which made all his hackles rise.

"Are you trying to imitate the way I speak?" he said to the next child who attempted it.

Naturally there was no audible response to this, but from their looks he perceived that the whole class was guilty.

Jonathan laughed. (Perhaps, he reflected afterwards in the free period which mercifully followed, there had been just a trace of bitterness in this laugh.)

"Well, try harder," he said.

The class was silent for the remainder of the dictation, but they looked glum and suspicious; they imagined, Jonathan saw too late, that he was deriding their own accents.

Their reading was atrocious.

The six lessons and one free period of the day were over at last. In the afternoon Jonathan had two consecutive periods with a section of the sixth form. With these twelve lads, only a few years younger than Jonathan, and interested in him, because his Oxford career was exactly what they wished for themselves, as well as in his subject, he had unqualified success; the time sped by, the response was all that he had hoped. He left them with confidence restored, feeling happy. Unfortunately, for the last period of the day he had to cope with the thirteen-year-olds of Form III. The result was chaos.

Jonathan came home to Stanney Royd feeling that the dearest ambition of his heart—to realise which, he felt, he had fought Morcar tooth and nail for years—was totally out of his reach; he was totally unsuited for, incapable of, teaching.

28. Chuff and Jonathan

"Well, how did it go today, Jonathan?" enquired Morcar comfortably, as they all sat at coffee in the den that evening.

"Not too well, I'm afraid," said Jonathan, putting on a cheerful air.

"I wouldn't do teaching for the world—standing up in front of a lot of little boys and messing about with chalk on a board," said Chuff.

"Well, nobody is asking you to teach," said Jonathan with some asperity.

"I don't think it's your line at all, Jonathan," continued Chuff.

"How would you like it if I said I didn't think textiles were your line," cried Jonathan angrily, his temper, frayed by the events of the day, suddenly giving way.

"Are you saying that? Eh?" said Chuff, turning crimson.

"Nowadays managerial competence is the essential, not family inheritance," snapped Jonathan. "I don't think you're particularly well qualified to take over Syke Mills."

"Ah, hell, man, you're jealous," said Chuff contemptuously.

Jonathan laughed, and Morcar said: "Now come, Chuff. You know perfectly well that Jonathan declined to enter textiles."

"More fool he," said Chuff.

"I'd better go, or we shall quarrel," said Jonathan, rising. Susie at once rose too.

"We *have* quarrelled," said Chuff.

"Now that's enough. Stop it at once, you two," said Morcar sternly. "Each of you owes the other an apology."

After a pause Jonathan said in a stifled tone: "I agree. I apologise."

"Oh, so do I," said Chuff, offhand.

Jonathan went out into the garden by the window, and Susie followed.

"All the same, I don't think teaching's Jonathan's line at all," persisted Chuff.

"Just because it's not your line, doesn't mean it isn't a fine career," Morcar reproved him. "It's what Jonathan wants to do and I respect him for it, and you have no right to interfere."

"I still don't think it's Jonathan's line."

"But you know nothing about it," said Morcar crossly.

"He cares too much about everything. He's not tough enough."

"I disagree. He goes in for these marches and has brushes with the police."

"He just sits down, and they carry him off. Oh, it takes courage, I expect," said Chuff, "but it's rather, rather—"

"Passive?"

"Yes. He's not aggressive. He doesn't stand up enough for himself. He's not tough."

"And you are tough, I suppose."

"Toughish," said Chuff with a grin.

He rose, but remained where he was, standing and gazing at his grandfather. Morcar looked at him enquiringly.

"I get a bit tired of it, you know, grandfather," said Chuff at length.

"Tired of what?"

"Everybody liking Jonathan so much better than they like me.

You do, and Aunt Jennifer of course, and Mrs. Jessopp. And even Susie. And Mrs. Mellor, and G.B."

"What about Ruth?" blurted Morcar, alarmed.

Chuff smiled. "Oh, Ruth's all right," he said. He paused. "The trouble is," he added with a rather nervous grin: "I agree with them."

"Chuff, you're all right," said Morcar. He felt guilty; he had never given a thought to the boy's possible jealousy of his cousin.

"Ha!" said Chuff. "Not to worry, grandfather. As Jonathan would say," he added sardonically.

He laughed, and bounced out of the room.

29. Jonathan and Susie

MEANWHILE SUSIE AND Jonathan paced round the garden.

"Just once more," said Jonathan. "Then I must get to work on tomorrow's lessons." He sighed. "I'm sorry I was rude to Chuff, Susie. I wasn't really accusing Chuff. It was just the principle of the thing. I'm really very fond of Chuff, but he annoyed me."

"He's fond of you. But he feels you're sort of superior."

"He dances better than I do—everything physical he does better than I do," expostulated Jonathan. "It was just that—"

"You're disappointed with school," said Susie softly.

"With myself. It's not easy to take when one's efforts have always succeeded before."

"I suppose teaching's as difficult to learn as anything else."

Jonathan laughed rather harshly.

"I mean, if you wanted to be good at playing in an orchestra, you wouldn't expect to be at Hallé standard on your first day," said Susie.

"You're right," exclaimed Jonathan. He reflected, then said: "Teaching is more than just exposition, Susie."

"What is it, then?"

"I don't know—yet. Pussy, I ought to have gone to that Training College."

"You can go next year," said Susie, comforting.

IV

TEXTILE

IV: TEXTILE

30. Ring Road

ALL OF A sudden Morcar felt deadly tired.

His Scandinavian agent was an excellent agent and an honest and agreeable man, but they had been together for five days and had nothing more to say to each other. They had talked of the rose and lemon, of worsted plans for next spring, of the rose and lemon, of the sales of the rose and lemon, of the iniquities of competitors, of the changing market, of the rose and lemon, of what was to replace the rose and lemon next year. Morcar felt sick and tired of the rose and lemon, and at the same time uncomfortably conscious that he had nothing else as good to replace it. Some inspiration would probably come in a few months, but it could not be forced. Inspirations did not bubble up in his mind nowadays as often as they used to do twenty or thirty years ago. The head of his designing department, though admirable in development, had not a very original mind—or if he had, he'd forgotten how to use it in his long years of service under a man who always provided the necessary originality himself. Morcar did not wish his Scandinavian agent to know that he had no brilliant idea in mind for next season. The agent naturally wished to probe into Morcar's plans. There was therefore a friendly tussle, a conflict of aim, between them. Morcar was well able to keep his end up in a tussle of this kind; in a genial, forthright manner, without one definite word, he conveyed the impression that he had a first-class design on the point of emerging from his sleeve, but preferred not to particularise it just yet. The agent—a shrewd man, or he would not be Morcar's agent—was not quite convinced and not quite unconvinced, but found Morcar too good and reliable a provider to annoy. They therefore tussled amicably. But now, all of a sudden, as they were on their way into lunch at the Palace Hotel in Copenhagen where Morcar was staying (his agent had come to meet him there) he suddenly felt that he simply could not bear any more of it. He was tired *out*. He had booked a seat on a plane leaving for Manchester the following afternoon, but the thought of spending another afternoon, evening and morning in his agent's company was suddenly intolerable. But what hope was there of avoiding it without hurting the man's feelings?

As they passed the receptionist's desk the clerk gestured to him. He approached and took the proffered letter from the man's hand. Almost he stuffed it into his pocket without opening it, for from the stamp and the typescript of the address he knew it would be Chuff's daily screed. He had commanded from Chuff a daily account of what was going on at Syke, Daisy and Old Mills. He knew that this was a chore Chuff loathed, he knew that the information thus too frequently collected had a bulk out of proportion to its value. He knew also that mainly it was Nathan who supplied it and mostly it was Ruth who put it into shape. But after what had happened during his South African absence he was not taking any chances, and if Chuff could be taught in this way to dictate a decent business letter, the experiment was well worth while.

He opened the envelope. The letter, beautifully laid out—of course by Ruth—spread into two pages. (This, again, thought Morcar with a chuckle, was a device of Ruth's to make Chuff look important.) It contained nothing needing urgent attention. As he turned to the second sheet, however, Morcar perceived in a flash how he could use it to free himself—or at least, to make the attempt.

"Ha!" he exclaimed, turning back with a serious look to the front page.

"Bad news?" queried the agent.

"No. Good news," said Morcar, smiling. He folded up the letter and tucked it away in his pocket, with a great air of satisfaction. "In fact, the possibility of very good news. But it would be wise for me to be in Annotsfield tomorrow morning." He paused and frowned, as if considering.

"There is an afternoon plane. Let us try for a booking," said the agent, naturally wishing to appear efficient and helpful.

"Yes, I should be grateful. Do your best," said Morcar.

The agent approached the head porter, and after a good deal of telephoning and possibly a little bribery—though the Danes were not much given to that kind of thing, reflected Morcar virtuously —Morcar had a seat on this afternoon's plane.

"Sorry to cut short my stay. But I think we'd pretty well finished, hadn't we."

"I think yes," said the agent. He ran rapidly and accurately over what they had agreed, Morcar nodding at appropriate moments. "I regret we miss our free time together, but for a big deal—"

"Exactly," said Morcar. "Pleasure to deal with a man who understands."

The result of all this was that they parted on excellent terms, and that about midnight Morcar found himself driving his car, which he had left at the Ringway airport, over the Pennines.

His satisfaction was immense. Merely to be in England, in a country where what he said was always understood, was a great relief, but there was more to it than that. He had a deep feeling for his native Riding, and to be thus coming home to it gave him a sense of comfort, of content, almost as great, he thought, as if he were sinking into the arms of a woman he loved. The September night was clear and pleasant; there was a moon almost at full and quite a spangling of stars in and out of slender clouds which drifted slowly before a quiet breeze; the hills were alternately black and silver; the air was fresh. The feeling of fatigue, impatience and frowstiness which had suddenly afflicted him in Copenhagen and increased in the plane, dropped away; he felt vigorous and happy. When he passed the county border into Yorkshire he felt so exhilarated that he actually burst into song. Pausing a moment to discover what he was singing, he was rather disconcerted to find that he had given voice to a tune which Jonathan often whistled lately about the house. It was a fine tune, and Morcar had once asked the lad its name. Jonathan had replied that it was a song much sung by negroes and their supporters in protest marches in the southern states of the U.S.A. (At this Chuff had looked extremely sulky.)

> "How many roads must a man walk down*
> before you call him a man?"

sang Jonathan in friendly defiance. Morcar liked this; to be a man, he thought, took some doing, some enduring, some experience.

Then there came a couplet which Morcar could not remember:

> "Yes, 'n' How many seas . . ."

* BLOWIN' IN THE WIND: Copyright © 1962 by M. Witmark & Sons. Used by permission.

No, he had forgotten it. Then:

"Yes, 'n' How many times must the cannon balls fly
before they're forever banned?
The answer, my friend, is blowin' in the wind, The
answer is blowin' in the wind."

Morcar let these words roll out on the breeze, humming the lines he had forgotten. He was occasionally surprised by a sudden shrill note in his voice—"an old man's pipe," he thought with rueful amusement—but on the whole his baritone still sounded strong enough and warm enough to give him pleasure.

He came down out of the hills into the Ire Valley, humming more quietly now, and reached Stanney Royd.

The house was quite dark, naturally, for the hour was after one, and he was not expected until tomorrow. He rolled the garage door up and down very quietly, so as to disturb no-one's sleep, inserted his latch-key into the front-door lock and let himself into the house very quietly. The picture of his own comfortable bed rose up before him entrancingly, and he chuckled to himself with glee at the remembrance of his Copenhagen stratagem. So long as nobody ever knew of it but himself, he thought, no harm could come of it to anybody. He trod softly across the dark square hall, opened the kitchen door, put on the light, wrote a note announcing his arrival to Mrs. Jessopp, and took a bottle of milk out of the fridge. While pouring a glassful from this, it occurred to him to wonder whether there were any letters awaiting him; he made his way into his den and sat down at his desk. A few circulars, a few invitations, a few bills. The evening's copy of the *Annotsfield News*, loosely folded as if it had been read, lay to one side. He picked it up and opened it out.

The awful shock of what he saw almost killed him.

The top half of the front page was devoted to a diagram, a map of the new Ring Road from Yorkshire to Lancashire which was to bypass Annotsfield and join the Ire Valley road (which was to be enlarged) just above the Ire bridge. The new road, marked in thick heavy black, cut across Syke Mills.

"But it's impossible, it's absurd, it's not so, it can't be, don't be such a fool, they would have told you," muttered Morcar. He traced the road with his forefinger from its origin in the A1 (M) in the east, along to the south of Annotsfield, up the Ire Valley and over the Pennines to the west. Although buildings were shown only as small grey squares and the orientation of the map was unusual, Morcar knew the landmarks of this part of Yorkshire so well that he could not be mistaken. The proposed road took not merely a corner but a whole substantial block, or rather, halves of two substantial blocks, off Syke Mills. Remembering the breadth of the new motorways, and the open verges which bordered them, Morcar saw that the whole mill would probably have to come down.

"What an idiotic thing to do! They can't really mean it. Why on earth not shift the road a few feet to one side?"

He gazed at the plan again; it was clear that to avoid Syke Mills the road would have to take a considerable bend; between the hills and the river Ire, there was not room for such a bend.

His heart sank. An awful hollow seemed to expand in his stomach. His body trembled.

"It can't be true. This can't be happening to me."

He sat for a long time with his hands stretched out in front of him, resting on his desk, the map lying between. He was not thinking. He was beyond thought. His mind was merely full of pain.

After a time he roused himself. He stood up, swaying a little. He folded the *News* in three, so as to leave the portion of the map which showed Syke Mills, exposed. Leaving the glass of milk untouched on the desk, he staggered from the room—forgetting to turn off the light—and with the newspaper under his arm, hauled himself upstairs, clinging to the bannisters.

Once in his room, Morcar, usually the tidiest of men, threw off his clothes in all directions and flung himself into bed.

But of course he did not sleep. The map kept rising over and over again in his mind, that awful black line burning itself into his brain. His incredulity was so great that he could not bear to keep still under it, but threw himself from side to side, muttering protests. Presently it occurred to him that the map had been accompanied, of course, by explanatory text; with a feeling of relief he rose and put on the light and read the *News'* description of the scheme. Syke Mills was referred to as one of four or five important buildings which were to be demolished, along with several acres (it seemed to Morcar) or small houses and shops. A leader in the middle page confirmed this statement, and directed attention to the merits of the scheme, which had not yet, it appeared, been submitted to the appropriate Ministry. Morcar groaned; the laudatory tone of the leader showed the attitude which would be generally adopted. But demolish Syke Mills! No, no! He wanted to make his protest now; to telephone the whole Town Council, to write a letter, to shout and thump the table and argue. His whole being was so full of opposition that he felt as if the organism would break apart from its pressure.

After a time, from exhaustion both mental and physical, he drowsed uneasily—to wake again to the same agony, the same fury of opposition. This alternation seemed to continue all night long, but probably he had slept more than he imagined, reflected Morcar, waking again to find his room full of daylight; people always do. He rose, put his head under the cold water tap of his wash-basin, and sat down to study the *News* more carefully. It seemed there was a model of the new road on view, in the Annotsfield Town Hall.

"I must see that at once," decided Morcar. "Then the Town Clerk ... The Mayor ... the Highways Committee, I suppose ... What time is it?"

To his surprise, his self-winding watch said nine o'clock. He must bestir himself, be out and about at once. But now that the time for action had come, an immense discouragement weighted his limbs.

A loud knock sounded at his door.

"Come in," said Morcar irritably.

The door opened, and Jonathan appeared with a look of horror on his face. The sight of him recalled at once to Morcar's mind the song he had sung on his happy journey home last night; he had been in a state of—"euphoria" he thought was the word. From far out of the past a line from a play came up in his mind—*my bosom's lord sits lightly in his throne*—yes, *Romeo and Juliet*, he had seen it long ago with Christina and her husband. Romeo said that and felt jolly, when in a few moments he was to be confronted with news of Juliet's death. Last night he, Morcar, had felt the same cheerfulness, and then met this news. Fool, fool, said Morcar cynically to himself; you should have known that life has always one more frightful trick in store for you, waiting round the corner. It's been the same tune all the time. When Winnie had agreed to a divorce, a V.One killed Christina. And now this. He found he was staring at Jonathan with blank eyes, not seeing him, and with an effort focussed his gaze. Behind Jonathan in the distance Chuff could be seen hovering, looking white and dis-

172

traught, as totally wretched as he had appeared when Morcar met him at the docks. It was clear that Jonathan and Chuff both knew about the threat to Syke Mills, thought Morcar with relief; at least I don't have to tell them.

"Come in and shut the door," he said.

Jonathan obeyed. "Mrs. Jessopp thought you might like a cup of tea," he said, setting this down with a hand that shook.

"Why aren't you at school?" said Morcar roughly.

"When we realised that you had come home and—seen the paper," said Jonathan: "I thought I ought to be—I wished to be—here. I've telephoned school to say I shall be late."

Morcar took a sip of the hot liquid and to his surprise felt better.

"Has there been anything printed about the scheme before last night's paper?"

"No, that's the first announcement."

"There's a model on show, I see."

"Yes. We've seen it. As soon as we read last night's paper we went down to the Town Hall. I'm afraid the road does—"

"Go through Syke Mills?"

"Yes. Compensation, of course," said Jonathan, "is statutory. But not rehousing, except for domestic premises. They'll give you big compensation, Uncle Harry."

"Don't insult me, Jonathan," said Morcar hoarsely. "Syke Mills means far more to me than money. It's my life's work. Now it's to be demolished."

"I know. I understand."

"No, you don't understand. You don't care about textiles. You don't feel as I do."

"I can experience empathy," said Jonathan, looking aside.

"What does that mean?"

"I can understand your feelings and regret them for you, though I do not feel the same myself."

Morcar snorted and felt rather more himself.

"It's as empty as it sounds," he said.

"This happening gives you the opportunity to retire, to shed some of your responsibilities, if you wish."

"I don't wish," said Morcar.

"I'm very sorry about it, Uncle Harry," said Jonathan.

"Well, don't let's get lugubrious about it," said Morcar. "I don't want any sympathy, Jonathan. I can't stand it."

"Susie," began Jonathan.

"I don't want to see Susie—yet. I mean that. Keep her away from me for a while, Jonathan. Well, I must get down to the mill," said Morcar, resuming his rough outward tone. "They'll be having kittens there."

"Nathan rang up last night. We sent you a telegram. We tried to telephone but they said you weren't there; you seemed to have left."

"I had. I hope your telegram was discreet," said Morcar, thinking of the agent, who might see it.

"Of course. We simply said: *urge immediate return important developments.*"

"That showed sense, at least."

"It was Chuff's wording."

"Tell Chuff to telephone Syke and say I'll be there in half an hour. He must wait and drive me," said Morcar, admitting to himself that he felt a trifle shaky. "And a car smash-up for me now would just about put the lid on," he told himself.

"I'll tell him. Is there anything else I can do, Uncle Harry?"

"No." Morcar, reflecting that the lad had shown courage and affection in breaking in upon him after such news, made a great effort, and said: "Thanks for coming in, Jonathan."

Jonathan muttered something inaudible, and withdrew.

It was only when Morcar, having gathered his forces to rise and dress, came to shave, that he perceived the extent of Jonathan's courage and the reason for his horror, for it was then that he saw himself in the mirror.

His hair, bushy and turbulent as ever, had turned completely white.

"Well, when *you watch the things you gave your life to, broken,*" he thought to himself, "it's not surprising, after all. How does it go on? *And stoop and build 'em up with worn-out tools.*" He paused for a moment, savouring to the full the anguish of his situation. "Kipling, my God!" exclaimed Morcar. The Liberal in him revolted. "Come on, Harry," he said to himself. "That's enough of that."

He buttoned his jacket and pulled it down sharply all round so that its fit was perfect, then went off with a composed air to Syke Mills, beside Chuff, pale and silent.

The lamb on his desk looked almost unbearably poignant that morning.

31. *Jonathan at School*

"GIVE THESE MAPS out, Shackleton and Lister."

"Why are you so late this morning, sir?" enquired Grim-shaw.

"Shut up and sit down, Grimshaw," said Jonathan, offhand. "I've no time for whimsies from you this morning."

"Have you had bad news, sir?" enquired Shackleton, who as top of the class had a certain official standing.

The image of Morcar, white-haired, his face lined, distorted, twitching, his eyes full of perplexity and anguish, sitting limply on the edge of a dishevelled bed, rose before Jonathan's eyes, and he replied shortly:

"Yes."

At this from mere decency all the class fell silent except the irrepressible Grimshaw, who cried:

"What's a whimsy, sir?"

"Look it up. Get a move on with those maps, boys."

"I haven't got a dictionary, sir."

"Sutcliffe, have you got a dictionary? Lend it to Grimshaw for two minutes, please."

"I've found *whimsy*, sir."

"Then come right out here and read the definition aloud.

"*Whimsy. Whim, crotchet, fad.* What's a crotchet, sir?"

"A whimsy. Is there any more? Continue, then."

"*Whimsical: capricious, fantastic.*"

"Old Grimmy's fantastic," cried a voice gleefully from the back of the class. This was repeated in various quarters, and there was laughter.

Grimshaw crimsoned painfully.

"Sit down now, Grimshaw. Give the dictionary back to Sutcliffe. No more whimsies today, Grimshaw?"

"No, sir," said Grimshaw, very quiet.

Jonathan, having forgotten his ambitions, his learning, his failure, his desire to please, in a word himself, in his grief for Morcar, gave a good brisk lesson. It was listened to with silence, with respect, and presently even with interest. There was not a word out of Grimshaw.

At the end of the period Jonathan could not help but feel a certain elation.

"I got on top of them that time," he thought.

Immediately he felt ashamed. He had always promised himself never to hold a pupil up to derision, and he had performed precisely this despicable trick with poor silly young Grimshaw.

"The world's slow stain," he rebuked himself.

Nevertheless he thought he began dimly to see, or perhaps only to feel, what had been wrong previously with his teaching.

32. *Highways Committee*

"I THINK YOU might have given me warning in advance, gentlemen, and not let me learn the proposed destruction of my property from the evening newspaper."

Morcar had composed this sentence on his way to the meeting with the officials of the Highways Committee of the Annotsfield Town Council, and he delivered it now with sonorous emphasis.

"We can't play favourites, Mr. Morcar," said the chairman. "A great deal of other property has to come down in addition to yours. A great deal of domestic property. We've let you know all at the same time by a public announcement of the scheme in the press."

"I don't consider an announcement in the press as, legally speaking, information."

"You're wrong there."

"Well, you know the scheme now."

"Aye! I know now. And I've survived the shock. To my surprise."

"It's an even worse shock to house-owners."

"I doubt that. I'm the largest property-owner on the proposed route, I believe."

"Yes. Well," murmured the Borough Surveyor, "we can't make favourites."

"I shall fight it tooth and nail. There'll be a public enquiry, I suppose."

"Now, Harry, what's the use?" said the third member of the

committee, a fellow-clubman, soothingly. "There's no other possible route. The river Ire is on one side of you, and Emsley Brow on the other; there's no room to enlarge the present road except through Syke."

Morcar had worked this out for himself, but he felt sick to hear it thus openly confirmed.

"Take the new road along the other side of the river," he suggested hoarsely.

"That would be worse!" exclaimed the surveyor. "That side is crammed with mill property. Besides, higher up the valley, it narrows on that side. There's no room."

"What are you going to do about the Ire Bridge?" enquired Morcar, interested in spite of himself.

"Leave it where it is."

"Improve the angle a bit, of course."

"And widen it. It will join the new road—form one of the entrances from Annotsfield to the new road."

"The other entrance will be on the far side of the town—on the east. The town itself will be completely by-passed."

"You've worked it all out, I see," said Morcar with as much disagreeable sarcasm in his voice as he could manage. In reality he felt daunted, for the plan was, in fact, a good one, considering the situation of Annotsfield and the lie of the Ire Valley land. The Pennines always made things difficult, he admitted to himself.

"Of course we have. We've tried and tried to cause as little disturbance to existing property as possible. But there it is. The property on both sides of that stretch of the Ire Valley road will have to come down. We're told that in ten years' time the road traffic will be twice as great as it is at present. We've got to by-pass Annotsfield with a road from Lancashire to join the A1, or the town won't stay in existence at all; it'll just be a mass of traffic lined by empty shops and houses, because nobody—no pedestrian, I mean—will be able to get across."

"In fifty years these huge roads will be empty and grass-grown, because everyone will travel by helicopter," said Morcar.

"Maybe," said the chairman, setting his jaw. "We've heard that before. But we have to do what's best for our own time."

"Has the Ministry of Transport approved the scheme?"

"It's only just been sent to them."

"And if it's approved, when do you mean to begin work?"

The chairman cleared his throat.

"As soon as we've acquired the necessary property," he said firmly.

"This is going to cost Annotsfield a pretty penny, gentlemen!" exclaimed Morcar.

"Compensation is statutory, and according to fixed scales."

"But moveables are not compensatable," put in the Borough Surveyor hurriedly.

Morcar gave an exclamation full of bitterness, thinking of all his modern electricity installations, on which he had spent so much, of which he had been so proud. Looms and presses could be moved, but at what a cost.

"Is re-housing statutory?" he enquired. "Have you to find me a new home, eh?"

There was a pause. The three men looked at each other sadly.

"Re-housing is only statutory for domestic property," said the Borough Surveyor at last.

"Of course we shall be as helpful as we can," ventured the chairman.

"You're going to lose my Syke Mills rates, too! I hope you'll enjoy that—they're heavy enough!" cried Morcar with vicious enjoyment.

"We're going to lose a lot of rates, Mr. Morcar," said the chairman.

"But future re-development may restore some," said the Borough Surveyor.

"It's all nonsense! Bloody nonsense!" exclaimed Morcar in agony. In spite of himself, his voice broke.

"I won't insult you by saying we are as distressed as you are, Mr. Morcar," said the chairman. "But we are deeply distressed by this necessity."

"You experience empathy, do you?" enquired Morcar sardonically.

"I don't know what that means, Mr. Morcar," said the chairman with dignity. "But we are deeply distressed on your behalf."

"Much obliged, I'm sure," said Morcar roughly.

But in his heart he felt more kindly to them and at the same time more despairing. They were men as honest and as determined as himself, he thought; men caught between contemporary pressures, who were genuinely striving for their town's good; they grieved sincerely for his trouble and had dreaded this interview almost as much as he had himself. Against such men there was no hope; they had after honest anxious thought honestly made up their minds to the honest best of their ability; they were Yorkshiremen as stubborn as he was, they would not budge.

"You've got two mills beside Syke, Harry," said the member, Smethurst by name, who knew him at the club.

"They work in with Syke."

"You could retire, Mr. Morcar," suggested the Borough Surveyor—who was, of course, reflected Morcar after a quick flash of anger, not a West Riding man.

"No, no," said the other two hastily.

"If Syke is pulled down it will mean three hundred Ire Valley men out of work," said Morcar. "Of course three hundred is nothing compared with the millions people talk about nowadays, but the Ire Valley isn't going to like it."

The chairman, holding his head down, was heard to murmur something about fresh premises.

"That's something I meant to mention to you, Harry," exclaimed the third member. "If you should think of—building anywhere, or adapting a building—well, of course in any case you would have to get planning permission, so perhaps that would be taken care of—but there are certain areas of Annotsfield which are scheduled for rehabilitation. It would be useless to seek accommodation in such areas, as you can see. Because they too will be pulled down shortly."

Morcar groaned.

"And everything outside the town's in a Green Belt area, I suppose," he said.

"Now, Harry, that's not fair."

"I don't feel in a mood to be fair," said Morcar.

"We understand that," said the chairman quietly.

"Well, I can see there's nothing more to be said," said Morcar. He rose and picked up his hat. "Except just one thing. If this is the method taken to increase production and send up export figures, it's not one I recommend. Goodnight, gentlemen, I suppose I shall hear when the scheme's approved, from the evening paper. Thank you for receiving me."

The chairman stood up and offered his hand, and the other two followed his example. Morcar solemnly shook hands all round, and left.

"This is as bad as 1931," he thought, plunging down the Town Hall steps.

33. *Premises*

MORCAR MANAGED TO keep a composed face at the breakfast table next morning, but could not eat. To distract attention from his lack of appetite he found it useful to talk a good deal.

"I don't know whether I altogether like that new fringe of yours, Susie," he said.

Susie burst into tears and rushed from the room.

"Really, Uncle Harry," said Jonathan reproachfully, throwing down his napkin and rising to follow her: "I think that was unkind. You know how much Susie cares for your good opinion."

"I don't, as a matter of fact," said Morcar gruffly.

"Of course you do. Surely she has a right to dress her hair as she wishes."

"And I have the right to like or dislike it," snapped Morcar.

"Well, yes. That's a rational view," said Jonathan, somewhat mollified. "But Susie's rather young to appreciate it."

"And I'm rather old to like change."

Jonathan exclaimed crossly and left the room.

"They're always pretty gloomy on Friday, Grandfather," said Chuff soothingly.

Morcar reflected. Friday, was it? Yes, he supposed this awful week had reached its last working day. Since Jonathan had begun teaching in Annotsfield and settled for the time being at Stanney Royd, he dined on Friday nights with the Nat Armitages; on these occasions Jennifer sometimes invited other young people to meet her son. (The Sunday excursions to Emsley Hall by Morcar and Susie were slipping into disuse; Morcar walked over sometimes but Susie usually went out with Jonathan on Sundays; Chuff still divided the day between his grandmother and his girl.) On Friday evenings Chuff had a class at the Technical College. On Friday evenings therefore Susie sat alone in Morcar's den, conscientiously clearing off her weekend's homework. On Friday evenings Morcar went down to the Annotsfield Club. To go to the Club tonight would be about as uncomfortable for him as being bound to the cylinder of a carding engine, he thought. The proposed demolition of Syke Mills had created a *furore* throughout Annotsfield, and every man who entered the Club would offer his sympathy to Morcar, either genuinely or with his tongue in his cheek at the misfortune of a competitor—a continual series of sharp painful stabs. On the other hand, nothing in the world would induce Morcar to stay away from the Club that night. He would face it out—with a cheerful face, too—if it killed him. But what should he say if they asked him what his plans were?

He took a decision which he now perceived had been forming in his mind all night.

"Are you at Syke or Tech this morning, Chuff?"

"Syke."

"Tell Nathan I'll be late. Get the car out for me, will you?"

"Where are you going, Grandfather?"

"Never mind."

Chuff scowled but flung obediently away.

Jonathan and Susie now returned, smiling, Morcar felt, rather artificially. Susie had parted her fringe to each side, leaving her temples bare; the result, with the strands of short hair protruding, looked rather odd.

"Well, now, Susie," said Morcar in his friendliest tone: "You misunderstood me, you know."

"Yes, Grandfather," said Susie brightly.

Oh, lord, they've remembered that I'm in trouble and have to be handled like glass, wrapped up in cotton wool, thought Morcar in disgust.

"I only meant that I couldn't make up my mind about the fringe for a few days—until I got used to it, you know," he pleaded.

"Yes, Grandfather," said Susie as before. "Shall I give you some more coffee?"

"Yes, do, dear," said Morcar with a sigh.

She took his cup, Jonathan the while reseating himself at the table and smiling approval. When she bent down beside Morcar to replace the cup, he put up one finger and gently drew the short gleaming strands back across her forehead. Susie smiled at him, and this time, thought Morcar with relief, the smile was genuine.

When he went out he found that Chuff had not only opened the garage and extracted his car, but driven it down the drive past the awkward turn and placed it in the road, facing down towards Syke Mills.

"I don't want to go down the valley—turn it round for me, there's a good lad," said Morcar.

181

Chuff, who was a good driver, neatly and skilfully did so, but he had to back up the drive quite a distance to obtain the necessary space at the side. Meanwhile Morcar stood by the gate and meditated. Ah, if only old John Hardaker were alive, he thought—for he had made up his mind to go and take a look at Ramsgill—if only we were partners, if that merger had gone through! At least I should have someone on my side to talk to about the Ring Road. I could have built an extension to Ramsgill; it would all have been natural and easy. What a shame, what a shame for the old man to have been struck down like that! And for what reason? A paltry few hundred pounds that he could have given those lads outright without feeling it! If only they'd told him the mess they were in! There was no confidence between those three. If only people confided in each other! It struck him suddenly that he was making exactly the same mistake himself. Chuff had now turned the car to face up the Ire Valley, and left the driving seat. He looked sour, and scowled.

"Can you keep a secret, Chuff?" asked Morcar.

"Yes," said Chuff, brightening.

"You've heard of Ramsgill Mills, I daresay."

"Where the Hardakers were? Yes—Jonathan told me."

"Well, I'm going to see it. If we're to be turned out of Syke Mills we must find other premises."

"Goodoh!" exclaimed Chuff. "But isn't Ramsgill occupied?"

"It's let to a lot of small firms."

"You'd buy it over their heads?" said Chuff approvingly.

"Yes!" said Morcar with emphasis, though he felt a pang of conscience. "They're small; they can find other places easier than I can. They're not in cloth, they haven't looms and such. But listen, Chuff. It's absolutely essential that nobody hears about this yet. Understand me? Not one word to anybody. Except Jonathan, perhaps," he added. "But warn him to keep it quiet."

"I understand what you say, and of course I won't say a word, but I don't see why."

"Because I don't want to look a fool if it doesn't come off," said Morcar sharply. He started the engine. Chuff stood beside the window, glowering. "Would you like to come with me?" said Morcar on impulse.

"Yes!" exclaimed Chuff, leaping round the car.

"Go and telephone Nathan, then, or he'll think—" began Morcar. He left his sentence unfinished; he felt that Nathan (who had wept at the news of the proposed demolition) would think that this disaster had knocked Morcar completely out if Morcar did not turn up on time at Syke Mills; but this was not a thought he wished to express to his grandson.

While he sat waiting, the Minicar with Jonathan and Susie came down the drive. (The arrangement nowadays was that Jonathan had the car one day, Chuff the next, whoever had it dropped Susie at school on his way to work. On alternate days Chuff drove his motor-bike and Jonathan took the bus.) They waved cheerfully as they drove off down the valley. Chuff came out, smiling, and seated himself beside Morcar.

"You didn't say a word to Nathan?"

"Not a word. I think he heard in my voice that I was feeling more cheerful, though," said Chuff honestly.

Morcar snorted and drove off.

Presently he turned across the Ire and turned up the steep lane (now, he noticed, officially signposted Scape Scar Lane) which led up the flank of the Pennine ridge separating the Ire Valley from Ramsgill. Further east, this broad ridge divided into several slopes with intervening valleys, which made the low-lying route from Annotsfield to Ramsgill considerably longer; here they were at the neck of the system, as it were, and the distance from Stanney Royd to Ramsgill was not great. Morcar explained this carefully to Chuff, who listened with interest.

"This is where the murder took place," said Morcar, drawing across the road so that he could look down the steep rocky slope where old John Hardaker's car had burst into flames.

"Look out!" cried Chuff suddenly.

A large lorry had suddenly bounced over the brow of the lane and was rushing straight down upon their car, which was of course standing on the wrong side of the road. Morcar instantly accelerated and swung the wheel, and they found themselves safely on the grass verge, a few inches from the brink and the steep drop, while the driver's mate on the lorry, and the driver of a following car, shook their fists and shouted imprecations at Morcar.

"That was a silly thing for me to do," exclaimed Morcar, as he swung the car back to its proper side of the road. "I hadn't realised how much this road is used nowadays. A few years back it was a mere rough lane."

Chuff gazed ahead and said nothing, rather markedly.

"A very fine view of the industrial West Riding," said Morcar as they topped the brow and turned into the main road.

"Yes. It's kind of—complex, all these hills and valleys criss-crossing each other."

"Nobody has ever been able to find the right word for it," said Morcar with satisfaction.

"Where's Annotsfield from here?"

"Oh, Annotsfield's out of sight over that way," said Morcar, nodding his head in a southerly direction. "We're not in the Annotsfield borough now; we're in Hudley."

It was difficult for him to say this, and he could not keep the pain from his voice. He had nothing against Hudley, of course; but he was an Annotsfield man, and the thought of moving into another borough, of having a Hudley address on his business notepaper, was a deep grief to him. But it was no use being sentimental about the matter; if there were suitable premises for him in Hudley, to Hudley he would have to go. Chuff looked at him sharply, but was mercifully silent.

They reached Ramsgill Mills and dismounted.

The paint was shabby. Morcar remembered having urged the lawyers entrusted with the Hardaker affairs to give the building a new coat of paint to increase its purchase value, but they had declined to incur this expense. The excuse they offered was that a purchaser might have his own views on the colour of the paint; but in Morcar's opinion this was nonsense, for by custom the window-paint of all West Riding textile mills was white. "There are doors and railings, Mr. Morcar," objected the lawyer. Morcar let the matter drop, with the result that the white paint was now dirty and flaking, and the doors wore a dingy green. The *J. L. Hardaker and Company* brass plate was gone from the front door —the screw-holes were still visible—and a sheet of inadequate cardboard instead announced a firm of beauty products. Various other placards and posters about the frontage told of various other activities, none of them, as Morcar knew, textile. Morcar strode under the archway into the yard. The boiler pit had been filled up, the engine-room doors were closed and looked as if they had not been opened since the sale a couple of years ago; the paving of the yard seemed to have disintegrated, it was uneven, full of potholes and mud. Rubbish lay about in heaps: cardboard, paper, rags, sacking, shards of pottery, ragged and rusting sheets of iron. Morcar, who remembered this yard

184

clean, spick and span, warm from the boiler fires, humming with the great flywheel of the engine-room and the distant sound of the looms, felt profoundly saddened by its present decay.

"We should have bought it and kept it going," he muttered. He crossed the yard. "Well, let's see the loom-shed," he said.

He entered. The once vast space was now cut up by thin wood partitions into half a dozen rooms, each occupied by what was no doubt some useful activity, thought Morcar, trying to be fair. But what a waste to use such an acreage thus! A small spare harassed-looking man in shirt sleeves and waistcoat came out of one of the rooms and looked interrogatively at Morcar.

"Can I help you?" he said suspiciously.

"Young and Young," replied Morcar in a casual tone. "Just a matter of some repairs."

"Oh," said the man, nodding in apparent understanding, "Well, there's nothing wrong here."

"No, it's not you I'm looking for," said Morcar cheerfully, and passed on.

They crossed the yard back to the beauty product quarters, and made a thorough tour of the whole mill.

"I suppose you didn't want to give your own name," said Chuff as they drove away.

"He wouldn't have known it. This is Hudley, not Annotsfield, and he wasn't a textile man. Young and Young are the lawyers in charge. All of them will pay their rent to Young's."

"Oh, I see," said Chuff, relieved.

"I'll ring Young's up in a day or two," said Morcar. "Meanwhile, I think I'd better go to Scarborough tomorrow. Be sure you fill the car up tonight."

"Scarborough?"

"Young Mrs. Hardaker lives there."

"You won't make her an offer for Ramsgill tomorrow, though?" said Chuff quickly.

"Of course not. There'll be a lot of bother before I get to that point—valuations and counter-valuations and lawyers and deeds and heaven knows what. But I want to get Carol Hardaker on my side. She has children—a couple of boys and a girl—if she's any sentiment about keeping Ramsgill for the boys to start up again, I'd better know it now. It'll cost a lot of money to get Ramsgill in running textile order again—more money than she's ever likely to have, poor girl. She'd do best to sell it to me. We'll call at Old Mill on our way back," he concluded.

"Jonathan says Old Mill was the first mill the Oldroyds had," said Chuff as they turned down the lane off the main Ire Valley road towards the Ire.

"Yes, it was," said Morcar shortly. "It was called Syke Mill then," he added.

"It's a tumbledown old place."

"It has water rights, though," said Morcar as before.

Morcar could not but remember how Old Mill had been David Oldroyd's and Jennifer's and Jonathan's, and how it had fallen into his hands. But such griefs must just be forgotten, and Ramsgill's situation in Hudley must just be forgotten. A man who was a man put these things aside and went on with his work. The thought of the immense amount of work required to rehabilitate Ramsgill should invigorate him. It was not, no, not, he told himself, daunting. Once he got Ramsgill into his hands he would be too busy to indulge in any sentimental sadnesses. Tonight at the club, when asked his plans, he would be able to put on a secretive smile, and reply that he had one or two things in mind. He actually whistled as Old Mill, with the Ire flowing peacefully in the background, came into view.

"Well, at least we have an alternative, now," he said cheerfully. Chuff said nothing.

34. Available

MORCAR EXTRACTED CAROL HARDAKER'S address from his correspondence of a couple of years back; she had no telephone, it appeared, so he sent her a telegram requesting permission to visit her at noon on the morrow and inviting her to lunch with him at one of Scarborough's most celebrated hotels. He received no reply to this communication, but determined to make the journey all the same. Chuff disapproved.

"Suppose she's away, or out," he said.

"Well, I shall be no worse off. It's a pleasant drive," said Morcar. "I always enjoy a glimpse of the sea."

"Jonathan, do try to dissuade him," pleaded Chuff, making a private visit to Jonathan's room late that night. "Its all nonsense. What good will it do to see her? It's a matter for lawyers and surveyors. All that will matter is the Ramsgill price."

"If you think so, why don't you say so to him?"

"You handle him better than I can."

"I think he feels a feverish desire for action," mused Jonathan. "He's had a frightful blow."

"I know. But rushing off across the county won't make it any better."

"I think it might. In any case, the visit will occupy a day of this waiting period. Perhaps even two—you might manage to persuade him to stay the night."

Chuff groaned.

"You could telephone your grandmother not to expect you on Sunday."

"Jonathan, he isn't fit to drive all that way."

"I should have thought that by African standards ninety miles wasn't much of a distance."

"You should have seen him yesterday, calmly crossing to the wrong side of the road, below the top of a hill and before a bend. We were both nearly killed, I may say."

Jonathan looked alarmed.

"He's always been an excellent driver. He's just upset."

"That's what I'm *saying*, Jonathan. He's *upset*."

"You'll be with him."

"I will if he takes me."

"I might put in a word about that," said Jonathan thoughtfully. "But I should take it for granted if I were you."

Chuff grimaced and withdrew.

"Uncle Harry," said Jonathan, accosting Morcar as he came down the stairs to breakfast next morning—he looked very spruce and distinguished, Jonathan observed; the whitening of his hair had improved his appearance, though his face was lined and his once fresh complexion had faded. "I just wanted a word with you." He drew the older man into the den in an intentionally conspiratorial manner, and said in a low confidential tone: "You're taking Chuff with you to Scarborough, aren't you?"

"I wasn't thinking of it," said Morcar, frowning. "Carol Hardaker doesn't know him. She might find his presence embarrassing."

"I'm afraid he'll be hurt if you don't take him," urged Jonathan as before.

Morcar sighed. These youngsters have so many *feelings*, he thought irritably. You'd never guess it to look at them, but it's true. He had been looking forward to a long day alone, with no necessity to conceal the sharp agony and dull leaden ache of pain which he alternately experienced.

"Very well, I'll take him," he said crossly.

Jonathan wondered whether he could risk suggesting that Chuff should do the driving, but did not venture to do so. However, to his great relief, when Morcar came out of the house to his car—which Chuff had had cleaned and polished and filled with the necessary ingredients the evening before in a way even Jessopp could not have bettered—he said crossly to his grandson:

"If you're coming you may as well drive."

Chuff leaped instantly into the driving seat, and they went off into the main Ire Valley Road with all due care.

The day was crisp and bright, the leaves were turning to autumn gold, and although the day was Saturday, the morning was early and the roads towards the coast were not yet too full of traffic. Morcar from time to time experienced for a moment a feeling of enjoyment. But no, he recalled at once, there is some heavy reason why I cannot be allowed to enjoy. Then he remembered what it was: this heavy wearisome grief which lay at the bottom of his mind like a cannon-ball—yes, an old round cannon-ball such as you saw, in his childhood, piled in neat heaps on the ground in the Annotsfield park beside old snub-nosed, huge-wheeled, rusting guns. (Boer War, perhaps? Surely not the Crimea, though they looked old enough for Troy. No guns at Troy, however.) This cannon-ball in his mind would always in the future prevent him from whole-hearted enjoyment; if a balloon of happiness strove to rise, the cannon-ball would haul it down. Don't be so fanciful, with your cannon-balls and balloons and goodness knows what, Morcar adjured himself; and yet on the other hand it was rather restful and refreshing to let one's wounded mind flow free. Chuff was silent and drove with skill, so that Morcar was able to cease watching the road and let his mind roam. It was throwing one's hand in, however; he knew that well. He pulled himself together with an effort as they approached the coast.

They found Carol Hardaker's neat little brick house in a row in a small sloping street not too far from the sea on the north side of the town. The curtains and paint, the short stone path and steps, looked extremely clean but somehow a trifle grim, and this impression was strengthened when the door was flung open and Mrs. Hardaker appeared in severe dark blue, two young boys crowding at her side. The boys, dark-haired and red-cheeked, in high-necked sweaters and shorts of the same utilitarian navy shade, looked handsome but rough, and stared at Morcar and Chuff with a belligerent air. Mrs. Hardaker—a good-looking piece, middle thirties, fine eyes, pity there's grey in all that black hair, thought Chuff; her beauty had hardened with grief, thought Morcar—was also evidently not in a good humour.

"I didn't reply to your telegram, Mr. Morcar. I didn't want you to come. I've no money to waste on telegrams," she said angrily.

"You didn't forbid me, so I came. I very much want to see you. I don't bring bad news," said Morcar mildly.

"That'll be a change. Who's this, then?" said Mrs. Hardaker, nodding towards Chuff.

"He is my grandson." Morcar hastily ran over Chu's baptismal names in his mind, rejected them all, and concluded: "Chuff Morcar."

"He's like you. Is he coming in too?"

"Perhaps the boys would like to go for a short drive," said Chuff hastily, appalled.

At this the two boys gave a loud shout, rushed down the path and hurled themselves into Morcar's car, pawing and kicking the paint and the chromium fittings in a manner which Morcar took calmly but which maddened Chuff. He gave them a disapproving glance as he climbed in; at this they laughed derisively and wrestled with each other with a total disregard for the welfare of the handsome leather upholstery.

"Come in," said Carol, standing aside for Morcar to enter.

She closed the door behind him and led the way into a small front room, rather bare, spotlessly clean, decorated in hideous taste. She sat down and waved Morcar to a chair; immediately a little girl of three or four, dark-haired like her brothers and very pretty, with huge dark brown eyes, climbed on to her lap. Carol, hugging her, rocked her slowly to and fro; the child, one arm round her mother's neck, gazed out in alarm at Morcar. In spite of Carol's declared objection to Morcar's visit, it was clear that it had been half expected, for the little girl was wearing what was obviously her best white party frock, agreeably embroidered in pink and scarlet. Morcar could never remain insensitive to a colour scheme, and he observed this unusual combination keenly now. It gave him unexpected pleasure, and he smiled. The child, after a stare of surprise, smiled shyly in return, then looked at her mother for approval.

"I'm sorry if I was rude, but I hate seeing anybody from the West Riding," said Carol, somewhat mollified.

"I can understand that. How is—your husband?" asked Morcar.

"Lucius is dead. Last winter. Pneumonia."

"I'm sorry," said Morcar sincerely.

"I'm glad. So was Lucius, I'm sure. He wouldn't want to live. It'll be better for the children, with him gone. We'll go down south where the name of Hardaker doesn't mean anything. There's nothing to keep us up here now Lucius is gone. I shall put the boys into engineering, or electronics or something. Anything but textiles."

This last remark vexed Morcar. His unconscious reaction, a desire to wound, caused him to ask:

"And your brother?"

"Oh, *he's* all right. A model prisoner, I'm sure. Esteemed by all. What did you come to see me about, Mr. Morcar?"

"A new Ring Road is planned for Annotsfield, and my Syke Mill is to be knocked down to make way for it."

"Well! Fancy that! We all have our troubles," said Carol in a softer tone.

"I must find other premises, and naturally I thought of Ramsgill. If the road scheme is approved, I may want to buy Ramsgill."

"You should have bought it at the time."

"I didn't need it then." Suddenly the scene in empty Ramsgill when Jonathan revealed his aversion to textiles flashed before him, and he winced.

"I don't really care whether you buy it or not, so long as it brings me in the same income as it does now. Or more, of course. You see, there's a lot of us to keep, Mr. Morcar. There's old Mrs. Hardaker, Lucius's mother. Of course all this happening knocked her off her perch, and she's pretty much of an invalid, has to be waited on hand and foot, you know the kind of thing. Costs no end. That sort always live long. Well, they do, Mr. Morcar. Well, then, there's Elizabeth, Lucius's sister, married to my brother, poor girl. And their child, Edmund. Poor little thing, he's a wreckling; in spite of the health service he costs them plenty, I can tell you. Elizabeth keeps going back to nursing, but what's the good, Edmund's always being ill and she has to come out again to look after him. Then there's me and my three. I'm a shorthand typist, always have been, and I can easy get a job, but you see there's young Carol here. She doesn't like it when her mummy's away, do you, Carry, love?"

The child buried her face in her mother's breast.

"You could perhaps do some copy-typing at home," suggested Morcar.

"That means buying a typewriter. Where's the cash to come from?"

"Hire purchase?"

"No! Never will I get into debt by one single penny!" shouted Carol. "Look what it did to Lucius and Edward! And poor old Mr. Hardaker," she added in a lower tone. "Though he hadn't much longer to live anyway, I don't suppose. So you see there's seven of us to keep, Mr. Morcar."

"It might be more economical if you all lived together," said Morcar.

"It would! But I'm not going to do it. I'm not going to live with any Hardakers again. I've had enough, thank you. Of course there's nothing wrong with Elizabeth. Elizabeth's all right. A bit dreary, though. But you see, Mr. Morcar, with all the expenses of the trial, and auctioneer's percentages, and Lucius not allowed to profit—fortunately old Mr. Hardaker had left some of his money through to his grandchildren, as it were, but what a fuss of lawyers and fees to get it settled!—and our removals, and the way the cost of everything goes up and up, the price of coal, and food, and electricity, and gas, and even milk, you wouldn't believe, and the boys are very hard on their shoes—with all that, it makes things difficult."

"Yes, I can understand that," said Morcar gravely. "Now, listen, Mrs. Hardaker."

"Yes, you've had enough of my troubles, I don't doubt."

"I may want to buy Ramsgill Mills. But before I so much as think of it, I want to know that you have no objection. No, listen a moment," he said, raising a hand to stop her as she began to speak: "If you have any idea of ever getting Ramsgill back for your sons—"

"Never!"

"—I shouldn't want to buy it. If it becomes mine, it stays mine."

"It's very good of you to take my feelings into consideration, Mr. Morcar. It is indeed, and I appreciate it. But I never want to hear the name of Ramsgill again, or have anything to do with textiles. I couldn't care less whether you buy it or not, so long as our income from the rents or whatever they put the money into if you buy it, doesn't dwindle."

"Thank you, Carol. That's all I wanted to know."

"It was good of you to come yourself instead of just sending a cold letter. Would you like a cup of tea, Mr. Morcar? We don't have anything stronger here, you know. No fear. If ever you've seen anyone taking to drink, Mr. Morcar, you can't bear to touch it yourself, you know."

"But I'm sure Lucius—" began Morcar.

"No, it wasn't Lucius. Never mind. I can pop the kettle on in a minute."

"But you're coming to have lunch with me."

"No, I'm not. I can't leave the children, and I don't want to bring them with me. I don't want to give them a taste for rich hotels and that sort of thing. They'll have to be workers and they may as well start right. What about that cuppa, eh?"

"Well, I will have a cup, thank you," said Morcar.

He was still drinking it when his car drew up at the gate, Chuff very sulky and the Hardaker boys very merry. Carol, holding her little girl by the hand, came down the short path to see him off.

"Don't worry about me and my troubles, Mr. Morcar," she said kindly as he made to close the door. "We shall manage."

"What did she say about Ramsgill?" demanded Chuff as they drove off.

"She doesn't care whether we buy it or not."

"Ah!"

"Turn up into the town, Chuff," commanded Morcar. "I want an office-supply shop."

"Won't it do after lunch?" said Chuff, who looked slightly battered after his interlude with the Hardaker boys.

"No. The shop might be shut. It might be early closing day."

"Not on Saturday, surely."

"We won't risk it."

Chuff sighed and complied. Morcar purchased a handsome typewriter, inscribed a card *As a token of respect. H.M.* and ordered the machine to be delivered immediately to Carol Hardaker. He chatted in a lively manner over lunch, and afterwards sat out on a seat on the sea front with his hat off, smoking a cigar, and feeling better, more himself, than he had done since what he had come to call The Blow. The sun shone; far below at the foot of the cliffs the waves, light green in colour by the shore, though not large were sizeable enough to draw the eye agreeably. Pink, scarlet and an unusual light green began to weave themselves together in his mind.

"You're looking better, Grandfather. Your visit to Scarborough seems to have done you good," remarked Chuff.

"Aye, it has. There are people in the world with worse troubles than mine,' said Morcar soberly.

"I'm glad you feel that."

"Oh? Why?"

"Because I'm going to make your troubles worse," said Chuff.

His tone was so constrained that Morcar took alarm at once.

"Is it about Ruth?" he said in a tone of vexation which expected an affirmative reply.

"No, it is not!" cried Chuff with loud emphasis. "Why you should always suspect me of that sort of thing, Grandfather, I really don't know."

"Well, it often happens," said Morcar mildly. "But her mother's a dragon, of course. Go on, then, tell me what's the matter. Money?"

"No!" Chuff then dropped his voice and muttered: "I don't want us to go to Ramsgill."

"Why not, you silly boy?" said Morcar, amused. "You think so, because Ramsgill looked a mess when you saw it yesterday; you can't visualise how it can be restored and set on its feet again. Let me tell you, Ramsgill is a fine old mill."

"Old is the operative word," growled Chuff. "It's a dreary place, old-fashioned, out of date. With poor windows. On several floors. The processes would sprawl about all over the place. They wouldn't be properly organised," he concluded, his voice rising again in angry protest.

"Yes, they would. I should organise them," said Morcar calmly. "It would cost a bit, of course."

"But why should we go to Ramsgill?"

"Because it's available. If you think I like moving out of Annotsfield, where I've worked the best years of my life, I don't. But we've got to make the best of a bad job."

"Why not make a good new job?"

"Don't be silly, Chuff. Mills don't sprout like mushrooms. The fabric of Ramsgill is good. It's a well-built shell. Plenty of good cloth has been manufactured there."

"We want a place suitable for new textures."

"What is it you want me to do?" roared Morcar, suddenly losing his temper.

"Build a new one-storey mill, with large glass windows and sheds arranged in logical order."

"One of those low sprawling concrete things," said Morcar with contempt.

"Yes!"

"You're out of your mind. Have you any idea how much a thing of that kind would cost?"

"No, but I think we ought to find out."

"And where will you site this new *factory*," said Morcar, giving this word the scorn he thought it deserved.

"In the field by Old Mill."

"Well, there is a field there, certainly," said Morcar.

"It's your field."

"But getting planning permission to build there is another matter."

"Well, if you can't swing that, it's a poor do."

"We don't *swing* things in this country."

Chuff sniffed. "There are other mills along the Ire down there," he argued. "One more wouldn't spoil the skyline. There's a goodish road down to Old Mill. I don't see that it would do anybody any harm. The river curves away from the line of the main road there, so there's plenty of room for widening the road for the new Ring Road scheme. The new building would be just an extension of Old Mill. You could call it Syke Mill. You needn't change your business address. It's got water. Think of the water rights!" he urged.

Morcar thought of the water-rights.

"You're pretty cool, telling me what to do with my own mills," he said.

"I understood that my future lay in your mills, Grandfather," said Chuff. "Of course if it doesn't," he added, crimsoning painfully, "pray wash out everything I've said."

"Don't be a donkey, Chuff."

"*I'm* not being a donkey."

There was one good thing about Chuff, reflected Morcar; when you argued with him you could hit out, and he hit back—it was not like arguing with Jonathan, who always got hurt, so that you felt sorry.

"It might be a good thing," resumed Chuff, "to apply at once for permission to build an extension, and then—"

"Oh, shut up!" said Morcar, savagely. "Give me time to think." He picked up his hat. The sun had gone in, the wind felt shrewd, the sea, now a dull leaden colour, was beating against the shore in short choppy waves which sounded bad-tempered. "We'd better go," he said.

As they walked together towards the car park Chuff said slyly: "We haven't done so badly about Syke after all, Grandfather."

"How do you make that out?"

"Two ideas how to replace it, within a week."

Morcar snorted. "Oh, we're a grand pair," he said sardonically. He was silent till Chuff had completed the complicated task of negotiating the afternoon traffic of the town and brought them safely to the main road out of Scarborough, when he said:

"You seem to think I'm made of money."

"I think you know where to find it," said Chuff with a cheerful grin.

35. *Alternative*

"You see, Mr. Morcar," said the architect seriously, "unless you made *very* extensive alterations, practically rebuilt the place, you might well find your plans rejected, as not conforming to modern standards. Worse still, defects might be found by the inspector when you had completed your alterations."

"So much for Ramsgill. Now tell me the advantages of a new building," said Morcar with a surface mildness which did not deceive Chuff—nor, possibly, the architect, for he gave Morcar a shrewd glance and modified his tone.

"Well, it would *not* be a multiple-storey building," he said. "A one-storey building only. No problem of stairs, lifts, or differing levels. The various rooms or sheds would all open into each other —or if necessary swinging doors could be inserted to diminish inter-departmental noise. The departments would be arranged to conduce to the flow of material with maximum rapidity and ease. That is to say, all material would proceed in a one-way direction, and be wheeled or rolled from one process to the next. Large windows everywhere, in inner walls and doors if necessary, would facilitate personnel supervision."

"Personnel supervision?" enquired Morcar.

"It's very necessary nowadays, unfortunately," said the architect. "Production mounts when working personnel is under continual supervision."

"How disgusting!" said Morcar, outraged. "I regard that idea as an insult to my employees."

The architect pursed his lips and slightly hunched one shoulder, in simulated ruefulness. "It's been found very necessary in many cases, nowadays. I regret it as much as you do, but there it is."

"What about power? For looms and so on?"

"Each loom will have its own individual drive. Electricity will, of course, be secured from the appropriate authority, in this case presumably the Yorkshire Electricity Board."

His voice held a slight question, and he obviously hoped the question would lead to a disclosure of the whereabouts of the proposed site. Morcar, however, said nothing, and Chuff also appeared uninterested, as if lost in thought.

"He's got more sense than you'd think," approved Morcar silently. "Of course we should have to have a boiler as well," he said aloud.

"Why?" snapped Chuff, suddenly awake.

"For heat—for process steam," said Morcar. ("I can talk this modern lingo as well as they can," he told himself with a chuckle.)

"Another point you should consider—I am sure you have already considered it, Mr. Morcar," continued the architect, "is the local labour supply. It is well to build where this is abundant."

"Yes, you're right," agreed Morcar affably. "In this case there will be no difficulty." He had already had a talk with the Syke Mills shop steward, who was very anxious about the employees' jobs; he felt pretty sure he could take the whole lot with him if he built by the Ire. Old Mill was only a mile or so up the valley, and the weekday bus service was good. A mill bus down the lane might be useful. Ramsgill of course would be a different matter; it would mean two buses for most of the men, into Annotsfield and out again. Or he could run a mill bus, from Irebridge, direct over the brow, the route he and Chuff had taken, and poor old John Hardaker when he was murdered. There would be problems in either place, but none that was insoluble.

"Let's come to the important point," he said. "What would all this single-storey affair cost to build, eh?"

"We calculate it at three pounds a square foot, with heating," said the architect briskly. "So, a hundred feet by fifty, that would be a hundred and fifty thousand pounds."

"We should be a bit squashed up in that area," said Morcar grimly. (He observed with sardonic glee that Chuff looked staggered.)

"The area's for you to decide, Mr. Morcar."

"It is indeed. Well, thanks very much. I'm greatly obliged for all the information. I'll probably get in touch with you later."

"I hope you will," said the architect, ushering them out. "Pray feel free to ask me any questions you like, at any time."

"Well, what did you think of that, Chuff?" asked Morcar, grimly amused to see his grandson looking pale.

"It's going to cost an awful lot of money to build a new mill."

"It is."

"All the same there were advantages, he said."

"Flow of material and easy supervision of personnel."

"Exactly."

"He wanted the job," suggested Morcar.

"Of course he did! I know that," said Chuff impatiently. "I'm not like my father, Grandfather," he said, glaring fiercely at Morcar as they reached the foot of the architect's steps. "I know my way about. I'm tough."

"Good! You'll need to be."

"Grandfather," said Chuff to Morcar's back as he climbed into the car: "If you were my age—*when* you were my age—in these circumstances you wouldn't hesitate for a moment. You'd build a new mill."

"Perhaps I have more sense now as well as more money," said Morcar.

He spoke mildly, but raged within.

V

END OF AN ERA

V: END OF AN ERA

36. The Last of Winnie

"I've come to say I can't come today," said Chuff when Ruth, looking agreeably domestic in a small rose-coloured apron, opened the door.

They kissed.

"Oh, Chuff, why not?" said Ruth, disappointed.

"Grandma's ill. She's got jaundice, the doctor says. She's to go into hospital. There'll be a bed for her tomorrow morning. I couldn't get into the house when I arrived, there was no answer. I had to climb in through the bedroom window. Did I have a time getting in! It was wedged with a brush. She was in bed, more or less unconscious."

"You haven't left her alone!"

"No, of course not. I've got a neighbour to come in for an hour. The doctor's getting a district nurse or something for the night, but I don't know when she'll come so I must go back to Hurst Road and stay there. Of course I could have telephoned you," admitted Chuff, "but I thought I'd just like a glimpse." He grinned. "Where's your mother?"

"Chapel."

"And G.B.?"

"He's out canvassing."

"Goodoh," said Chuff, taking her in his arms.

They kissed more warmly.

"What are you wearing this for?" asked Chuff, touching the apron with a caressing finger.

"I'm cooking the Sunday dinner," said Ruth, smoothing it down. "I'm sorry about your grandmother, Chuff. It seems sad, doesn't it, to be ill all alone? Is she very bad? Did the doctor say?"

"I rather think it's all up with her."

"It's very sad to die alone."

"Oh, I don't know," said Chuff. "She might like it better that way. She has her own ideas, and they're not the same as anybody else's. She looked very small, shrunken somehow. And yellow, of course."

Ruth, with the intuition of love, perceived that beneath his bluff manner he was a good deal distressed. She kissed him again, gently. At this Chuff hugged her very tightly. He was a strong young man with muscular arms, as Ruth had discovered before to her enjoyment.

"Don't break my ribs," she said teasingly.

"I wish to God we could get married," said Chuff with emphasis. "I want us to be married *now*."

"It's no good till you're twenty-one and through your exams."

"Lots of people get married before they're twenty-one."

"Your grandfather would never allow it, even if Mother would."

Chuff groaned. "Why do we always have to do what older people say, instead of pleasing ourselves? Let's go off and get married."

"We can't till we're twenty-one, not without their consent."

"We could go off to Gretna Bridge, or whatever it's called, like you read about in the papers."

"Gretna Green. I shouldn't like that," said Ruth. "I think it would be silly. Excessive." Chuff growled. "Besides, I shouldn't like to do anything to upset Mother or hurt Mr. Morcar. He's a great man, Chuff."

"He has been."

"Oh, he still is!" objected Ruth. "Everybody thinks so. Even the men at the mill."

"Man-made fabrics are going to catch up on him if he doesn't look quick."

"He fought his way up alone to the very top of the industry. If you do half as well, Chuff—" She paused, dropped her belligerent tone, and concluded softly: "I shall be very proud of you."

This led to an even tighter embrace.

"Of course if Mr. Morcar would agree," began Ruth, weakening.

"He won't. He's always going on about the foolishness of early marriages."

"Well, it's not to be wondered at, when his own was such a failure."

"How they ever came together beats me. He never cared for Grandma, I'm sure. It's Jonathan's grandmother he cared for."

"Really?"

"Yes. You should see her photo on the stand in his bedroom. A real beauty, she was. Don't tell me they were only friends."

Ruth seemed disconcerted.

"Does Jonathan know?" she asked.

"Goodness, no. Jonathan's a babe in arms when it comes to that sort of thing. Far too high-minded to have such a thought in his head."

"But you like Jonathan, don't you?" said Ruth anxiously.

"Of course. Who doesn't? But he's a mug, you know, a sucker; he'll get done in all round."

"You must prevent it."

"I shall try, but it won't be any good. Meanwhile he's having a good influence on me," said Chuff with his good-humoured grin.

"Silly!" said Ruth fondly. "It seems odd to think of old people like Mr. Morcar being in love," she mused, "but I expect they were very different when they were young." The emotional temperature of the interview having sunk a trifle, she was able to free herself from Chuff's arms. "We shall just have to wait till we're twenty-one," she said consolingly. "It isn't long."

They compared their birthday dates, as they had done before, with satisfaction at their nearness to each other.

"You must go now, Chuff. I have to baste this loin of lamb."

"I'll help you," offered Chuff.

"Oh, no, you won't. You'll just buzz off pronto. Mother'll be hopping mad if she comes and finds you here."

"That's all nonsense nowadays."

"I know, but you know what Mother is. Besides, you must get back to your grandmother."

"Yes, that's true, I must," said Chuff, his face clouding. "Goodbye, Ruthie. I'll come along this evening if I can, but I'm afraid it's doubtful."

"Goodbye, love," said Ruth.

They kissed and parted.

37. Election

"JONATHAN," SAID MORCAR, as on the day of the General Election the two drove to the polling station together, to record their votes on differing sides, "I wish you would explain to Chuff that I cannot, I absolutely cannot, attend his grandmother's funeral tomorrow. I should despise myself if I did. My—wife—did me two very grievous wrongs, one of which involved my son, Chuff's father. She ruined my life, and Cecil had no happiness till he escaped from her to Africa. It wouldn't be decent for me to go into all this with Chuff, but I should be glad if you would give him a word of explanation on my behalf."

"Can't you forgive her even now when she's dead?" said Jonathan gravely.

"No."

"I'm sorry," said Jonathan as before.

"Of course it would look better if I attended the funeral," said Morcar. "But I'm not one who cares much for looks."

"No. Is it true, though, that she's appointed you as her sole executor?"

"Yes, it's true." (Confound her impertinence, added Morcar to himself.)

"I think that's rather pathetic," said Jonathan mildly. "Shall you accept?"

"I don't see how I can refuse," growled Morcar. "There's nobody else to do it. Chuff's legally too young. By the way, you might tell Chuff: I've been in touch with her lawyers and she's left him all her property, house and savings and so on. Nothing to anybody else. Chuff will get a formal notice presently. He'll get about two thousand pounds, I dare say."

"I didn't know she had any property of her own," said Jonathan, surprised.

"She hadn't. But the house was in her name—I put it in her name."

"In reality, she had nothing but what you gave her."

"That is so."

"It seems odd that she should bother to save," said Jonathan.

"She did it to annoy me," said Morcar angrily

Jonathan sighed and parked the car outside the Sunday School polling booth.

The borough of Annotsfield had been a Liberal stronghold since Mr. Gladstone's time and even in these latter twentieth century days had maintained the same political colour. Morcar as always voted Liberal, though he felt little enthusiasm for the Liberal party as at present constituted; Jonathan, exercising his vote for the first time in his life, joyously voted Labour. As they emerged into the October sunlight together, having performed this simple, secret and powerful rite, Morcar remarked cheerfully:

"If Chuff were a little older we should have had one vote for each party from Stanney Royd, I think."

"Yes, I'm afraid we should," said Jonathan gravely. "Chuff is a born Tory. Though how he reconciles that with his admiration for modern manners and customs, is a perplexing question."

"He likes the pleasant parts of both ways of thought," Morcar decided, but refrained from uttering.

Next morning, the early election results having given indications of a close electoral contest, there was a good deal of excitement in everyone's mind and a general disinclination to settle to work. Morcar however worked if anything rather harder than usual. He drove to Old Mill and to Daisy, had a useful row with his cropping foreman and dictated half-a-dozen letters to Ruth. Glancing up from this occupation in search of a word, he chanced to see the hands of the electric clock in his office click to twelve noon; it struck him with a sobering effect that this was the hour of Winnie's funeral. At this very moment her body was being lowered into the grave. He made an effort and finished his letters, put through a 'phone call or two, looked at some figures; but when the time was after one o'clock and the funeral must be over, on his way down to lunch at the Club in Annotsfield he turned aside to the cemetery.

It was easy to find the new grave by its very rawness. He stood looking down at its rather sparse covering of flowers. There was a handsome wreath of bronze chrysanthemums *from her loving grandson Chuff*, a cross of white carnations *from her granddaughter Susie* ("I hope that child isn't going to turn religious," thought Morcar), a pleasing cushion of pink and purple asters *from Mrs. Nathaniel Armitage and Jonathan Oldroyd* ("nice of them," thought Morcar), a neat circle of dry purple statice *from*

Mrs. Mellor and family ("suitably inexpensive," thought Morcar with a grimace), and one or two small sincere tributes from women, evidently Winnie's friends or neighbours. Of course—he might have known it, why had he been such a fool as to come, thought Morcar angrily—the idea of Winnie lying there, the names of her father and mother on the gravestone now laid to one side—for heaven's sake, there was even a tribute to Charles John Shaw, killed in action, Neuve Chapelle, 1915—all this started him off as usual. He saw his childhood, Mr. Shaw's dingy mill, the quarrel about the false weights, his employment with the Oldroyds, the trenches, the shell-hole, Charlie's death, Winnie announcing their engagement, the child, that darling baby Cecil lying in his shawl on Morcar's arm, the awful shock of Winnie's lie depriving him of fatherhood—all the frightful miseries of his life rolled through his mind, crushing it into agony. That pert, perverse, twisted girl who in addition to that frightful lie had for so long declined to divorce him or give him evidence for divorce, kept him from remarriage until it was too late—well, it was all over now, thought Morcar with relief. She was dead. No doubt her life had been wretched too. Well, of course it had. Could he pity her? Jonathan thought he ought to do so. He tried. Well, yes; Winnie herself, poor maimed spirit, he could pity and forgive. But her actions! The careless cruelty, the joyously barbed taunt, the gleeful revenge—no, those he could not condone.

Well, it was over now.

He flung away to the Club and took a double whisky with his lunch.

At Stanney Royd that evening Jonathan turned on the television set and sat watching keenly for the election results.

"I'm tired, I think I'll go up to my room," said Morcar after a while.

"Shall I turn this off? Would you prefer it to be off?" said Jonathan anxiously.

"No, no. Keep it on by all means."

"Well, it *is* rather exciting," said Jonathan. His eyes were positively starry with enthusiasm, for indeed the two main parties were running neck and neck. (The Liberals seemed to be doing even worse than usual.)

"Come up and tell me the Annotsfield result," said Morcar kindly.

A few hours later Jonathan knocked at his door.

"Labour is in with an overall majority of four," he said.

His manner was decorous and he was obviously trying to keep the rejoicing out of his voice in deference to Morcar's opinions, but his eyes glowed with happiness.

"Well, I hope they won't regard that as a mandate for all kinds of wild-cat schemes," said Morcar grumpily.

"We shall, Uncle Harry!" cried Jonathan in a sparkle of friendly defiance so youthful that Morcar could not but smile.

"How about Annotsfield, then?" he asked.

Jonathan sobered.

"Labour gain," he said.

The effect on Morcar was all that Jonathan had feared; his colour seemed to fade still further and his vitality to dim. Annotsfield not represented by a Liberal! He thought of the great days when the British Liberal Party, enlightened, progressive, generous, was the wonder and almost the ruler of the world. Everything seemed to be crumbling about him. The whole world looked strange. If he had not been Harry Morcar, a tough solid stubborn Yorkshireman, he told himself firmly, he would really have felt quite daunted.

"Well, goodnight, Jonathan," he said.

He wanted the boy to leave him quickly, for he needed to lie back in his pillows, and could not yield to such an expression of weakness while Jonathan was in the room.

"Goodnight, Uncle Harry," said Jonathan, closing the door behind him.

38. Chuff and Marriage

"I DON'T THINK it will be any use, Chuff," said Jonathan seriously. "But I think you are right in making your wishes known. Why not broach the matter to him tomorrow, when he'll be at home all day? Tomorrow afternoon. After he's had his nap, and before we have to dress to go out."

Accordingly on the afternoon of Christmas Day Chuff nerved himself to the encounter and presented himself in Morcar's den. The members of the Stanney Royd household had eaten a very light lunch without benefit of Mrs. Jessopp, who had gone off for the day to her eldest son, because they had all been invited to Emsley Hall for Christmas dinner that evening. The invitation pleased none of them. Chuff had hoped to escape for the evening to the Mellors, whose midday family party, with many aunts, would then be over. Jonathan did not enjoy seeing his mother as Nat Armitage's wife. Susie, though she had a delicious new white frock for the occasion which she could not help looking forward to wearing, did not enjoy seeing Jonathan with his mother. Morcar could have enjoyed dining with Nat and Jennifer well enough if the younger generation had not been about, but he guessed this generation's reactions and knew he would be on tenterhooks all evening lest Jennifer perceive them also and be hurt. When the time for dressing arrived, therefore, everybody would probably be in an irritable mood; but for the present, in the dead of the afternoon, good humour might still be hoped to prevail.

"Well, Chuff, what do you want?" said Morcar, waking with a start. "If you're trying to get off from your Aunt Jennifer's to-night, it's no use, so don't try it."

"I wasn't going to," said Chuff with an air of virtue.

"What is it, then?"

"I suppose it's no use, either, saying I want to get married."

"None at all till you've passed your exams," said Morcar, not taking him seriously.

"It's too bad!" cried Chuff, suddenly almost weeping.

To see his carefree, somewhat insensitive, by his own declaration "tough" grandson with his face thus distorted was painful to Morcar.

"Now, Chuff," he began kindly. "You know you're too young to marry yet."

"Lots of people get married at nineteen."

"The more fools they," said Morcar briskly.

"Why can't I do what I want? Why should I have to do what you say? I have some money of my own now," blurted Chuff.

"Don't insult me, Chuff," said Morcar angrily. "Money has nothing to do with it. If you're fool enough to run off and marry Ruth, I shan't do anything to stop you and I shan't cut you off with a penny, so don't make yourself into a martyr about it. I shall think you a fool, that's all."

"Why?" said Chuff in a milder but still tear-filled tone.

"If you marry Ruth now in a hurry, everyone will say you had to, for the usual reason. Do you want to expose Ruth to that slander? I hope it is a slander?" said Morcar sternly.

"It—is—a—slander!" shouted Chuff, crimsoning. "The maddening thing is," he added, "if it weren't, you'd give your permission and we could be married in a proper way."

"Yes, that's true," said Morcar, laughing a little at this admittedly absurd paradox. "With great reluctance and disappointment, however."

"It's no laughing matter to me," said Chuff, glowering.

"Society has its rules," began Morcar.

"They're all nonsense, hopelessly out of date."

"Maybe. If you want to break them, you can. But in that case you can't expect its support."

Chuff threw himself about the room, muttering angrily. "*You* do what you like; why can't I?" he said.

"Why do you want to gulp every pleasure down at once, in such a hurry? There'll be a lot of your life left still, after you're twenty-one."

"Maybe not," growled Chuff, sombre.

"What do you mean by that?"

"Atom bombs."

"Chuff, you never give a thought to atom bombs."

"Jonathan does, all the time."

"That's Jonathan's way. It's not yours. It's affectation to pretend you ever give them a thought."

"Why should I waste the best years of my life? I want to get married," said Chuff obstinately.

"Pass your exams first."

"I'd get through them better if I didn't have to go to the Mellors to see Ruth all the time. If she were at home with me, I should have more time."

Morcar found himself unequal to a physiological discussion with his grandson—as to which in any case there might be two sides to the argument—so he put that aside, but allowed himself to see a picture of Chuff walking a bedroom at midnight with a teething baby wailing in his arms. He sighed.

"I can't consent, Chuff, really I can't. You've two jobs on hand already, with the mill and the Tech. Marriage would be a third. Wait till you've finished your exams, do. It's only eighteen months, after all."

"Eighteen months!" wailed Chuff.

In a handsome dark green cardigan patterned across the shoulders in fawn (knitted for him, Morcar remembered having heard, by Ruth) Chuff looked very young. He also looked extremely unhappy. He still hung around in front of his grandfather, unable to abandon his hopes, moving uneasily from one foot to the other, his hands in his trouser pockets, his lower lip pouting. Morcar felt very sorry for him.

"How should you like to be engaged?" said Morcar kindly.

"What would be the use of that?" growled Chuff.

"Ruth might like it—ring and all that."

"Well, there is that, of course," said Chuff thoughtfully. "She might like it. Girls do. It would be easier at the mill."

"It would," agreed Morcar.

The black cloud on Chuff's face began to lift

"Well," he began again. "It's not what I want. I've asked for bread and you've given me a stone, that's what *I* think. But we'll get engaged now, and I'll pass my second exam in summer, and then," he concluded with triumph: "I shall broach the question of marriage to you again, grandfather."

"I shan't promise to give my consent," said Morcar, alarmed to find that he appeared to have made some concession.

"Ha!" snorted Chuff derisively. "I'll go and tell Ruth now."

He flung joyously from the room, but returned to put his head in at the door.

"I shall be twenty in July," he said consolingly.

39. Loss of a Great Man

"IF MR. CHURCHILL can stay in bed, surely you can, Grandfather," said Susie severely.

"If you don't you'll be down with pneumonia again and have to go to Africa," said Mrs. Jessopp.

Morcar hastily agreed to stay in bed. As a man who tried to be honest with himself and was fairly knowledgeable about his own motives, he enquired whether this quick agreement was due to his permanent reluctance to have Africa recalled to Susie's mind or to his desire to subside into bed. The weather this last week had been really awful even for January: gales, sleet, rain, snow, hail, thunder and again gales had made his customary winter visit to Copenhagen a real misery; planes had been grounded, ships buffeted, trains delayed. Hours spent on draughty platforms and in overheated airport lounges had resulted in a head cold so severe that even his agent's ecstatic approval of the new scarlet and rose design had failed to cheer him. He decided that he wanted to stay in bed but his aversion to references to Africa in Susie's presence was at the same time genuinely unselfish and a welcome excuse.

Being an invalid for a few days was agreeable. At first he lay supine, able to give his attention to nothing but sneezing, only too thankful to be alone, warm and under no obligation to take any kind of action. The family doctor was brought by Jonathan to see him.

"What have *you* come for? It's only a cold," said Morcar irritably, sneezing.

The doctor thumped his chest and took his temperature, then told him he was correct in saying that he was ill with a cold only.

"But if you'd gone about with it in this awful weather, you'd soon have had something worse," he said. "Stay in bed till the end of the week. I'm warning you: these overseas journeys are getting a bit much. You're not as young as you used to be, you know."

Morcar's angry growl was interrupted by a sneeze.

After a few days, however, he began to feel slightly better, and able to take an interest in life again. Jennifer came to visit him; he took pleasure in her sophisticated elegance and her happy face. The Stanney Royd household took pains to cosset him, and he now enjoyed it. Mrs. Jessopp proffered light savoury dishes which Susie placed, charmingly arranged, on an effective modern bedtable which Morcar had bought a few years before for his mother. Chuff with a look of pride in his own usefulness brought him cheques and letters to sign; he knew more about their import than Morcar would have deemed likely. Jonathan came up every evening and sat with him for a while, discussing the problems of his teaching career; he seemed easier to talk to, more approachable, than for some years past. On Thursday night two inches of snow fell, but thaw set in by Friday afternoon and Morcar felt cheered by the appearance of a few gleams of sun. He rose, and though still feeling tottery, managed to bath and shave and partly dress, and came down for an hour in the evening. His handsome dressing-gown and cravat of spotted dark blue silk were much admired—or at least, he thought with amusement, the children all played it that way—and this gave him undeniable pleasure. "Boosts the ego," he said to himself sardonically of their admiration; but all the same he enjoyed it.

"I shall be back at the mill on Monday," he said with satisfaction. This fifteen per cent imports tax had made overseas customers angry and reluctant; he felt he was needed at his post to tempt them out of this attitude by the fine quality of his goods.

Saturday was cold but sunny; Morcar dressed and came down to lunch. The effort tired him a little, however; he was glad to get back to bed in the early evening, slept heavily throughout the night and on into the morning. Mrs. Jessopp woke him with breakfast and the news that the weather, with customary English variability, had turned warm; it was a lovely sunny spring day, she said, and indeed Morcar could see through the windows, and feel in the balmy air, that it was so. The sunshine had tempted the young people to go off to the Lakes for the day, said Mrs. Jessopp; they hoped he would not mind being left alone for the day, they had looked in on him three times before leaving but he was fast asleep. Morcar said heartily that he did not mind (though he did). What were Mrs. Jessopp's plans? Mrs. Jessopp would of course be here to prepare his luncheon, she said; but if he did not mind, she would give him a hot meal in the middle of the day and then leave a cold one out for the evening, so that she could go to her eldest son's for tea and chapel. To this Morcar of course offered no **objection.**

He was therefore alone when, watching the evening news on B.B.C. television, he learned that Churchill was dead. The greatest heart in England, as one speaker said, had ceased to beat. Churchill had died, quietly and with dignity, soon after eight o'clock that morning.

Morcar's first feeling was of deep personal grief. He had loved this man, as well as admired and respected and trusted him. His next sensation was of shattering loss. This was indeed the end of an era. Morcar's world broke up into fragments, black and jagged, which whirled beneath his feet and round his ears. Daunted, suddenly bereft of all his strength, he went quietly to bed and spent most of the night re-living, with an aching sadness, the incidents of his country's finest hour. He saw the familiar pictures of Dunkirk beach, the flames of burning London, the families asleep on platforms underground, the flight overhead of the menacing V.Ones, with their short tails of fire; he heard the thud of anti-aircraft shells, the louder fall of bombs, the awful news of French surrender; over and over again he heard Churchill's voice, staunch, warm, sustaining, loveable, holding together the decencies of the world. He saw Christina's body lifted from the ruins of the Haringtons' house, and felt the sharp enduring pang of her loss.

But all this was old now, old and past and over; Churchill was dead, the era was ended; Morcar belonged only to the past; his tale was done.

40. Decisions Needed

HAVING LAIN LONG awake, Morcar was thankful when his bedside clock at last registered an hour when it would be decent for him to leave his bed. He rose rather in the mood of a man condemned to death on the morning of his execution—without hope, all interest in life over, but determined to see the thing through with a decent calm. He dressed with especial care—"so as not to let the old chap down," he said to himself—put on a black tie and went downstairs.

The hour was early, but to his pleasure everyone in Stanney Royd had clearly felt as he did. They were all up—even Chuff, too often a lie-abed; they were all very neatly turned out—Jonathan had a black tie, Chuff disappeared and put one on; they were all very quiet and wore looks of unaffected sorrow. The three men's political differences always necessitated the provision of several daily newspapers (Susie of course read Jonathan's); this morning they all exchanged their various sheets, anxious to see how each treated their hero. Mrs. Jessopp wept as she brought in the bacon. Jonathan began respectfully to enquire from Morcar details about Churchill; he must speak of him to his classes today, he said, and would be grateful for original anecdotes or accounts of what Morcar and other West Riding people had felt at the time.

Morcar was able to make an abundant response to his questions, and was glad to do so; yet he was chilled by the ignorance and misunderstanding of the war period shown unawares by Jonathan, a highly intelligent, well educated and sympathetic young man, son too of one of the heroes of the time. "They've got it all wrong," mourned Morcar privately: "It's history now and historians will make a mess of it."

This sadness was accentuated when as Chuff drove him down to Syke Mills he poured out—eagerly enough, Morcar granted—many further questions which showed all too clearly how appallingly he misconceived the actions of the time. From air raids to naval convoys, from Eisenhower to Belsen, his details were maddeningly mistaken—not grossly out of true but enough to distort the whole picture.

A deep sadness hung over the whole mill; men went about their work very quietly, without looking at each other. Morcar withdrew to his private office and surveyed the pile of correspondence awaiting him, with distaste. He felt he really had not the strength to cope with business, and toyed with the important letters which Ruth had displayed at the top of the pile, in a lackadaisical manner. The telephone rang in the outer office and Ruth put the call through.

"Councillor Smethurst," she said.

Morcar's pulse quickened. He remembered all too surely that Smethurst sat on the Highways committee. "This is it," he thought. "Good morning!" he cried, artificially cheerful.

"Harry, I just thought I'd let you know," said Councillor Smethurst quickly. "The Ring Road's approved. We've heard this morning. It'll be all in the newspaper tonight. My committee agreed that I should warn you. I just thought I'd let you know," he tailed off. Morcar was silent. "Harry!" cried the Councillor urgently.

"Well, it's only what I expected," said Morcar in a casual tone.

This was true; since Churchill's death he expected no more good from life. But had it not been true, he would still have replied in the same offhand style—no councillor need think to ruffle him into showing despair. Nevertheless there was a terrible sinking at his heart, a feeling of total emptiness, as though every drop of courage and energy had been drained from it. He was to be spared nothing, it seemed.

"Well, that's the way to take it," said the Councillor doubtfully.

"That's right. Thanks for letting me know."

He put down the receiver and looked up; Nathan and Ruth were staring at him anxiously.

"Well—the Ring Road's approved," he said.

Ruth exclaimed, and Nathan seemed to shrink and wither.

"Where's Chuff?"

"He's gone to Old Mill," said Ruth. "They just telephoned."

"They're having some trouble with one of their fulling stocks," explained Nathan mournfully, "so he's gone to see what's wrong."

"What!" shouted Morcar, bounding to his feet. "Get Old on the 'phone, Ruth—tell them Chuff isn't even to look at those stocks—I'll come along at once. Chuff is to do nothing—don't you remember, Nathan, we had to repair the shaft of that far stock, just after the war, with poor wood and an iron band, because there wasn't anything else available?"

"Oh, aye, I remember now," murmured Nathan, still only half alive after the awful shock of the Ring Road.

"It'll splinter—God knows what it'll do. Ruth, tell Chuff he's to leave those stocks alone, he's to wait for me. And see that he does so."

"Yes, Mr. Morcar," said Ruth meekly, snatching at the telephone.

Morcar ran down the mill steps. His car was not in the parking area; Chuff of course had taken it.

"Hi, you!" shouted Morcar to a member of the designing staff who was ambling across the yard carrying a bucket. ("Why a bucket?" demanded Morcar inwardly.) "Is this your car?" He struck the bonnet of a green Mini with his open hand.

"Yes," said the man, alarmed.

"Drive me to Old Mill," said Morcar, getting in.

"It seems they still need me," thought Morcar as they drove away. "I've got all this in a muddle; I shall have to think it out."

41. End of an Era

IT WAS NINE-TWENTY on the morning of Saturday January 30th, 1965. The five members of the Stanney Royd household sat

215

clustered about the television set in Morcar's den. Mrs. Jessopp, in the centre of the group, rocked herself slowly back and forth in the kitchen rocking-chair which Jonathan had carried in for her. It was a grey, dull, bitterly cold day and the fire had been heaped high with good Yorkshire coal and "made-up with small", as Mrs. Jessopp said—Stanney Royd was not yet in a "clean-air" zone, thank goodness, thought Morcar—so that they would not have to break off from watching Sir Winston Churchill's funeral to attend to it.

The half-hour struck; the scene changed to the outside of Westminster Hall, where a Royal Naval gun crew stood drawn up in faultless lines; the bearer party of Grenadier Guards came out from the Hall with measured step, bearing on their shoulders the coffin, covered with the Union Jack. The naval party received this with caps off and bent heads. The insignia of the Garter lay on a velvet cushion on the flag, and a row of officers now appeared, bearing Sir Winston's orders and decorations on velvet cushions before them. The bearer party placed the coffin on the gun-carriage, the gun crew formed up, the thick white ropes were adjusted, the Earl Marshal of England raised his baton; silently, with exquisite precision, the cortège moved off. Bands struck into a funeral march.

"But are they going to draw the gun-carriage by hand all the way to St. Paul's!" exclaimed Jonathan, aghast. "It's a considerable distance.'

"It tells you everything in the *Radio Times* supplement," growled Chuff, passing the sheets.

Morcar sympathised with his irritation at Jonathan's interruption. He was himself deeply impressed by the punctuality, the simultaneity of movement, the perfect alignment, the accuracy and dignity, of the proceedings so far.

"Nobody does this sort of thing as well as the British," he thought: "This is going to be a really great occasion."

He felt deeply moved and he hoped nobody would talk, for he wanted to take part in the ceremony in respectful silence. As the procession moved on through London at the same steady inexorable pace, however, on and on and on and on with unvarying tread, between lines and lines of silent mourners, the men standing bareheaded in respect, the women silently weeping, feelings of pride and sorrow overtook them all. Jonathan said no more, and his fine face fell into lines of grief and admiration; Mrs. Jessopp ceased to rock, Chuff lounged but did not stir, Susie sat as if frozen. Morcar, though enthralled by the solemn and moving spectacle, attending Churchill's funeral with all his heart and soul, nevertheless presently found his mind working. He thought about Churchill and his achievements, his passing and the termination of the era; he thought about himself, his problems, his early life, his relationship with Jonathan and Chuff, the decision about the future of Syke Mills which he had promised himself to take next Monday. It was in 1958, he thought, that life had begun to change for him. What, then, was his situation now?

At first his reflections were dispersed, chaotic, but presently settled into reasonable chronology. Throughout they were deeply true to his nature; it struck him that perhaps no better opportunity for thought would ever occur for him, than this time of silent watching, when the nobility of the spectacle he watched released his thought to a lofty level. Perhaps indeed no better tribute would be given by him to Churchill than a profound meditation, the best of which he was capable, on the meaning and purpose of his whole life. His memory roved over the past. On the whole he thought he had not acted too badly, though more by good luck than by conscious management—"better than old Hardaker, any road," he reflected sardonically—but that remained to be seen.

First he considered himself from the physical point of view. He was still a strong and active man, but not as strong and active as he had been of old. He now wore spectacles, he was a little deaf, he handled small objects clumsily, he had had a bout of pneumonia and now this appalling head-cold, he soon grew tired. Chuff was now a finer animal specimen than himself, and though Jonathan lacked Morcar's robust appearance, he was in a wiry way healthy enough. Physically, therefore, the young men had the advantage, and in all matters of physique should be allowed to exercise their judgment.

And mentally? Morcar remembered the letter he had dictated wrongly to Ruth, the mistake he had made in crossing to the wrong side of Scape Scar Lane. (He really must get himself a new chauffeur to replace Jessopp, by the way, and not allow indolence and sentiment to deter him; if not, either he would smash himself up by some carelessness, or he would become a nuisance to Chuff and Jonathan, relying on them to conduct his movements.) His memory, once infallible, now sometimes skipped a little and left blank patches. As regards design, the main theme of his life: last year the textile industry of Great Britain had achieved £169 million pounds' worth of direct exports; of this figure he had furnished one million pounds, almost entirely from his own designs. It was not bad, it was not bad at all. In truth, he still had excellent design ideas. But, he must admit, less frequently than of old—one a year instead of half a dozen. Yes, he was (naturally) far less fertile than he used to be. Chuff's powers were still growing to their height; Morcar's—though he ventured to think, indeed he knew, his powers greater than his grandson's—were on the decline. But when he looked back over his life he saw fifty years of experience in textiles, fifty years in which scarcely one day had passed without some textile thought, some business negotiation. This experience was an invaluable possession which ought not to be wasted. Look how things went wrong when he was away! Look at the Old Mill fulling stocks! (Now safely replaced by his instructions.) Inexperienced handling might have induced disaster. Then, too, Chuff had thought to replace one stock only, but Morcar knew that would make their beat uneven. Morcar told Chuff how to manage a funeral, he knew where to find advice for Jonathan about schools. (Though was it the best advice?) Yes, in some aspects of life, indeed in many, Morcar was still needed.

On the other hand, the young people had more experience of modern phenomena. Jonathan knew what kind of speech Morcar should make to young students; Chuff knew more than his grandfather about bowls, dances, motor-cycles—and what young people liked to wear.

Was Morcar, then, so much needed, so useful, as to be entitled to hold the power over the younger generation that he undoubtedly possessed? He had the power because he had the money; how far was he entitled to use it? Well, first of all, decided Morcar firmly: I think a man should uphold his own basic principles, even to the point of severity. I was right to rebuke Chuff over his poor reports, I was right to lay strongly before him what I thought about his behaviour with Ruth. To give in about basic beliefs, to yield wrongly against one's principles, is feeble and useless. The only way to obtain the respect of the young is surely to be worthy of it. Maybe that was all you could do for the young: show them a way of living as a standard with which to compare their own.

On the other hand—the procession was now entering the Strand, and a fresh band broke out in solemn music; gun salutes shook Morcar's thoughts—on the other hand, Morcar sympathised with the resentment of the young at always having to do what the old told them to do instead of doing what pleased themselves. Yes, it was more than empathy, it was sympathy, thought Morcar, smiling grimly; he himself was a man who liked to go his own way, a man who hated to be governed. When Jonathan said that a man should make up his mind what he wanted to do, and not be bossed out of doing it, Morcar agreed whole-heartedly. Indeed he had often said the same himself. (To change one's mind from rational consideration was a different matter.) But on the one hand, if the older generation did not pass down their ideas of civilisation to the younger—"we have heard with our ears and our fathers have declared unto us," thought Morcar—there would be no progress in civilisation at all, for each generation would have to start again from zero. On the other hand, unless the younger generation differed from the older, there would be no progress because no change, as Trollope remarked with his confounded woad, thought Morcar irritably.

Is the conflict between the generations more difficult to resolve than the conflict of interests between contemporaries, wondered Morcar. Yes, he thought so. There were the biological factors, Oedipus and all that, to begin with. On top of that, the lives of the young are inevitably shaped by the patterns made by the older generation. Myself, Charlie, Jessopp, Winnie, Christina, David, Jennifer, Fan: we all made patterns (not always willingly) in which these three youngsters, Chuff, Jonathan and Susie, are enmeshed. Even their characters, their faces, are handed to them by their elders. Naturally the young resent this curtailment of their free choice. The patterns are already made, and can't be unmade, but though the young must cope with them, we should not require the young to like them.

But because their environment is so different from that of the previous generation, their ideas cannot be yours, indeed must necessarily be different from yours. Everything your generation has added on to your childhood's way of life, has made their environment different from yours. Except when their ideas appear to run counter to your morals, you have not the right to forbid them. Morcar coloured as he remembered the instruction he had cheerfully given his two young dependents about their car: "A sober colour and not too many gadgets." To warn them that in his experience many gadgets made a heavy expense for impermanent benefits was sensible, but what right had he to curtail their choice of colour? That he was paying the bill? That was a tyrannous use of power, he reflected; such a gift was not a gift, but an extension of one's own personality. It was natural for young people to like new things, which sprang from the same impulses as themselves; new colours, new shapes, new clothes, new buildings. Had he the right to chain Chuff down for life to an old mill he hated? That a new mill could stand beside the Oldroyds' first mill on the Ire would be pleasant; he could call it Syke Mill, which was its original name, and Susie's modern lamb would look at home there. But the thought of all that glass and concrete was odious to him. Still, he must not allow himself to dislike new customs just because they were new; his bitterness against Beatle-cuts, beehive hairdo's, shift dresses and black stockings—did he just revolt against their unfamiliarity? He must try to judge, not by whether they were new or old, but by the criteria of taste he genuinely accepted.

In change, the old see decay; the young, new life. Both are right.

It was not much consolation, though perhaps a little, that the problem was not unique, but faced every generation. He remembered, not without a rueful chuckle, that the two Hardaker boys had treated Chuff as an old bore, that Jonathan was having a stiff struggle to make his school class respect him.

Now his meditation was broken: the procession had reached St. Paul's. With a perfect dignity and accuracy which Morcar admired with his whole heart, the bearer party lifted the heavy coffin and carried it safely, with measured step, up the long flight of steps and into the great cathedral. Morcar was not one who greatly loved ceremony; but "I like it if it's to do with something I believe in," he sometimes said. Now the spectacle greatly moved him; the rich blaze of colours in the uniforms, the superb pattern of human lines and curves—an orderliness not natural or easy, to be learned only with great effort, practised only with great control —the great ones of the world gathered to pay tribute to a commoner ("none of them a patch on him," thought Morcar), the true grief on every face.

"This is the climax of the affair, the highest moment," thought Morcar soberly.

He did not in the least believe in any bodily resurrection, but the sentences announcing it, as the procession moved up the cathedral, had a deep relevance to human longing. As for *To Be a Pilgrim*, which the vast congregation now proceeded to sing, it expressed Morcar's view of life exactly.

> *Who would true valour see*
> *Let him come hither;*
> *One here will constant be*
> *Come wind, come weather;*
> *There's no discouragement*
> *Shall make him once relent*
> *His first avowed intent*
> *To be a pilgrim.*

"That's Churchill exactly," thought Morcar, and he felt he owed it to Churchill to reduce his chaotic and muddled thoughts to firm practical conclusions. He struggled to do so.

All parts of a man's life, thought Morcar, were important to ones estimate of him as a man, the last ten years as much so as the first. Therefore one's standards must be maintained through one's last years: old age must be lived with dignity and honour. Dealings with the new generation must therefore be such as one's best judgment approved.

How to do this? How to withdraw gracefully so as to retain enough power of action to continue to be helpful, but little enough to give the younger generation full scope? He could not deny that he had been hurt when Old Mill had asked Chuff to advise on their broken stock instead of himself, and ignobly glad when his own knowledge was needed; yet his own knowledge was really needed. Again, there was more feeling beneath the apparently callous surface of the young than one would guess at first sight. Chuff suffered from Jonathan's mental superiority, and was sorry for his grandmother; Susie wept over her fringe and resented Jonathan's mother; Jonathan was hurt to have "prank" applied to his C.N.D. endeavours and sacrificed an easy future for the sake of his ideas. How to behave wisely and well towards them?

It struck him that this was one of the severest challenges, the trickiest assignments, of his whole career. How to meet it?

First, of course, one must love the new generation. For him this was not difficult: Jonathan he had always loved and indeed admired; Pussy was his darling; for Chuff he had grown to have a solid realistic affection. Of course love of this kind put one always at a disadvantage. It was a law of life that the older loved the younger more than the younger loved the older; to the older, the younger were a fulfilment, to the younger, the older were a hindrance to fulfilment. You cared for the young's happiness more than they cared for yours. This must just be accepted. It made you vulnerable, they tended to get their way by being unhappy if you didn't allow it, because you cared for their unhappiness more than they cared for yours.

How, then, to judge when to give them their way, when to yield?

Not to give way, weakly, for to do so was mere self-indulgence, sparing oneself pain. Not to refuse unthinkingly, for that was mere self-indulgence, pushing aside problems, enjoying the exercise of power. Decisions must be taken after a rational consideration of all the factors concerned.

True; but one of the factors was that it was the young's lives which were at issue. Morcar had perhaps ten years, of diminishing participation, to live; Chuff had fifty or sixty. He had the right to decide how he should live for that long time. Wherever possible the young should be given their choice. Lay before them one's own view, one's own wishes, one's own experience, but let them choose.

It is natural and right that a man should wish to be a man of his time, not a stale leftover from a previous age, thought Morcar, remembering Jonathan's phrase, and G. B. Mellors' estimate of himself. Well! True enough! Nobody can take your past achievement from you, so don't try to grab the future too. Churchill was dead, but his deeds would not be forgotten. There was more in it than that, thought Morcar, but he could not quite fathom its meaning.

The service was over. The national anthem was sung; the last post and reveille were sounded, piercing, unbearably poignant, from the silver trumpet; the dead march was played, the last hymn rolled out. The coffin was borne out of the cathedral and down to the Thames' side; the launch left the pier; planes flew in formation overhead; the tall cranes bowed their heads in the drivers' last tribute; the great man's coffin was entrained for the quiet country churchyard.

The era was over.

To the new age, then.

Stiff and dazed from four hours' concentrated watching of the solemn and moving ceremony, the Stanney Royd household stood up and moved their chairs. They all looked pale and subdued, and it was evident that Susie and Mrs. Jessopp had shed tears.

"Well, he was a great man of his time," said Jonathan with respect, sighing.

"Nay! There's more to it than that. He *made* his time," exclaimed Morcar strongly.

"I suppose we all do that to some extent," mused Jonathan.

"Aye, that's so," said Morcar. He was well pleased, for this idea was what he had been looking for. "Well—I did what I could for my time; see you make a good one of yours. You shall have your new mill, Chuff," concluded Morcar pleasantly.